The Necromancer's Smile

Book One

By Lisa Oliver

The Necromancer's Smile Book 1

Copyright © Lisa Oliver, 2018

ALL RIGHTS RESERVED

Cover Design by Lisa Oliver

Cover model and Image by Paul Henry Serres Photographer, Montreal.

(FD1_182)

First Edition March 2018

All rights reserved under the International and Pan-American Conventions. No part of this book may be reproduced or transmitted in any form or by any means, electronic or mechanical including photocopying, recording or by any information storage or retrieval system, without permission in writing from the author, Lisa Oliver. Yoursintuitively@gmail.com

No part of this book may be scanned, uploaded or distributed via the internet or any other means, electronic or print, without permission from Lisa Oliver. **Warning:** The unauthorized reproduction or distribution of this copyrighted work is illegal. Criminal copyright infringement, including infringement without monetary gain, is investigated by the FBI and is punishable by up to **5 years in federal prison and a fine of $250,000.** Please purchase only authorized electronic or print editions and do not participate in or encourage the electronic piracy of copyrighted material. Your support of the author's rights and livelihood is appreciated.

The Necromancer's Smile is a work of fiction. Names, characters, places and incidents are either the product of the author's imagination or are used fictitiously and any resemblance to any actual persons, living or dead, events or locales is entirely coincidental.

Dedication

To those of my readers who understand that sometimes my muse just takes me off to do wild things, like write stories that aren't in a current series.

To Pat and Amanda for brushing up my words.

To Phil for telling me he loves this one – made my day.

To Mary for showing me new things and keeping me on track.

To everyone who has filled my last month with sexy pictures, cute animals, and most of all their loving support.

Thank you.

Table of Contents

Chapter One 7

Chapter Two 25

Chapter Three 43

Chapter Four 57

Chapter Five 67

Chapter Six 81

Chapter Seven 99

Chapter Eight 113

Chapter Nine 123

Chapter Ten 133

Chapter Eleven 147

Chapter Twelve 167

Chapter Thirteen 187

Chapter Fourteen 201

Chapter Fifteen 217

Chapter Sixteen 235

Chapter Seventeen 247

Chapter Eighteen 261

Chapter Nineteen 277

Chapter Twenty 293

Chapter Twenty-One 301

Chapter Twenty-Two 321

Chapter Twenty-Three 333

Chapter Twenty-Four 347

Chapter Twenty-Five 377

Chapter Twenty-Six 393

Chapter Twenty-Seven 409

Chapter Twenty-Eight 421

Chapter Twenty-Nine 449

Epilogue 465

Other Books By Lisa/Lee Oliver 475

About the Author 482

Chapter One

"Head's up, the Captain's here," Brad muttered as he put himself between Dakar and the oncoming posse. Dakar groaned as he quickly loosened the leather tie from around his wrist and caught his long hair in a messy but "would have to do" manbun. It was bad enough he'd been yanked away from the full-lipped blond who'd been giving him a bathroom blow job on his first night off in weeks to attend a crime scene but dealing with the Captain was last on his list of things to do.

Taking one last look at the body to make sure he hadn't missed anything obvious, Dakar straightened his legs, ignoring his boss until he felt the unmistakable presence at his back. There were times he would swear his Captain was a full demon but since paranormals were outed some fifty years before, it wasn't considered polite to ask unless you planned on dating someone and wanted to ensure your genetics were compatible.

Not that there was anything wrong with demons per se. Those that worked among humans were no different from any other paranormal in that they respected human/paranormal laws, and generally went about their business like anyone else. However, his Captain wasn't the type to blend in and whatever blood was running through his veins, the man agitated his wolf and the man's scent singed his nose in an unpleasant way.

"This is the fifth body in as many weeks," the Captain snapped as if Dakar wasn't already consumed with the damn cases twenty-four seven. Dakar stayed silent, keeping his eyes on the poor wretch sprawled at his feet.

The harsh lights set up hastily by the uniformed officers first on the scene did nothing to camouflage the horror of the situation. The young man's nude body had been gruesomely staged. His curled hands failed to contain his entrails spilling from a wide gash across his abdomen; large v-shaped cuts bisected his pectorals and while his cleanly shaved groin area was untouched, his thigh and calf muscles had been slashed to ribbons. Two feet away, his head sat on the gravel, nothing but holes as eye sockets and his mouth propped open in a silent scream.

Dakar knew without looking that the man's heart would be missing, just as it was from the other victims. The scent of blood mixed unpleasantly with the stench of vomit left outside the crime scene area, thank goodness. Unfortunately, the rancid scents combined with the anxiety Dakar always felt in the presence of his boss and was threatening to leave him with a nasty headache.

"Tell me you've found something tangible at least." The Captain was studying the body and this time

Dakar knew he was expected to reply.

"The victim was discovered during a routine police sweep of the area at 2.45 am." Dakar flashed a sympathetic glance at the rookie who'd left the remains of his dinner not twenty feet from the body. The young man's face was still green. "Previous patrols hadn't picked up anything unusual suggesting the incident occurred anything between ten pm and two am. This time frame has been tentatively verified by the M.E. who'll confirm this once he's processed the remains. The victim has no unusually identifying features and given the staging of the body, the M.E. asked we not take fingerprints until after he's been moved to the morgue."

"In other words, you have nothing. Again." Dakar would swear he could see steam coming from the Captain's nostrils although given the temperature was dipping below 20 degrees, it could just be the cold. "Scents, gut feelings. Damn it man, you must have something. What did I hire you for if your enhanced senses are useless?"

"Police regulations state it's not prudent to shift in the vicinity of a crime scene due to the possibility of foreign hairs contaminating evidence," Dakar said stiffly suddenly longing for a hot coffee doctored with a stiff whiskey. "Neither Brad nor I detected any unusual scents beyond the victim's blood and this is a high traffic area during the day. All scents around the body are hours old and there are too many of them to determine anything specific to this case." He understood his Captain's frustration – he felt exactly the same way, but it's not as though he'd been given leave to say so.

"Five cases in five weeks. All the victims are young men aged between twenty and twenty-five, from what we can determine because so far, none of the bodies have been identified. For fuck's sake, how is this possible?" The Captain's eyes were glaring hard enough to burn.

"Sir," Brad said hesitantly, "our team has gone through all the missing person's reports for every city in a two-hundred mile radius dating back over the past five years. We've run the fingerprints through every database possible both paranormal and human, and dental impressions have been sent to every dentist along the west coast."

The Captain harrumphed and turned to the M.E. who was hovering on the other side of the body. "Don't move him," he ordered.

"Captain, it will be light in a few hours and this park is commonly frequented by the jogging fraternity. The young man deserves some dignity in death and the sooner you allow me to get him on my table, the sooner I can make my report." The M.E.'s concern was accompanied by the shiver than ran through his thin frame. Six months from retirement, Dr. Barker's sparse gray hair peeked from beneath a thick red woolen hat, matching the end of his nose. The poor man looked as wretched as Dakar felt and that was saying something.

"I've got the local authorities breathing down my neck for closure in this case. The papers are going ballistic because of the lack of ID on any of these victims, claiming there's some sort of cult at work and my best detectives," the Captain's glare raised the hairs on the back of Dakar's neck, "can't sniff out a single clue. The publicity on this is getting out of control." He pointed to the two uniforms. "Call in extra troops, screen off this area and make sure no one comes within camera distance of the scene. You will all remain on guard until the consultant gets here. You two," he turned back to Dakar and Brad, "will ensure our consultant is treated with the utmost respect or I'll have your balls for breakfast."

"Fucking hell, I didn't think he'd go that far," Brad whispered as the Captain strode away, his aide Roger struggling to keep up with the taller man's strides as he spoke urgently into his phone.

"What do you mean? What freaking consultant?" Dakar had only been in Pedace three months having transferred from the East Coast looking for a quieter life. "I thought the Pedace force relied on shifter powers rather than magic users." All law enforcement consultants were magic users – lower level witches and wizards who supplemented their consultant wages by running apothecaries that never failed to stink out an entire city block. Dakar hated magical consultants, seeing them as nothing more than a leech on society and a drain on police resources.

Usually attractive, the magic users swanned around and spoke in riddles, never coming right out and saying they didn't have a clue what they were doing. Dakar had made the mistake of scratching a carnal itch with the one attached to his last department. In typical wizard fashion, the young man seemed fine with the "no-strings sex rule" Dakar employed since puberty and willingly polished Dakar's cock with his tongue. Unfortunately, as soon as the young man swallowed Dakar's come, he started spouting off about stars alignment and being true mates. Dakar flashed his fangs to scare him off and was left with a nasty itching rash on his balls that took over a week to heal. One of his reasons for moving to Pedace was there was no local coven within a hundred miles of the place.

"What does the Captain mean by consultant if there're no magic users around?"

"Oh, there's no coven here," Brad said with a grimace. "None of them would dare dip a toe past the county line unless they wanted it to go black and fall off."

"Then what? Do they come in from another county?" Dakar was edgy enough as it was and he wished Brad would just spit it out. He needed sleep, his balls still ached from the aborted blow job and his last cup of coffee left his system hours before. Being nice to anyone, even under orders, wasn't on his agenda.

"You didn't know?" Brad wiggled his eyebrows and grinned. "You're in for a treat. The Pedace Police Department doesn't have to call in an outside coven for their consulting services. The contract is already held by a Necromancer. The brass rarely calls him in because apparently his fees run to hundreds of dollars an hour, but clearly the Captain wants this case solved and fast and he expects this man to do it."

A Necromancer? Dakar had never met one but had heard enough about them to know he and Brad were going to be in for a rough night. The strongest of all magic users, Necromancers were known for their elitist attitudes, goth clothing and bad tempers. If the Pedace Necromancer took a dislike to him or Brad ball itch would be the least of his problems.

/~/~/~/~/

Sy surreptitiously glanced at his watch. It was almost four am. Thirty minutes more and he could say with all honesty he'd fulfilled his social requirement for the week. Staring out at the thinning crowd; most revelers were well past the point of drunk and heading for lunacy. He flickered his fingers and increased the strength of his wards as another muscle-bound alpha lurched in his direction with lust in his eyes. The man bounced off his wards, just as Sy intended, his eyes already scanning the crowds for his next fuck. Sy sighed, his skin itching for the solitude of his house.

But he had to stay. Sy and Brock had an agreement. He would deign to visit a club, restaurant or other such sociable establishment for four hours a week. Brock believed at the time, that Sy would break those four hours into four separate events. Sy always felt as though he was breaking out in hives if he was in anyone's company for longer than an hour, so the assumption was understandable. But Sy hadn't spent more than fifty years studying contract law to be taken in so easily and his dalliance at this current club was meeting all the contract requirements. He was in a place where people gathered to meet others and he was now twenty-seven minutes away from completing this week's tedious assignment. That would give him six gloriously peaceful days until Brock reminded him he had to do this all over again.

He quirked an eyebrow as he saw the man in question effortlessly parting the crowds, coming towards him looking completely unruffled as he always did. Brock had worked for Sy's father and his father before him, and it was as if nothing short of an erupting volcano would shift the broomstick out of his ass. He was tall even among paranormals and built like a linebacker. His clipped straight black hair was never out of place as though no single hair dared rebel against the others. Brock's face had a classically handsome yet timeless quality that belied his advancing years. Sy lifted a hand to hide his grin. The way Brock wore his suit attracted a lot of attention, especially in a gay club. But Brock waived aside lewd suggestions and the occasional grope as though they were nothing more annoying than flies.

Sy flicked another glance at his watch. "I still have twenty-five minutes to go," he said as Brock looked in disapproval at the single glass sitting on the table. "I've spoken to three different people as per our contract and as you can see, there is nowhere more sociable than a place like this." He waved his hand to indicate the dancers lurching around the floor. At this late hour, alcohol had robbed most patrons of their grace and those that weren't already clinging to another body were ravaging the crowds with fevered gazes desperately looking for someone to end the night with. Thanks to his wards, most of the gazes swept right past Sy as though he wasn't there, which was Sy's intention.

"Sir," no matter how much Sy pleaded, Brock refused to call him by his preferred name. "You are well aware you are stretching the boundaries of our agreement in a most unsatisfactory manner. Ordering a drink from the barman does not constitute a conversation. However, I don't have time to debate that with you now. You've been called in on a job."

"A job?" Sy rubbed away the furrow he felt between his eyes. "Who on earth would dare to call me in at this time of the night?" *Twenty-three minutes and counting.* "Tell whoever it is my office hours are between ten and twelve and they need to make an appointment."

"It's the Pedace Police Department, sir," Brock's rigid military stance never wavered even when the persistent alpha Sy noticed earlier fell against his back and then lurched away as though burned. "You are requested at a murder scene."

Sy was even more confused. "I thought the force was full of predatory shifters – wolves, bears, and the like. What in blazes name do they expect me to tell them that they can't tell for themselves with their uber noses and super sharp eyesight."

"None of them can speak to the dead, sir," Brock replied as though the words were perfectly obvious. "From what I understand, the Captain is concerned they have a serial killer on their hands who must be stopped at all costs."

"Who's the victim?" Sy gathered his coat and gulped down the watery remains of his whiskey. In his experience he was only ever called when the victim of a crime was someone with money or power or both. Fortunately, those crimes were few and far between in Pedace.

"They have no idea, sir. I imagine that's one of the things they want you to find out. Shall we go?"

"It's not as though I have much of a choice," Sy grumbled, his familiar annoyance with the contract his father signed for his services with the local law establishment flaring once more. To his knowledge, his family were the only magic users in the area for good reason; most covens refused to have anything to do with what they considered black magic users. Not that Sy used anything of the sort, but he'd given up trying to educate the magical community years before. It was easier to leave others to their erroneous assumptions. At least he wasn't forced to attend magical ceremonies that included dancing around a pole sky-clad before collapsing in an orgiastic heap afterwards. Sy's lip curled at the very idea. Being considered a powerful freak was preferable to having to mix with magic folk or anyone else for that matter, on a regular basis.

Following Brock's commanding presence through the crowds, his wards flowing with him, protecting him from unwanted attentions, Sy checked his watch one more time as they reached the front door. Eighteen minutes left. Damn it, he was so close. But then a random thought had Sy grinning as he stepped onto the pavement. "So, I imagine I can work off the rest of my social requirements for the week at the crime scene. After all, I will be meeting new individuals and its definitely somewhere people congregate."

Brock's lips tightened as he opened the passenger door of the limo blatantly double parked out the front of the club. "We seriously need to renegotiate the agreement," he said tersely as he closed the door after Sy was seated. Leaning back against the plush seats that still held that new leather smell, Sy's smile grew as he recalled the exact wording of their contract:

Meeting place definition: Any place where it can be considered likely that three or more people might congregate for the purposes of sharing ideas, thoughts or common interests, and where conversation is encouraged between all parties.

Brock had added the last part when Sy spent his first month's worth of social engagements at the local library.

Although it had been years since Sy had attended a crime scene he'd bet a drop of his highly coveted blue blood it would still fit within the terms of their contract. With luck, Sy could cut his social requirement for the following week by half again if he employed the "carry over" clause. He didn't often get one over on his loyal butler but when he did it was worth celebrating.

Chapter Two

"He's here," Brad said, nudging Dakar hard enough to cause the hands around his disposable cup to squash the cardboard and almost causing him to drop his coffee. "Look alert. According to the gossip, this guy doesn't miss a thing."

"You've never met him before either?" Dakar asked as he took the final swallow from his cup before crumpling it and putting it in his jacket pocket.

"I've never had the chance," Brad chuckled. "I told you, the contract signed by this man's father is ironclad and costs the Captain a fortune every time he's called out. When the son took over the area after his father retired, I'd heard the previous captain tried to renegotiate the terms. But this guy must study law or something in his spare time because he ended up with the sweeter end of the deal. With the council watching every cent spent, I'd say the only reason our friendly neighborhood Necromancer is here now is because the council have approved an increase in our budget."

"He certainly wears the money well," Dakar muttered, taking in the tall being striding towards him dressed in a suit worth more than a year's worth of Dakar's wages. The man carried himself with the air of someone who'd never been denied, never come across a problem he couldn't solve, and his power nudged at Dakar's wolf from the moment he stepped over the police tape. He was followed by an adorable twink with a mass of dark curls who was dressed for a night on the town.

Dakar's eyes narrowed, and he surreptitiously sniffed as the tall man approached. Most magic users in his experience smelled of sage, basil and a hint of hemp. The few more powerful ones charged the air around them with subtle electricity jolts. This guy had no electrical charge and smelled more of fire and brimstone than herbs. In fact, scent-wise he could be related to the Captain although Dakar's gut told him that wasn't the case.

Stepping forward, Dakar inclined his head enough to show respect and kept his expression professional. "Necromancer, I apologize for disturbing your evening plans. If your boy toy would care to wait by the car, I can show you what we've found at the scene so far."

The tall man's spine got even straighter if that was possible and the temperature around them dropped ten degrees. Dakar got the impression he'd caused offence even if he couldn't work out what he'd said wrong. Then he remembered what he'd said and winced. Shit, what if the boy toy was the Necromancer's mate, significant other, or whatever the hell a necromancer calls his partner? Opening his mouth to offer yet another apology he was thwarted by cutting tones delivered with a decidedly British accent.

"Far be it for me to offer advice when you've not even offered your name and designation," the haughty tones dripped with ice, "but may I suggest you should never judge a book by its cover. As you pointed out our evening plans have been interrupted so our attire should be excused. But then," dark eyes reflected the scorn in the man's tone, "I imagine it's been some time since you've bothered to pick up a book of any kind so perhaps you're unfamiliar with the cover analogy."

Dakar bristled under the insult and his wolf growled in his head. "Now look here," he snapped, "I…."

"Don't let them bother you, Brock, you know it will only give you heartburn." The boy toy hurried past the three men, walking straight up to the body before curling his legs so he ended up sitting cross legged on the ground beside the head. To Dakar's shock the young man caressed the blood splattered hair before closing his eyes.

"What the hell?" Dakar shared a look with his partner before turning to the one called Brock. "Look Necromancer, I get its late and you aren't the only one who got cock-blocked by this murder but get your pet away from our crime scene. He's contaminating evidence."

Dakar admitted, to himself at least, the boy toy was definitely worth spending fifteen minutes with. His mass of curls shone like a sinful halo under the harsh police lights, his slender face crafted by an angel. His lips were dark pink and full enough to stretch delightfully around his hardening cock. The club clothes the boy wore highlighted an ass taut enough to bounce a roll of quarters on and he had a lightly defined torso any twink would be proud to show off. But the boy's innocent air would have stopped Dakar from approaching him if the circumstances of their meeting had been any different.

"Detective," Brock's lips curled, and the brimstone edge of his scent increased. "I would appreciate it if you would stop eying that young man as though he was your last meal. That man you callously insulted suggesting he was both my boy toy and my pet is the Pedace County Necromancer, Prince Sebastian York of the York clan; only heir to the York fortune and the strongest and most able man of his craft in the America's."

Just dig my grave and leave me in it. Dakar's cheeks heated as he stumbled for something to say. "And you are?" He managed when his brain finally hit the right gear.

"I'm Brock, Prince York's butler," Brock announced as if he was the President.

"It's a pleasure meeting you," Brad intervened as Dakar tried to merge

Brock's imposing presence with his idea of a crusty British butler as portrayed by random television programs he rarely watched. "Forgive me if I'm being impertinent, but what is the Necromancer doing? Doesn't he know he shouldn't touch the deceased?"

Brock peered around Dakar's shoulder and huffed. "I imagine he's attempting to talk to the young man's spirit," he said dismissively. "It's what a Necromancer does, among other things." The clipped tone suggested Dakar would find out just how powerful the cute young man was if he didn't find a way to extract his size fourteen boots from his mouth.

/~/~/~/~/

If Sy had a dime for every time someone confused Brock with the Necromancer position he'd be able to build a tower taller than the Statue of Liberty. Not that he'd craft the tower with dimes, of course. He much preferred the basic metals like silver and gold. It always warmed his heart when Brock jumped to his defense so strongly. Lord knows, no one else did. But after the Detectives' swift dismissal of him simply because of his looks, Sy just wanted to do his job and get it over and done with. He'd already counted seven officers at the scene, so this would qualify under his social engagement contract which was the only positive of the evening so far. *Hopefully, no one will interrupt me.*

Keeping his eyes closed, Sy started identifying and then blocking from his mind the elements of the scene unnecessary to him. The first layers – the brightness of the lights, the feel of the wet grass under his butt, the sounds of voices – they were easy to dismiss. Next, he recognized the rustle of the leaves in the tall trees surrounding the park, the wail of a distant siren, and the low thrum of a plane flying overhead. He blocked them too. Deeper and deeper he went, stripping out the trappings of the physical world in his mind until he reached the veil between the living and the dead.

Sliding through the veil, Sy immediately sensed a presence. He wasn't surprised the spirit hadn't wandered far considering the callous nature of the young man's death. Sy was conscious of a white glow, but nothing more. The victim was an innocent in every sense and hadn't been dead long enough to create the semblance of a physical form. Sy would have to work fast if he was to get any information at all. Chances are, the spirit was only hanging around because he didn't yet fully realize he'd passed beyond the veil and if the young man was taken into the hereafter quickly, it would require more than a force of will to contact him.

Where am I?

Good, at least he's recognized my presence. Sy knew that wasn't always the case and sometimes he could waste precious minutes yelling to get a spirit's attention.

"You're dead," Sy projected bluntly. There was never any point in sugar coating an obvious truth. "Can you tell me who you are?"

Don't you know already? Aren't you an angel? You shine like an angel. I thought they knew everything.

Oh, you poor sweet kid, Sy kept that thought to himself. "I'm not an angel sweetheart, but one will be coming for you very soon. I can wait with you if you like?"

That will be lovely, thank you. This is all very confusing. Someone had taught the kid impeccable manners, not always the case with the younger generation anymore. The white glow got closer. *Ew gross...Is that what's left of me?*

Sy realized the innocent spirit was watching the scene going on around the body. Brock and the two detectives were conferring in low voices; the detectives throwing loaded looks his way every few seconds. The garish blood on the body was dried but no less shocking against pale limbs that held a bluish tinge.

"Our body is simply a vessel that allows our spirits to experience different aspects of life," Sy replied feeling the need to offer some kind of comfort. "If it is meant to be, you will reform in another life but that's dependent on a number of different factors. Try not to worry about it now. Can you tell me your name?" Instinct told Sy that information was important. At least if he had the victim's name he could call on him again if he needed to at a later time.

He called me Peter, the young man's voice was faint and Sy struggled to hear him. *But I wasn't the first and I won't be the last. They are all Peter.*

Shit. Sy thought fast. He could feel the layers of life intruding, pushing at the veil. That damned detective probably wanted to conduct an interview or something equally unhelpful. "What name were you given at birth?" He asked. "Do you remember?"

The white glow wavered and Sy held fast to his powers. He was suddenly aware of everything that was going on. Brock was trying to stop the sexy detective from interfering and…what? Clenching his teeth, Sy focused on the light once more. "Your birth name," he prodded.

Warren. The glow got brighter. *Warren Peterson but he said that meant I was a Peter.*

"Who said," Sy projected desperately as angry voices from the real world pierced his ears. "Who said you should be Peter?"

"Stop! Don't touch him. You sir, are a damn fool," Sy heard Brock yell in tones far louder than his stoic butler usually employed. A wolf snarled, and a heavy hand landed on his shoulder. Sy lost his connection with the innocent spirit. Layers of real life piled in, one on top of the other as his concentration fractured. A familiar darkness curled over the edges of his mind and as Sy succumbed as he knew he must, he saw the white glow joined by another. *At least he got his angel escort*, Sy thought as he slumped back on the wet grass, barely aware his fingers were still entangled in the ends of the dead man's hair.

/~/~/~/~/

"Have none of you read the damn manual provided when the Prince's father entered into the contract with your department? Now look what you've done."

Dakar's retort died on his tongue as he took in the sight of the pretty young magic user slumped at his feet. All at once he was struck with a feeling of dread as he imagined the Necromancer as the victim. His wolf howled in his mind and growls bubbled up through his chest, spilling from his throat as if he were in his furry form. Ignoring him completely, Brock pushed him aside and in one graceful move plucked the young man from the ground, cradling him in his arms.

"How the... what are we...did he even *do* anything?" Dakar yelled as Brock brushed past him, heading for the waiting limo. Brock stopped and half-turned, his sneer fully formed.

"The Necromancer *was* performing his duties. If you'd read the manual provided you would know that when a Necromancer is yanked back through the veil between the living and the dead before he is done, he falls into a deep sleep while his brain reorients itself. On previous occasions, when your predecessors were as ignorant of the process as you've proven to be, they were always gracious enough to make an appointment at a more civilized hour to hear what he has to report. I suggest you do the same."

Dakar was getting more and more frustrated with the constant referrals to a damn manual he didn't even know existed. His heart was still trying to pound its way out of his chest over the way the Necromancer went down so quickly and the knowledge it was his ignorance that caused it. "This is the fifth victim," he insisted. "If we don't move quickly on this, the killer could get away."

"The killer has already gotten away," Brock said in his clipped tone. "Otherwise the person who perpetuated this awful crime would still be here, in handcuffs I imagine, being subjected to the wonders known as the justice system. Now, if you'll excuse me."

"How do I make an appointment to hear what the Necromancer has learned?" Dakar was seized with the feeling his best lead was being placed with gentle care into the back of the Limo.

"Read the manual, Detective." Brock didn't even bother to acknowledge the others at the scene as he slid into the driver's seat and the Limo moved down the driveway.

"Looks like you were caught with your pants down, Dakar. I take it, I can remove the body now?" Dr. Barker grinned as he waved at his assistants carrying black body bags towards the corpse.

"You knew who he was, and you let me make a right fool of myself. Thanks a fucking bunch. Do what you have to do. I have a manual to find and read before tomorrow's meeting." And he did need to read that manual. That was the only thing Dakar was certain of.

Everything else – the rising body count, the lack of clues and his captain's ire were all subject to change – but one fact engraved itself on his psyche. He owed the Necromancer an apology and he didn't want to go into a second meeting unprepared. He only hoped the young man wouldn't make him eat too much humble pie before he made his report. At this stage, Dakar was prepared to believe in fairy dust and true love if it meant he could get a lead on the killer...and maybe a chance to see the Necromancer smile. He imagined that would be something worth seeing.

Chapter Three

Sy stretched and snuggled further under his feather duvet. The clink of the tea cups, the smell of freshly buttered toast and then a blast of light he could see even with his eyes closed all let him know Brock was in the room and it was time to get up.

"Sir, I know you're awake. Those detectives will be here within the hour and if you wish to bathe the stench from last night's activities from your body and hair, you'd better sit up and eat your toast."

"Tea first, you know the drill." Sy pushed back the covers and wriggled into a seated position, pillows already waiting to support his back as a cup was handed to him. Chamomile. He was being spoiled this morning. Sy took a grateful sip and managed a smile. "I know you won't allow me to be late and even if I was, that is no more than those detectives deserve after last night."

"Sir, you can't...."

"I know, punctuality is a sign of professionalism and with my curls and youthful exterior I have enough trouble being respected as it is." Picking up a piece of toast Sy wasn't surprised to see it was perfectly cooked and smeared with just enough butter to make the inners soft. He winked at the staunch man standing at parade rest by the bed. "I also know, without resorting to magic, that my bath will already be run to a regulation four and a half inches from the rim. It will contain precisely twenty milliliters of bubble bath; likely lavender today as I had a rotten night. My towels will already be heated and waiting for me when I step out and while I am bathing you will lay out my Necromancer garb ready for me to step into. You know, it would be quicker if I took a shower."

"Don't even joke about it." The horror on Brock's face was worth another chuckle. Sy knew his butler was never happier unless he controlled everything he could down to the last inch. If he searched the man he'd likely find a thermometer stuffed in some secret pocket; its sole purpose to ensure the bath water was at precisely the right temperature designed to be soothing without burning him.

"Can we forgo the goth garb today, at least?" Sy asked, placing his toast crust on the plate sitting on the bedside table and giving up his cup. "The visitors have already seen me in club gear. Surely a button-down shirt and smart pants would suffice?"

"Absolutely not." Brock's eyebrows were at least half an inch higher than normal. "A Necromancer's position, including the wearing of...."

"I know, I know." Sy climbed out of bed, unconcerned with his nudity. Brock would have been the one who put him to bed after all. "But honestly, look at me. The long black coat, all black shirt and pants and even the soft leather gloves for goodness sake. They were designed for someone a lot taller and more imposing than me. They make me look like I'm playing dress up in my father's clothes."

"You make a very fine Necromancer. You've got more power in your little finger than you father has in his whole body," Brock said firmly. "Now let's have no more arguments. You have forty-seven minutes left before your appointment."

"Can I at least make a fiery entrance?" Sy batted his eyelids. "That seems to attract respect."

Brock sighed and Sy knew he'd do as he asked. "I'll put them in the smaller dance hall then, sir. That will make more of an impact than if we use the larger hall. The marble floors will be easier to clean the scorch marks from than the wooden one in your office."

"You are too good to me, thank you." Sy hurried through to the bathroom to save Brock having to hide his embarrassment. The man had been in service for so long, he'd forgotten how to accept a compliment.

/~/~/~/~/

"You need a map and a compass to find your way to the bathroom in this house," Brad whispered as they followed Brock's upright form through an ornate mansion. Dakar agreed. It wasn't his first time meeting an important personage in their private home, but generally the office was handy to the front door. So far, they'd been walking the hallways for what seemed like ages and Brock showed no sign of stopping.

The inside of the home was filled with light; surprising, given the gothic architecture of the outside. Fresh flowers arranged in tall vases were spaced periodically along the halls and every room Dakar had managed to sneak a peek at was immaculately decorated. The ceilings loomed well above his head and came complete with plaster moldings, elaborate cornices, and sparkling crystal chandeliers. Dakar would assume it would take an army of people to keep the place clean but apart from Brock, they hadn't seen a soul.

"If you gentlemen would wait inside, I will arrange refreshments." Brock stood by an open door, his arm indicating they were to enter the room beyond.

Stepping across the threshold, Dakar expected to see another office, or even a small sitting room, but the room they'd been ushered into was huge. Large bay windows completely covered the far wall, lined with rich dark red velvet curtains. Dakar's boots clicked on the cool white and gold marble floor. Grecian pillars framed a fireplace large enough to swallow a Buick. Apart from a collection of ferns in large pots in one corner near the window the room was empty.

"Your seats, gentlemen, and refreshments. The Necromancer will be with you directly. For your own safety, do not move from the chairs provided." A wave of Brock's hand and two large red armchairs appeared complete with a table holding a carafe of coffee with the fixings and a plate of biscuits. Dakar wasn't one for eating sweets, but he quickly poured himself a large mug of coffee. Brad added sugar and cream to his and the two men sat in silence awaiting the Necromancer's arrival. It wasn't a comfortable silence, given how Brock was still standing at attention not five feet away.

"What do you think all that's about? Not being allowed to move, I mean," Brad leaned over to whisper. "Do you figure the floor is booby-trapped or something?"

"Probably worried we're going to pocket some of the family silver."

Dakar knew he looked rough but after only three hours sleep, grooming wasn't high on his priorities. His two-day scruff was reaching irritation point and he'd barely had time to run a brush through his long hair, worn loose for the occasion. Okay, he might have splashed out on a new shirt, but he wasn't admitting the why of it to anyone. It had nothing to do with a sexy young Necromancer who had yet to make his appearance.

The air suddenly hummed with magic and Dakar's nose was filled with the scent of honey and jasmine with the tiniest hint of lavender. The smell infused every cell in his body and his wolf sat up in his head and howled. His cock pounding, Dakar ran his eyes around the room, searching for the source of the compelling scent. He half rose, only to be interrupted by Brock. "I said don't move. The Necromancer is on his way."

Where? Nothing had changed in the room but just as Dakar finished the thought, a burst of flame erupted in the middle of the marble floor. Splitting in two threads, twisting and turning, the flames moved with purpose, etching a design on the marble. A pentagram. Dakar shivered. As soon as the two flames met at the far side of the symbol there was a loud boom that left Dakar's ears ringing. Another circle appeared inside the pentagram, the flames leaping ten feet into the air.

And there, sitting in the middle of it all on an ornately carved throne was the Necromancer. Gone was the party boy from the night before. His curls were slicked back, making his high sharp cheek bones more prominent. Dressed entirely in black leather, Prince Sebastian York epitomized power, yet as large gray eyes caught his, Dakar swore he saw the hint of a smirk on the Necromancer's lips.

"Your audience with the Necromancer has begun," Brock intoned as the young man clicked his fingers and the flames died down to a gentle simmer. "Please state your full names and purpose of your visit."

"Detective Brad Summerfield and Detective Dakar Rhodes from the Pedace Police Department asking for the results of last night's enquiry from the Necromancer," Brad said formally as Dakar struggled to find his voice. Everything about the young man called to him with an instinct older than time. *Mate? It's not possible* and yet Dakar couldn't take his eyes off the younger man. It was as if the Necromancer could tell his every thought.

"The victim's name is Warren Peterson, however the killer called him Peter." The Necromancer's tone was giving nothing away.

"You talked to him? You talked to our dead victim?" Dakar's brain was on overload and his wolf, who was running around in excitement, wasn't helping the situation.

"It's what I do, Detective Rhodes." There it was again, that slight twitch of the lips as if the Necromancer was reliving a private joke. "Your victim had not been dead long and was an innocent. It was fortunate you called me as quickly as you did, otherwise communication would have been more difficult."

"Does this mean it's too late for you to communicate with the other victims?" Brad asked, scribbling furiously in his note book. He looked up quickly. "We haven't managed to identify the four other victims. Having their names would be extremely helpful to us."

"No one has claimed any knowledge of the previously deceased?" The Necromancer shared a look with Brock that Dakar couldn't interpret. "Warren was far too innocent to be a homeless person; someone must be missing him."

"We've turned up nothing so far," Dakar said, his lust temporarily dampened by the thoughts of the dead men. "I believe that's why the Captain asked for your help. We've found no evidence to suggest these victims ever existed in the time leading up to their deaths."

"And yet now their bodies are lying in your morgue, unnamed and uncared for. Those poor souls." The Necromancer went quiet, seemingly lost in thought. Dakar was just about to ask him if he'd learned anything else, when the young man jumped to his feet. With a wave of his hand, the flames and throne disappeared.

"Brock, is my bag still in the boot of the limo?"

"Of course, sir, freshly stocked."

"Very good." The Necromancer appeared to pluck a staff almost as tall as him from thin air. It was fashioned from a tree limb; Oak, Dakar would have guessed, and was crested with a very realistic life-sized skull. "Come along then, Detectives, we've got work to do."

"Where are we going?" Dakar asked as Brad hastily stuffed his notebook and pen into his jacket pocket.

"Why, the morgue of course. Unless you happen to have any personal effects from the victims on your person?"

"No personal effects were found on any of the victims. They were all in the same state you saw last night." Dakar tried not to inhale as the Necromancer swept past.

"Then the morgue is our only option. Come on, chop, chop. The dead wait for no man."

Chapter Four

"Detective Dakar Rhodes has lustful thoughts about you," Brock said as he pointed the limo in the direction of the city morgue. "He stunk of arousal."

"A lot of people lust after me when I'm dressed up like a comic book freak. It's got something to do with my power levels." Sy wasn't worried that Brock might disapprove. Heavens, if he actually had sex with someone his stuffy butler would probably throw a party or at least celebrate quietly with a glass of hundred-year old whiskey.

"His wolf believes you are his mate."

"Are you certain?" Well, that put an unusual spin on his day. Sy wasn't sure how he felt about that idea.

"Animal spirits are rarely wrong about these things. It has something to do with your natural scent."

"I took a bath; maybe he's reacting to the smell of my soap. He didn't notice me in that way last night or you would have said so."

"The only thing anyone could smell last night was that poor victim's blood and the smell of vomit." Brock eased the limo around a large, ugly red brick building and brought the car to a stop in the lot behind it. "This will certainly change some things. Your father will have to be informed for one thing and it will mean we'll have to make changes in the house."

"Now hang on a minute. There's nothing in my social contract about taking a mate." Sy would have known about it if there was. "You just wanted me to go out and meet people and I do that four hours every week without fail. I don't need anything else."

"The mating issue is a done deal. It's only a matter of timing." Brock turned and rested his elbow on the back of the driver's seat. He was worried, Sy could tell, but he wasn't sure what his butler was so concerned about. "Shifters can be quite pushy about such things. I imagine if the Detective hadn't been so worried about this case, he would've stated his claim already."

"His stating it and me going through with it are two entirely different things." Sy wasn't sure he liked the idea of someone just claiming to be his mate. In his observations, mating or bonding as it was known among magic users was usually the result of failing to prevent a pregnancy after a solstice celebration. True matings were something other paranormal types did.

"Just try and keep his shifting to the non-carpeted areas of the house please." Brock opened his door and made to get out.

"Wait, you're accepting his claim? How will I...what will I...I don't even know him." Sy was feeling just a tiny bit panicked, or at least he thought that was what he was feeling. The churning in his stomach and the pounding in his right temple were reminiscent of when his father used to berate him for setting fire to his bedroom curtains as a child.

"Sir," Brock came around and opened his door but instead of standing back and letting Sy out, he leaned in. "It will be all right." Sy looked into Brock's deep dark eyes and saw nothing but concern. It lightened his heart to know it was for him. "If you want to take the time to get to know Detective Rhodes first, then as your mate he will respect and accept that. My biggest concern is going to be your father's reaction. His last communication to us suggested he's been negotiating a mating contract for you with the daughter of a powerful coven leader in France to take place sometime next year."

"You never told me about that. Why didn't you tell me?" Not that Sy was surprised. Even from Transylvania the man still believed he could control every move he made. Then Sy had another thought. "Is that why you insisted on that silly social contract?"

"There was nothing silly about me wanting you to experience normal life before you got dragged into your father's politics. But it seems I needn't have worried. Now, you are going to put this out of your mind until we're safely home again. We will need to come up with a plan to thwart your father and keep him on his side of the ocean. I don't believe he and your detective should meet until your bond is firmly established."

"We weren't expecting a visit from Father, were we?" Sy slipped out of the car and saw the Detectives had already arrived and were waiting by the door.

"With that man you can never tell. You know how he likes to keep us on our toes." Brock straightened Sy's coat collar. "Let's deal with one thing at a time. Help your detective solve these murders and then we'll discuss your personal life."

Sy wasn't sure which aspect of his day was going to bother him more.

/~/~/~/~/

Apparently, Dr. Barker and the Necromancer were at least passing acquaintances because the Medical Examiner had no problems arranging the remains of the previous four victims in what he called the viewing room. Dakar watched the proceedings with a mixture of awe and dread. The Necromancer, who Brock insisted preferred to be called Sy, had been absolutely focused from the moment the bodies had been wheeled in on their stainless-steel gurneys. Sy and Brock moved the two couches and coffee table aside, placing the four men in the shape of a cross with their heads pointing towards the middle.

What struck Dakar, as he watched Sy pull assorted items from a black leather medicine bag and place them around the heads, was the care and respect he'd shown the victims. As a shifter, Dakar understood the cycle of life. Death was a crucial part of the fabric of existence and with his nose full of the smell of decay, it was clear any resemblance the bodies had to the men they'd been in life was long gone.

But Sy didn't treat the corpses that way. He stroked their hair, even on those heads no longer attached to their bodies. He spoke softly, a language Dakar didn't understand, taking his time with all four of them, before letting out a long sigh.

"Are you ready sir?" Brock asked from his position by the door.

Sy nodded, his eyes glazed over as though in a trance. His head was tilted back slightly as though he was seeing something no one else was aware of.

"Gentlemen, I understand you are legally required to view these proceedings, but I must insist that from this moment on, you do nothing to impede the Necromancer in his job. Once he's established contact with the spirits, he might advise you of such and you might be able to ask questions quietly if the spirits allow. That privilege is not guaranteed and is totally dependent on the spirits. No matter what happens, no one is permitted to touch the Necromancer until he is finished and if anyone yells or expresses intense emotions I will remove that person immediately."

Brad raised his hand hesitantly. "Yes, Detective."

"What might happen if intense emotions are displayed while the Necromancer is doing his thing. Is it dangerous for any of us?"

"Necromancy is not a game or trickery. There are no smoke, mirrors or fancy tricks involved here. Necromancy is the oldest form of magic and only a handful of people are ever blessed with the ability to handle it. To speak to anyone who departed some time ago is a risk both to the Necromancer and anyone in the immediate vicinity. Not all spirits have to be invited into a space; they come if they see an opening, intent on causing harm. Anyone expressing intense emotions are likely to become a target."

Brad gulped, and Dakar's anxiety increased. Even if his human half hadn't quite got a handle on Sy being his mate, his animal half was already committed to the slender man, so his protective instincts were riding high. His erection hadn't truly gone down since the night before and he was sure his Alpha pheromones were fighting for dominance over the smell of death.

There was another part of him that was proud he would soon call the pretty young man his own. Alphas respected power of all kinds and Sy had that in spades. Dakar had never considered there might be a dangerous aspect to using magic – frankly, he didn't know anything about it at all and he made a vow to change all that as he felt the buzz of magic in the air. The Necromancer, *his* Necromancer had begun.

Chapter Five

Bracing his feet firmly on the cold tiled floor, Sy grasped his staff with both hands. A single hair from each victim was laying on the skull that adorned what he privately called his secret weapon. The magic behind Necromancy required something tangible from the person they wished to speak to. A hair from any being contained traces of an individual's life from the day they died back until the last time they'd had a haircut. Judging from the length of the hairs he'd collected there was at least a month's worth of experiences harbored in the strands.

Sliding through the veil had gotten easier with practice. Sy focused on the residual life force in the hair and pushed out his magic. In his mind's eye, he was calling for "Peter" even though he knew there was a chance none of the dead men actually went by that name. But that was all he had to go on and he'd contacted spirits with a lot less in the past. The hairs he'd taken would ensure he was communicating with the right spirits.

The gray mist of the veil swirled around him teasing him with glimpses of restless souls. Focusing on a clump of them, Sy pushed harder. He'd hoped that the victims had some connection when they were alive and would gravitate to each other in death. Sure enough, after a short while four young men floated towards him, followed hesitantly by Warren who'd found a partial physical form.

"Warren said you talked to him yesterday," the most fully formed of them said, standing protectively at the front of the little group. "He said you were kind to him which is the only reason we answered your call."

The first victim. Sy recognized the sharp facial features. He smiled and inclined his head. "I only want to talk, to hear your side of what happened to you."

One of the others snorted. "We were tortured and murdered. I thought that was obvious."

"The police want to catch who did this to you. Surely you want that too?" Sy had spent his teenage years alone and had precious few skills when it came to talking to young people. But this interview was important, and he had to try.

"There's no point in us talking to the police. No one will catch the Master," another one spoke up. "He lives in the shadows, see. Like you, he comes and goes even here, although he looks different here. We've seen him since we died, but he doesn't stay here and never tries to communicate with us."

Sy stilled. There were only a handful of beings that could navigate the veil, but most weren't human and on this side of the veil those traits were obvious. Only another Necromancer could move about like he did but if the boys noticed a change in the person on this side of the veil he could be anything from a demon to a ghoul.

"The police need your names," he said quickly. "Your real names, something so they can trace your life."

"I barely remember my life before the Master," the second victim whispered. "I could barely walk when I was taken. He told me my name was Peter. All I remember from before is a kindly woman with bright red hair. She used to sing to me."

"You only passed three weeks ago," Sy really wished he could convince the boys to talk to the Detectives directly, but he didn't want to argue with them. If they felt it was helpless, he was bound to accept that. "Can you tell me where you've been all this time? Where did you live?"

"It was a big place. Lots of concrete. We were never allowed out," the first victim said, looking at the others who nodded. "I'd never seen grass until he took me out that night."

Oh, mother of God, this is worse than I thought. Worst still, Sy could feel their connection waning. "Are there others? How many, how many more are still there?"

The second Peter looked at Warren who held up both hands, his fingers splayed but his thumbs tucked into his transparent palm. "Eight more, there are eight more men like you being held?"

Warren nodded. "There were thirteen of us in total," the first victim said. "For the thirteen disciples the Master said."

There were only twelve disciples in the bible. But Sy didn't have time to discuss religion. The apparitions in front of him were wavering and his knees were shaky. He clung hard to his staff.

"Please," he begged. "Anything you can tell me about who you were, or where you were held. We have to save the others."

"I was Peter Johnson," the third victim said, his voice barely heard above the rising wind. Sy's spell was fading and he pulled on everything he had to push forward with his magic one last time. "The Master called the camp he kept us in the Sanctuary. Please tell them to hurry. My little brother is Peter number eight. His name is Thomas Peter Johnson."

"You're being killed in the order you were taken?"

But even as he asked the question, Sy knew it was too late for him to get an answer. The boys' spirits were picked up and whisked away and the veil closed around him, leaving him in the land of the living. Leaning his head on the skull of his staff, Sy panted as his brain quickly sifted and sorted the information he'd been given.

"Sir, sir, are you all right?" Brock came close but didn't touch him. Only when Sy nodded did he push through the gurneys and supported him as Sy stumbled to the nearest couch. He could feel the barely repressed fury and anxiety from the bear and the wolf shifter, but for the moment he needed to get his breathing under control. Raising one spirit was difficult. Four at the same time, well, five if he included Warren was the Necromancer equivalent of running a sub-four-minute mile. Taking a sip from the cup Brock shoved in his hands, Sy turned his eyes to Dakar who was hovering.

"We have to work fast. The killer is holding at least eight others."

/~/~/~/~/

With three names to go on, finding their records should have been a simple task. But the knowledge the boys were snatched as children complicated the issue. Most departments only started keeping electronic records five years before and a lot of cold cases, especially in incidences of considered runaways, hadn't been entered into the new system. Which meant Dakar and Brad had to slog their way through thousands of dusty files.

"What's going on with you and the Necromancer known as Sy?" Brad asked as Dakar sneezed for the tenth time. The file storage room was nothing more than a concrete box and with no through draft the air was thick with dust. Brad's voice was huskier than usual, probably for the same reason. Dakar looked over to see Brad watching him intently. Although he'd only known the bear shifter for three months, since joining the department, he already considered the big bearded man a friend.

"My wolf thinks he's my mate." Dakar knew there was no point in lying to another shifter. "But that can't be possible, can it? I thought magic users and shifters didn't mix."

"Who's been filling your head with that baloney?" Brad laughed, heaving another box of files onto the table they were using. "The Fates have been known to have a sense of humor. My cousin Tommy mated with a fairy, can you believe it? It took him a week to get the little guy to settle down long enough to get his fangs in his neck."

"A fairy as opposed to a fae?"

"Oh yeah, I don't think Pippin would know one end of a sword from the other. He's like a little sex-bomb with silvery wings."

"Tommy will be smitten then." Dakar grinned as his fingers flicked through the tabs on the top of the files. Paterson, Patrick, Peterson. Peterson! "I found one, I think." His fingers trembling, Dakar opened the file. A photo of a young blond boy with buck teeth fell out. "Warren Peterson, human, aged 8, went missing from the Pedace park twelve years ago. His mother said he'd never had any trouble at school, he was well liked, blah, blah, blah. The uniforms thought he was a runaway because his mother had recently remarried. They suspected the step-father initially, but he was cleared. Marked as a cold case six months later. Fuck."

"Yeah, no better here, I found the Johnson file. More humans, which fits with our victims so far." Brad slapped it on the table. "Their mother was killed in a single car collision ten years ago; her car hit a power pole. No one realized the two children, Peter aged 12 and Thomas aged 8 were even in the car until the neighbor claimed she saw them get into it before the accident. The police tracked down the father who was on business out of the county at the time. He committed suicide three months later. With no leads the case was shoved into storage."

"Double fuck." Dakar cursed. "So, what do we do? Visit the Petersons and see if we can find out anything there? They'll need to be advised about Warren's death although after twelve years I'm not sure how forcing the mother to do an ID would do any good. We'll have to get a photo and use that. Are there any DNA records on file?"

Brad shook his head. "Nope. Happened too long ago for that sort of thing. I wonder if your Necromancer could offer any closure for the family. He did speak to Warren."

"After he died. Shit." Dakar tugged on his hair. "You know this is going to make us look bad. They don't hear anything from us for twelve fucking years and then we show up and tell them Warren's dead and the only reason we found him is because he was left out like an altar offering for us to find."

"We're going to need to chase up the Johnson family and see who dealt with the estate. We have Peter's body, but Thomas still hasn't been found. What the hell's going to happen to him when we do find him alive?"

Dakar appreciated Brad's confidence. Since Sy had come onto their team, he really felt they had a chance at solving the case. "He's an adult now, hopefully someone left him enough to build a new life for himself. But gods, this sucks donkey balls." The alarm going off on his watch made Dakar jump. Six thirty. Dakar grabbed the files and stood, stretching his legs.

"Where are you off too?" Brad looked at his watch. "Shit, is that the time? I suppose there's nothing more we can do until tomorrow. The Peterson's have waited this long to hear about the fate of their son. They can wait one more day, unless you want the uniforms to do it tonight?"

"That might be for the best. I know it sounds weird, but I feel they should know. At least the Captain will be happy we've found something. Make sure the uniforms know to make an appointment for us to see the mother tomorrow sometime and get them to run the usual checks." Dakar looked in the file for the last known address. It was only five minutes from town. "She can come in or we can go there. Either way doesn't bother me. Whatever she feels more comfortable with."

"So, do I get to ask why you're hell bent on getting out of here tonight? Do you have a date with a certain Necromancer by any chance? I didn't remember seeing you speak to him after he did his thing at the morgue. Knowing you're mates has me commending your control."

"Even I'm not kinky enough to go thinking about mating in a morgue. Brock informed me my presence is required at dinner tonight before they left," Dakar quirked his brow at his friend. "He gave me the impression Sy is shy. I think this is the butler's way of letting me know I have been approved for social contact with his charge."

"Rather you than me, buddy, although I wouldn't mind seeing what that butler looks like stripped out of his starchy suits. I'm guessing there's some powerful muscles he's hiding under that buttoned up uniform of his." Brad winked. "I'd wish you luck, but I figure a cocky guy like you believes he doesn't need it."

"Yeah," Dakar laughed, "get out of here and take these files with you. See you bright and early in the morning."

Hurrying through the department basement, Dakar's wolf perked up, his excitement at seeing Sy again almost causing Dakar to sprout fur. His wolf really needed a run, but Dakar didn't have the time. Dinner, he'd been informed, was at seven thirty sharp and the last thing he wanted was to create a bad impression by being late. His mother had also taught him that he should never show up for a meal empty handed. But what on earth did you get a Necromancer who lived in a mansion?

Chapter Six

"Don't hover Brock, I'm busy." Sy looked down at the notes he was making. Perturbed about the spirits' comments about thirteen disciples, he was in his extensive library, researching all he could about disciples and the significance of the number thirteen.

"It's time to get changed for dinner, sir. You are having company this evening."

That statement was shocking enough for Sy to look up. "Company? We don't have company. We don't get visitors except during office hours and it's not as though I have a social life. The only time we share a meal with.... Oh no, tell me it's not my parents. I'm too busy to spend time with them. Father will just stick his nose in where it doesn't belong and piss me off while Mother will lecture me about my monkish habits."

"Your mother might have a point, but I'm sure that is about to change." *Did Brock's lips actually twitch?* Sy blinked rapidly. Maybe he'd been staring at the books for too long. "Detective Dakar Rhodes has been invited for a meal at your invitation. He'll be here at seven thirty."

"I didn't invite him. I barely said anything to him." Sy's heart started to pound in his chest. Sure, he might have had stray thoughts about the detective since they left the morgue but burying his head in musty volumes had a way of suppressing any desires he might have had in that quarter. Desires he really didn't have a clue how to handle.

"I took the liberty of passing on the invitation in your name." Brock was unruffled as ever. "The man believes you are his mate. The least you can do is sit with him and share a meal."

Sy's breath quickened; his heart was in danger of bursting out of his chest. "My research," he said quickly latching onto the one excuse he had. "Warren told me the man who took them called them his thirteen disciples, but I know there was only twelve or fourteen depending on which bible gospel you read, but then I clicked when I realized the men described in the bible were actually apostles, so I started researching what the number thirteen meant in magical terms, thinking the number was significant. Did you know all covens have thirteen members and that there are thirteen weeks between the equinox and solstice or vice versa depending on what hemisphere you're on?"

"I did know that, yes." Swizzle sticks. Sy should have known Brock could see right through his distraction ruse. "Friday the thirteenth is considered unlucky because the Knights Templar were arrested on that date in October 1307. You have thirteen major joints in your body. There are thirteen lunar cycles a year and perhaps more relevant to your enquiries the thirteenth rune is known as Eiwaz, which is the balance point between Heaven and the Underworld. The ancient Egyptians believe there are thirteen steps on the ladder to eternity and that the number itself represents immortality. The fact that the thirteenth card in tarot is the death card is also important I imagine."

"That's it. That has to be it." Sy scrabbled among the numerous pieces of paper on his desk. "Thirteen steps, thirteen deaths. All of them innocents, I'd stake my life on it. This guy's trying to become immortal."

"And I'm sure with further digging on your part and the detective's, you will find the source of this nasty business in due course. In the meantime, you need to get changed for dinner." Sy found himself pulled out of his chair and frog marched out of the library. He tried to brace his heels on the carpet, but Brock didn't even notice.

"I don't know what to talk about at dinner," he whined as Brock propelled him into his bedroom. "I never took a class in small talk, you know that."

"I know you're scared," Brock held him by the shoulders, forcing Sy to look at him. "That's perfectly understandable, given your upbringing. I've already hinted to the detective you are shy. You're not expected to have anal intercourse with him on the table. It's just dinner."

"He's going to want to do that too? Shoots, of course he will. He's a shifter. They're dominated by the basic instincts of their animal form. Brock, I can't do this. Tell him, I'm sick. I have a headache. Reschedule. Do something." Sy looked around the room, desperate to find another excuse to get out of dinner. It didn't help that his stomach was letting him know it was empty but going without a meal was easier than talking to someone who was virtually a stranger.

"Your bath is waiting," Brock was firm. "I'll lay out smart but comfortable clothes. As for conversation topics, mention a few of your more interesting cases and if you can't think of anything, ask him questions about himself. Most alpha types love that sort of thing. Now go on. Get in the bath."

"I'm going to drown myself in it," Sy muttered as he gave up and stomped towards the bathroom. Brock had been like a father to him his whole life; better than a father he was a friend, his protector. Growing up in a house where appearances meant everything, Brock was his one buffer against cold and verbally abusive parents. The only time Sy had ever seen Brock refuse an order was when his father retired and moved to Transylvania.

His father insisted Brock was to go with him. Brock said "no". To this day

Sy didn't know what Brock said to make his father change his mind. But when his parents finally left in a flurry of packing cases, orders, and admonishments to behave, Brock was there to ease his anxiety and run his household.

"And so now," Sy mocked himself as he dropped his clothes on the floor and stepped into the bath. "Now, I will go and make nice with a detective who probably wants to eat me in more ways than one." He poked at his dick which was unusually hard. "What do you think you're doing up? It's not Friday."

Like everything in his life, masturbation was scheduled. Sy didn't see a need for what he considered a useless appendage, but in attempts at being perceived as normal, every Friday night at ten pm, he fisted his cock until it made a mess. It's not something he ever told anyone about, but the action was something men did, so he did it to.

His weekly wank session was the sum total of his sexual experience. Personally, he didn't know why sex seemed so darned important. Brock referred him to books, movies and more internet porn sites than he could shake his dick at, when he realized that was one part of growing up his parents neglected to mention, but Sy was unmoved by all of it.

And now his dick was bobbing about in the water as if looking for a play date. "Go down." Sy poked at it again but it just bobbed about all the more. Huffing a sigh, Sy decided to ignore it. He didn't have a clue why it stood up on its own and he wasn't about to encourage that sort of behavior. Oh, he understood the biology behind it, but he'd always supposed some sort of stimulus was required to make it work. Sitting in a bath didn't count as stimulus as far as he was concerned. Huffing out a long breath, Sy reached for his wash cloth. He just hoped his outfit would include a shirt long enough to hide the darn thing if it didn't go down before dinner. He refused to consider the possibility his dick was reacting to the idea of seeing the sexy detective again.

/~/~/~/~/

At precisely seven twenty-eight, Dakar ran a sweaty palm down his trousers, before rapping sharply on the front door of the Necromancer's home. He was freshly showered; his facial hair was smartly trimmed, and he'd left his long hair down for the evening. He'd even taken the time to rub one out while he was showering, in the hopes he could control his urges over dinner. Urges that were already threatening to bring his wolf out.

As the front door opened, he managed a tight smile for Brock who looked him up and down before letting him inside. "It's nice to see you are on time, Detective."

"It's not always possible in my line of work, but as Brad and I spent the day going through records, it was easy to get away early." Dakar stamped his feet and wiped them on the mat provided while Brock closed the door. But instead of leading him through the maze of the house to wherever Sy might be waiting, Brock held up his hand.

"Please. There are a few things you should know about Sy before we go into dinner."

"Is it a butler's place to talk about their employer with a guest?"

"I'm sure you're already aware I am no ordinary butler. You are a detective."

Dakar frowned. "Do you and the Necromancer have some sort of a relationship? Are you banging my mate?" His wolf leapt to the challenge. No one should be touching their mate.

"How dare you suggest such a thing." Brock's fury was so intense Dakar felt he could reach out and touch it.

Considering they were standing chest to chest, it wouldn't be a difficult thing to do. "Prince Sebastian York has been under my protection since the day he was born seventy years ago. I have been in the York's family service for more than three hundred years. To even suggest there is anything remotely inappropriate going on between me and my employer is an insult to us both."

Dakar's protective tendencies backed down as he absorbed the butler's words. "Fair enough," he said, taking a step back, "although you have to admit I can't be the first person who would think that. You hover over him like a mother hen; from what I hear, he goes nowhere without you and it certainly looked like you and he were on a date when we met."

Brock relaxed his posture. "It was never my intention to give that impression to anyone. For the last year, I've insisted that Sy spend a minimum of four hours a week pursuing social activities. Otherwise he'd spend all his time in our library except for the two hours a day he spends on appointments. On that particular evening he picked a club. The entire evening the little toe rag had his wards up so no one could get close to him and he spent the whole time watching other people have fun. What does that tell you Detective?"

"Sy's not comfortable around people?" Dakar was guessing, and his analytical brain was already trying to work out why someone so attractive and with so much power had an issue being around others.

"Consider it a form of social development disorder, if you want to slap a label on it, Detective. Sy doesn't handle crowds and is only comfortable around others when he's fulfilling the duties of his position. He was told repeatedly by his father that the only people who'd want to get close to him would take advantage of him and his power. So, he doesn't mix at all."

"Surely, he must have had friends when he was a kid? What happened to them?" Dakar couldn't imagine growing up totally alone. He was raised as part of a pack, and while he'd long since distanced himself from everyone he grew up with, he still had friends on the force, the occasional hookup when time allowed, and he rang his parents every Sunday.

"Sy is the sole heir of the York empire. His father didn't consider anyone in this town of suitable social standing to allow in the house on a friends' basis."

"The poor kid." The words fell from Dakar's lips unintentionally, but Brock's harsh expression softened despite his gaff.

"I can assure you, Detective, Sy is no child. He is far stronger than his father or grandfather before him.

However, I simply wanted to warn you to be patient with him during dinner. Finding out he has a mate isn't easy for him."

Brock started to move down the long hallway and Dakar followed. "Do Necromancer's even have mates? Do they feel the mate pull like shifters do?"

"Sy feels it," Brock stopped outside of a door, lowering his voice. "He just doesn't have a clue what it is. Your mate is entirely innocent, Detective which is why I'm asking you to be patient with him."

After dropping that bombshell, Brock opened the door ushering Dakar into a small dining room. Sy was already sitting at the intimate table set for two. As Sy stood, a hesitant smile on his face, Dakar drunk in every detail. Dressed simply, in comparison to his Necromancer garb, Sy was wearing a light gray shirt that matched his eyes and plain pressed black pants. White sneakers peaked from below the pant cuffs and the only concession to his craft was the skull on his belt buckle. His damp curls framed his head in a casual effect and yet, Dakar could sense his tension and immediately wanted to put the young man at ease.

Young man? He's seventy. He's older than me by twenty years. Nevertheless, Dakar stepped forward holding out the gift he'd sweated over. "Sy," he kept his voice low; the same tone known to have men dropping to their knees at twenty paces. "Thank you so much for your dinner invitation. I brought a small gift; it's not new; it's been in my possession for some time. I thought you might like it."

Sy took the proffered book, his smile widening. "The Legends of Fenrir. Thank you. I've heard about this, but never read it. And it's an early edition," he added, opening the cover and reading the first page. Carefully shutting the book again, he looked up. "Are you sure you want me to have it? I imagine this is something special to you."

"It's a family piece," Dakar chuckled. "My mother always told me never accept an invitation to dinner unless you took along a gift. I didn't want to insult your chef by bringing wine or chocolate when I wasn't sure what we'd be having, and your house is already full of flowers. I thought this might be more suitable."

"It's very thoughtful, thank you." Sy laid the book beside his place setting. "Please, sit down. Perhaps you can read some of your favorite passages to me after we've eaten. If you can spare the time, of course."

"It'll be my pleasure." Dakar sat in the chair Brock pulled out for him and rested his elbows on the small table. This close, he could feel his knees brushing against Sy's under the table and his cock reacted accordingly. He didn't think Sy could smell the arousal coming off him in waves, but from the wrinkle of his nose, it seemed Brock could.

"I'll serve dinner," Brock said formally. "Would you like anything to drink, Detective?"

Dakar quickly scanned the dinner table. There were no wine glasses. "A bottle of your local beer if you have one, or just a glass of water will be fine."

Brock nodded and disappeared. Dakar noticed he didn't ask Sy what he wanted. Sy's tension increased slightly the moment Brock was gone, but seconds later he mirrored Dakar's pose and managed a smile. "Tell me about yourself, Dakar. I can call you Dakar, can't I?"

"I'd like that. What would you like to know?"

Chapter Seven

Sy was sure he was coming down with a fever. That was the only rational explanation he had for his clammy skin and the way his heart raced and his cheeks were burning. It was impossible of course. Necromancers never got sick. But that wasn't his most embarrassing symptom. Oh no. His dick was so hard it ached right through dinner and was showing no signs of going down. It was only Wednesday. This had never happened to Sy before.

"Sy, are you feeling all right?"

Damn, it twitched again. At this rate it's going to make a mess in my pants. Dakar's a wolf shifter. He'll smell it!

"I'm fine," Sy said out loud, putting on a brave smile. He was a York. He could handle a bit of discomfort. "You have a lovely speaking voice. I could listen to you for hours." *See, I can say nice things.*

"It's been hours." Dakar laughed and closed the book, putting it down beside him. "It's very late. I really should think about going."

"Is it?" Sy looked at his watch. 2:07. "Oh, my goodness, I'm sorry. You have to work in a few hours. Why didn't you say something?" He jumped to his feet, sure etiquette demanded he do something towards the end of a date although he didn't know what exactly.

"I didn't realize it myself." Standing, Dakar straightened out the creases in his pants, highlighting a healthy bulge in his crotch. "I've had a lovely time this evening, thank you."

Damn, that man's smile would melt my boots. But wait, he's leaving. Oh no. I have to say something. "Will you come again tomorrow? Or sorry, that's probably too soon for you. Can you come again at your convenience?" *That should be all right, shouldn't it?*

"Sy, you know we're mates, don't you?"

Batwings and swizzle sticks. He's holding my hand. When did he get so close? Sy looked up and nodded. "Brock told me your wolf thinks I'm his...your mate. Is that why I feel like I'm getting the flu?"

"Hmm." Dakar looked serious but Sy could see the twinkle in his eyes. "Let me see."

He put his hand on Sy's forehead and Sy's spine tingled. "A little flushed but well within the bounds of normality." He lowered his hand and cupped it around Sy's neck, his finger running up and down Sy's jugular. "Heart rate is running rapid, but it is warm in here."

Why is my dick responding to his voice? What kind of magic is this? Then Dakar did the unthinkable, at least to Sy. He put his hand right over Sy's groin. His hard dick! "Oh, my stars, don't." Sy pushed Dakar's hand away. "I'll embarrass myself." But it was too late. Sy's whole body shook as his balls unloaded and a warm stickiness developed in the front of his boxers.

His mouth fell open as Sy's mortification was complete. He didn't even have time to appreciate the afterglow. "I'm so sorry. I didn't mean...I have to go. Come again tomorrow." Turning sharply, Sy ran out of the room. Brock was lurking in the hallway and he almost ran into him. "See my guest out, please," he yelled over his shoulder. Sprinting up the stairs, Sy slammed the door of his bedroom behind him, tugging down the zipper of his pants and peeling the soggy boxers away from his groin.

"How could you do that to me?" He yelled at his unrepentant dick that was now all curled up pink and cozy. "I was having a lovely time and you ruined it."

His dick didn't answer. No. It was probably already taking a nap after enjoying a post-coital cigarette. "Fucking dick!" Sy fumed as he tore off his clothes and went into the bathroom to find a clean wash cloth. "You've never done this before," he scolded as he ran the water until it heated up. Scrubbing furiously at the semen stuck in his curls, he continued to rage. "Seventy years I've been alive. Seventy freaking years and not once, not ever, have you misbehaved so badly. I don't get hard when I'm out. I don't get hard when I'm with other people. What were you thinking? That is not appropriate dinner behavior."

Catching sight of his reflection in the mirror, Sy groaned. "He's going to think I'm a right nut job. The one time, my first ever date, if you can call it that, and you had to go and spoil it." He flicked his dick and then winced and grabbed his groin because doing that shit really hurt.

"I thought it was a lovely date," Dakar's voice came from behind him.

Sy froze, refusing to turn around. "Please tell me I'm hearing things. Please tell me that lovely voice is just a figment of my imagination." He carefully moved his hands away from his groin, hoping not to draw attention to it.

"Can't do that, I'm afraid sweetheart, but damn, I'm glad Brock told me where you were."

I'm naked! Sy clicked his fingers only to find he was dressed in his favorite pajama pants. The soft ones with bunny rabbits on them. "My humiliation is now cast in concrete," he said burying his face in his hands.

"Hey, hey, don't be like that, sweetheart. It's all okay." Big warm hands pulled his from his face. With no other option Sy buried his face in the chest standing right in front of him. There was a lot of it and it smelled really good. Sy might have nuzzled a bit, but he stopped himself as soon as he realized what he was doing.

"How much do you know about mates, sweetheart?" Dakar asked quietly.

"Well, I know that when a man loves a woman and they get married and…." Sy desperately tried to remember the birds and the bees talk his mother gave him when he was twelve.

Dakar's chuckle sent that darn shiver down his spine again. "I don't think any of that applies to us, do you? True mates don't care about gender and neither one of us are likely to get pregnant."

"Is that what we are? True mates?" Despite what his butler had said, Sy thought true mates were fairy tales like the ones Brock used to read to him before he learned to do it himself.

Dakar nodded. "Come on, let's find someplace to sit down. We've got a lot to talk about."

"But we have, we did, talk I mean." Sy let Dakar lead him out of the bathroom and over to the bed. Shell-shocked and embarrassed about his behavior, Sy still had time to notice *both* sides of the bed had been turned down. Brock had never done that before. A slight push on his shoulder and Sy sat down, Dakar sitting heavily beside him. Sy noticed they were still holding hands and was about to ask about it, when Dakar started to speak.

/~/~/~/~/

The last thing Dakar ever expected when he found his mate, was that he'd need to explain the sexual attraction that automatically thrummed between two people fated for each other. Sy's mini meltdown, which was so darn cute, let him know this was the first time in his whole life, Sy had got hard being around another person. No wonder the poor guy was so confused about his body's reactions.

"Sy, what's going on with your cock is perfectly natural. I've had a hard dick since I walked into your house."

"You have? You did?" Dakar was pleased when Sy peeked down at his crotch. He didn't have anything to be embarrassed about.

"Yes," he continued. "It's what happens between mates. The fates give all mated people a way of recognizing when the one they are fated for is near. With shifters, I just have to catch a whiff of your scent and my dick perks up."

"All the time?" Sy's eyes were huge. "How do you get anything done? Isn't it uncomfortable? I couldn't stop wiggling in my chair while we ate."

Dakar had to swallow his chuckle. His adorable mate was serious. "Didn't you get hard-ons when you were a teenager, just for no reason at all? Or wake up sticky from a wet dream?"

"No." Sy's frown caused a cute furrow between his eyes. "I know my teenage years were a while ago, but I'm sure something like that would've been remembered."

Making a note to talk to Brock about Necromancer physiology later, Dakar decided his mate needed reassurance more than anything else. "What you're going through is perfectly normal. It encourages us to get closer to each other, physically. When two people claim each other, it's done through sex. As a shifter, I will want to bite you, to leave my mark on you. I'm not sure what magic users do to claim someone, but you'll find yourself instinctively doing it while we're intimate."

"I'm not sure I know how." Sy rubbed his free hand on his pajama pants. "Is there some sort of rule book or etiquette manual for this kind of thing? Step-by-step instructions?"

"It's instinct, babe." Dakar gave into the urge he'd had all evening and pulled Sy into his arms. The poor man was trembling, and he wasn't sure how much of it was nerves and how much of it was arousal. The scent of it was intoxicating. Inhaling deeply, Dakar managed to say with a growl, "you can't do anything wrong if you follow your instincts."

"Like this?" Slipping one arm around his neck, Sy half climbed, his mouth hot and clumsy, but fuck he smelled and tasted so good. Using both hands, Dakar cupped Sy's head, trying to slow him down. Then he squeaked, he actually damn well squeaked and it all had to do with the foreign hand groping his crotch.

"Did I do something wrong?" Sy's eyes were wide and there was a touch of hysteria in his voice. "You touched me like that."

"Nothing wrong," Dakar swallowed hard. "It's just, your touch; it's so...so...so makes me want to come.

I'm having real trouble not throwing you on the bed, ripping those pj's off and claiming you right now."

"Don't you want to claim me? I thought that was why you followed me to my room." Seventy-year-old Necromancers who pouted should not look so sexy.

"Sy, babe, have you thought about this?" Sy hadn't moved his hand and Dakar was hard pushed not do to some hard pushing up against that warmth. "Once claimed you'll never get hard for anyone else again..."

"I don't get hard for people now except you, apparently."

"We could never get divorced, you could never be with anyone else except me..."

"I haven't been with anyone. Why would I start looking now I've found you?" Then Sy stopped and his mouth formed the perfect 'O'. "It's *you* who's not sure. I bet you've been with lots of people. You don't want to tie yourself down to a social reject like me."

"Don't say things like that about yourself...."

But Sy scrambled off him, his gorgeous face a mask. "It's fine. I understand. I apologize for my appalling behavior. You should go now." Sy waved his hands and Dakar felt a blast of magic before he found himself sitting in his car.

"Well, damn." Dakar thumped his head on the steering wheel. "That didn't go the way I expected." He looked up at the tall, dark house, imagining his mate curled up on his huge bed. Brock's words after Sy ran off flittered through his mind. *The boy is stronger than he knows, and fragile enough to break with one kiss. Don't fuck this up. Go slow.*

It was those last two words that had Dakar turning the key in the ignition. It was late. He had to be at work in four hours and he needed to sleep.

Sy needed time to come to terms with having a full-time mate because there were still a lot of other things Dakar hadn't mentioned. Like how he'd become like Sy's shadow and be hellishly protective. How that was going to work when he had such a demanding job still needed to be determined. With one last look at the lit top floor window, Dakar headed home.

Chapter Eight

Sy ignored the familiar light clinking of bone china tea cups, the smell of toast and the sound of Brock opening the curtains. He wasn't getting up and no one was going to make him. After his embarrassing behavior the night before, he didn't think he'd ever get out of bed again. *How could I have been so stupid?*

"I know you're awake and for the three thousand and sixteenth time this year, you are not stupid."

Flinging back the covers, Sy glared at his unflappable butler. "Do you know what I did? Do you know how badly I behaved? I used magic on him."

"And it was nicely done. He landed safely in his car. It could have been a lot worse." Brock handed over his tea cup. Passion Flower. Brock was worried about him.

"He doesn't want to claim me." That was the part that upset Sy most of all. If he was honest with himself, he'd admit he wasn't sure how he would cope with a mate in his life, but the feelings Dakar invoked in him were new, exciting, and addictive. Apart from Brock he'd never been able to converse so freely with another person and Brock didn't make his cock hard. Sy wanted to see what else happened between fated mates. If last night was any indication, his life promised to get a lot more exciting.

"Did he use those exact words? That he didn't want to claim you?" Brock deftly took away his cup and handed him his toast.

"No." Sy munched in silence for a moment, reliving what ranked as his second most embarrassing memory so far. "He was going on about how I wouldn't be able to, you know," just thinking about it made him blush. "Be close to anyone else if he claimed me and that he didn't believe in divorce." Looking up, Sy met Brock's quiet gaze. "I didn't know we were getting married. I thought he was here for dinner."

Brock sighed and then in a move that shocked Sy almost as much as Dakar did the night before, he sat on the edge of the bed. "I thought your parents told you about mating habits of other paranormal species when you were young."

Flicking his mind through various conversations he had with his parents, Sy shook his head. "My mother instructed me on how babies were conceived when I was twelve and apparently considered my sex education complete. My father told me that anyone who got near me would never be interested in me as a person and would only be getting closer to me to take advantage of my powers. I remember him telling me sex was a powerful leverage tool and to never let anyone get close to me like that. At the time I didn't even know what sex was. He never mentioned anyone might want me for any other reason, like mating. I didn't even know we could have mates."

"Every person has a mate," Brock said softly. "How did you feel when you were with the Detective?"

"Like I had the flu, or a fever, or something." Sy rubbed his chest. It'd ached from the moment Dakar flew out of his sight. "Maybe you should take my temperature. I think I'm sickening with something."

"You're not sick. What did you think about the Detective when you were talking to him at dinner?"

Sy handed back his toast plate and reached for his cup again. Leaning back on the pillows he considered his answer carefully. If Brock was asking, the answer must be important. "He's clever, comes from a big family who seem to care about him. He rings his mother every Sunday." Sy caught the wistfulness in his tone and quickly reined that in. "He made me laugh and he has a lovely reading voice."

Nestling further into his pillows, Sy sighed. "I could listen to him for hours," he said, thinking of the hours Dakar spent reading to him. Dakar didn't just read directly from the book. He shared stories of his own life and how they related to the shifter tales he was reading. Sy was fascinated at how passionate wolves seemed to be about every part of their life.

"Sir, shifters have rigid rules when it comes to claiming someone," Brock said slowly. "One of the cardinal rules is that they have to explain the ramifications of what it means to be mated to a shifter, before they mark you in anyway."

"You mean, that's why he was telling me those things about not being able to be with anyone else?" *Oops.* Sy was beginning to think he'd made another mistake.

"Wolves in particular, are very impulsive creatures. One sniff and they are completely smitten with the object of their desire." Brock's tone suggested he thought such a lack of control was beneath him. "After a spate of 'forced' claimings back when humans became aware of our existence; and I use the term forced lightly because every partner claimed that way was perfectly happy afterwards; the shifter council decreed that from that moment onwards, shifters planning to claim their true mates had to explain what that claiming would mean to the other person, even if that mate was another shifter or paranormal."

"Like not being able to be intimate with anyone else, and that there'd be no divorce?" Sy was starting to see that scene in the bedroom in a completely different light.

"Exactly. If you hadn't sent him to his car, he would have also told you that wolf shifters are extremely possessive, tend to growl a lot when other people are around, and they literally can't live without their claimed mate. Your Detective would die if something happened to you."

"Would he have to be faithful to me, do you think?" Sy hadn't realized what Dakar meant because no one had ever wanted him that way before. At least not to his knowledge. He knew people lusted after him sometimes; Brock often told him so, but as Sy never felt anything for the person concerned, he didn't see that as important. Dakar was big, powerful and strode around like he owned the world. Everyone would be falling at their feet for a chance to be with him and while Sy had never been with another person intimately, before last night, he didn't like the idea Dakar might share his sexual favors with other people.

"He would want to be faithful and yes, once he bites you, he will never want anyone else." Brock stood and straightened the wrinkles his butt caused in the covers. "Once claimed, you'll be his world. He won't ever hurt you, won't ever stray, and he will make it his life's mission to ensure you're always happy. How many marriages can you think of where partners can say that with any degree of honesty?"

"None." Sy spent his lifetime knowing his parents couldn't stand each other. Theirs was an arranged marriage and they'd made each other suffer for it for the hundred years since. The infrequent relatives he'd met over the years were all in the same boat.

"Which is why being claimed by your Detective is so much better than being forced into the marriage your father has planned for you." Brock patted the bed. "Come on. Get up. Time for your bath. You have three appointments this morning and then we have an appointment at the police station. Your Detective phoned this morning and said he and his partner are visiting Warren's mother this afternoon. He asked if we could attend."

"Is that a good idea?" Sy scrambled out of bed. He was still wearing his bunny pajamas and he couldn't help remembering Dakar's smile when he saw him wearing them. "You know I'm not good with too many people around. Usually family members visit me if they need something."

"You are the Necromancer," Brock said, his firm mask back in place. "It is as much your job to comfort those left behind after a death, as to talk to those who've passed."

"I'm not going to be able to do that with Dakar watching my every move." Sy's cock started to unfurl as he headed for the bathroom. *Swizzle sticks. I've got to contend with that too.*

Chapter Nine

Dakar looked at his watch. 11:59. Brock explained Sy had three appointments between ten and twelve. Apparently, not all people were in awe of a Necromancer's power, especially humans who probably weren't aware of the different things he could do. The Necromancer was often called upon to contact the dead to find everything from jewelry to missing last wills and testaments. Sy had revealed some of the stranger requests he dealt with during their dinner, like the time someone insisted he bring back an old man from the dead, just so his wife could yell at him for being caught dead with another woman.

Dakar sighed and looked at his watch again. With nothing left to do until Sy arrived, he and Brad spent the morning updating the Captain and were now back in the records room, looking for possible matches for the three unidentified victims. The relevance of the name 'Peter' was all they had to go on; searching for any missing child with some element of Peter in their names. There was a depressing number of them and as all the children appeared to have been taken at different ages, they started from the records dating back twenty years ago and worked forward.

It was a long and thankless task; not to mention a dusty one. He and Brad had exhausted their conversation over his unusual date within the first hour and now the two men worked in silence, flicking through and slowly adding to the growing mountain of files sitting in a pile on the floor. By the time one of the young uniforms came to tell them the 'scary one' had arrived, Dakar was on the man's tail before he'd even left the room.

Grumbling behind him, Brad whispered, "aren't you going to wash up first?" He pointed to Dakar's dust covered hands; his were just as bad. *Shit.*

"Oi," Dakar yelled at the uniform who was in just as much hurry to leave the dark basement. "We're going to wash up. Make sure the Necromancer and his aide are given refreshments. Put them in our office."

"Me?" The rookie barely looked twenty, his pale face bright red. "But what if he does some hoodoo or stuff that makes my hair fall out or my balls drop off?"

Dakar quirked an eyebrow. The young officer was a cat shifter who should know better. "Can you think of any reason why our visitors would even bother to do that?" Then his eyebrows came together. "Did you upset our guests?" He let out a small growl.

"No, Alpha, I'm sorry, I mean Detective." The young man backed up and tilted his neck. "I was just told to come and get you. Don't make me go near them, please. My grandmother told me they can read your thoughts and then if they don't like you...they do stuff to you." His voice dropped to a whisper and he looked around as if worried he'd be overheard.

Dakar decided his dirty hands would have to stay that way. *No wonder poor Sy doesn't go out much. How does he cope with this shit every time he leaves the house?* "Get back to your duties," he snapped, "and if I catch you spreading stupid rumors like that around the precinct about our respected consultant, I'll cut your balls off myself. Got it?"

The rookie didn't even answer; just took off running like the hounds of hell were after him. As he and Brad made their way up to the main office area, he could see things weren't any better there. Sy and Brock sat stiffly in two chairs by an empty desk and the seven or so other people in the room were all keeping their distance.

"You'd think cops would know better," Brad grumbled under his breath before smiling widely and striding over to shake hands. "Brock, nice to see you again. Necromancer, thank you for coming."

Dakar didn't even bother with niceties. He was pissed. Sy was here to help and they hadn't been offered a cup of tea. "Sy, sweetheart," he grinned and hurried to Sy's side, lifting one of Sy's hands in his and kissing the palm. "Please excuse the mess I'm in, I couldn't wait to see you. I'm so looking forward to our date tonight. Do you think Brock would mind if I took you out for a meal?"

His wolfish ears caught the rumble of surprise and muttered comments from the people in the room, but he ignored them. He was too busy being captivated by the blush on Sy's pale cheeks. It was a stark contrast to his black Necromancer garb. For a moment it looked like Sy would leave him hanging but then his mate straightened his spine and gave a regal nod. "I'd like that. Brock can take the night off for a change."

Brock made a muffled strangled noise – could have been a protest, or shock; Dakar didn't have a clue and didn't care. Offering his arm to his Necromancer, he winked. "Work first, honey, and then I can have you all to myself."

Oh, the gossip mill around the precinct will be running hot tonight.

/~/~/~/~/

After so many years in his position, Sy was used to the nervous glances, muttered comments (most of them unpleasant) and pure fear that seemed to bloom the moment he walked into a room. Brad's reaction was a complete surprise, but when Dakar did everything short of claiming him, at his work, in front of his colleagues, an unfamiliar warmth spread through Sy's body and lingered. Slipping his hand in the crook of Dakar's elbow, he felt like a king with his consort as they made their way through the busy building.

"We can take the limo, if you like," he offered as they stood outside. "There's ample room for all of us and I know Brock won't mind, will you Brock?"

"Of course not, sir." Brock opened the back door to the limo, ensuring Sy was comfortable, before sliding into the driver's seat.

"I could get used to traveling like this," Brad grinned as he managed to slide onto the wide bench seat across from him with surprising grace. "Oh wow, you have a small refrigerator, a screen and everything back here."

"Please ignore my partner's lack of manners," Dakar's grin was still firmly in place as he maneuvered himself into the car, sitting so their thighs were rubbing together. "We think he was dropped on his head as a baby."

"That was you," Brad laughed as the car started to move. "I'm not ashamed of being raised in a trailer. A lot of the best people were."

Sy sat silently as the two men bickered and joked with each other. It was clear they were good friends. His body was uncomfortably hot in his leather coat and he wished he'd taken the time to remove it. But then evidence of how affected he was by Dakar's presence would have been obvious to everyone. As it was, he hoped the smell of leather and some of the pungent herbs he had in his bag would overpower the scent of his arousal. Not that it was likely. Shifters were notorious for having good noses.

The trip wasn't long enough, at least in Sy's opinion. While he was uncomfortable around banter, simply because he didn't know if or how he should join in, he was acutely conscious of the heat rising from Dakar's body and the strength in the man as the Detective leaned into him; and not just around corners. Sy could almost see their connection and while he knew nothing about being in a relationship, he knew he wanted to explore all he could with the hunky wolf shifter.

But not now, he thought, keeping his mental sigh to himself. He almost laughed as Brock and Dakar jostled for position beside him as he climbed out of the limo. Brock was used to being his only form of protection; if Dakar claimed him then that position would have to be shared.

If? When, Sy decided. He'd do his job, that was something he was well trained for, but later…he wanted to explore more of the physical side of life with his detective.

Chapter Ten

Mrs. Peterson's red rimmed eyes and sniffs indicated she hadn't taken the news of her son's death well. There was a glowering man lurking behind her as she sat trying to control her trembling in a large easy chair. No one introduced the lurking stranger, so Sy concluded he was there for support purposes only. He remembered Dakar told him the mother recently remarried just before Warren was taken.

I wonder what surname Warren's biological father used? Could it be Warren was only taken because his mother had the misfortune to marry a man with Peter in the surname. Sy clicked his fingers and Brock handed over a pad and pencil. Magic users had trouble using any of the new electronic gadgets available, and while Sy had a secret fascination with them, if he wanted to make notes he could retrieve at a later date, pen and paper worked best.

"Mrs. Peterson," Dakar's voice was full of compassion yet tinged with the authority only a shifter could pull off. "I know you've been through this a hundred times since your son went missing, but is there anything you can remember now that could be relevant?"

"He was playing in the yard. Someone stole him. It's what I said back then and it's what I'm saying now." Okay, so Mrs. Peterson had teeth. "Maybe if you assholes had paid more attention all those years ago, then I wouldn't be sitting here having this conversation with you now."

"What was Warren's biological father's name?" Sy asked when Dakar went quiet. Probably trying to control his temper if the tic twitching at the side of his jaw was any indication.

"What's that got to do with anything?" Mr. Peterson had a snarl but nothing like the one Dakar used in reply. Mr. Peterson flicked a wary look at the detective but didn't retract the question. It was at times like this Sy appreciated the power of his position, even among humans.

"Mrs. Peterson," Sy said, purposefully ignoring the husband. "These detectives are doing their best to show some respect for your recent bereavement. I have no such compunction. I deal with the deceased every day. The bald facts of the matter, madam, is your son was taken because he had recently taken the surname Peterson. Whether his name change was legal or not is irrelevant. That is the name given on the missing person's report you filed twelve years ago and clearly it was the name he was known as among your associates or people he came into contact with."

"They fucking put me through hell when young Warren was taken," Mr. Peterson snapped. "I had nothing to do with it. If all you're going to do is slander my good name…."

"The Necromancer is right, Mr. Peterson," Dakar interjected smoothly. Sy wasn't sure if he was referred to by his title because Dakar wanted to remind the Petersons just how powerful he was, or if he was implying a threat to Warren's stepfather who hadn't stopped glowering. "Thanks to the Necromancer's efforts we've uncovered facts that indicate a rash of young boys who were taken years ago and are now turning up dead, all have names that include a derivative of Peter."

"Warren was one of the serial killer's targets the papers are all talking about?" Mrs. Peterson looked at her husband in horror. "He was taken because I married you?" Her voice rose.

"I'm sure it's just a coincidence, Nancy." If looks could kill, then Sy would be six feet underground. He traced a random symbol with his thumb over the fingers of his left hand and Mr. Peterson's face went bright red and he swallowed hard.

"What was Warren's biological father's surname, if you please?" Dakar's tone was more insistent this time.

"Jenkins," Nancy's glare at her husband was a clear indication their discussion on surnames was far from over. "Mr. Jenkins died just before Warren was born. Lloyd and I met when he was six years old."

"I looked out for him." Mr. Peterson looked as though he wanted to say more, but a glance from Sy and he stayed silent.

"This could be really important, Nancy." Brad leaned forward with the glimmer of a compassionate smile. "Who would have known about Warren changing his surname to Peterson."

"Well, lots of people I suppose." Nancy focused on Brad, ignoring her husband completely. "I was happy for

Warren to keep his father's surname. But Lloyd can be quite persuasive." Her faint smile illuminated features that would be considered pretty if she wasn't going through such a difficult time. "He felt that as a family we should all have the same surname, especially if Warren was blessed with siblings."

"Anyone in particular, non-family?" Dakar pressed the issue. "Lawyers, teachers, work colleagues?"

"Making up a list like that would take ages," Lloyd grumbled. "We had over a hundred people at our wedding, including everyone we worked with and friends of the family."

Sy could have slapped himself as he realized where Dakar and Brad's thoughts were going. "Excuse me, Mrs. Peterson. I realize Warren's room is unlikely to be in the same state as it was when he left...."

"But it is," Nancy said quickly as her cheeks took on a pink hue. "Lloyd agreed, even if he took fifty years to come home, we wanted Warren to know he'd always have a place with us."

"Do you mind if I see it?" Sy stood, holding out his hand for the bag Brock was carrying. Brock's lips tightened; a minuscule movement but one Sy was used to seeing. "I'd like to get a sense of your son and it's easiest done if I'm surrounded by his things."

"We don't hold with weird shit in our house. Now Warren's dead, his room is all we have left of him." Lloyd's voice contained traces of grief, but his arms were crossed over his chest in his best impersonation of an immovable object.

"As you said, it's our house but we're talking about *my* son," Nancy said firmly, getting to her feel slowly. "Come young sir, I'll show you to his room."

/~/~/~/~/

Dakar's wolf bristled as Sy followed Nancy out of the room, closely shadowed by Brock. *That'll be my job soon,* he promised himself and his wolf. Commonsense told him Sy was perfectly safe, especially with his ever-present shadow, but the scent of Lloyd's antagonism was challenging his wolf. Brad's bear clearly wasn't feeling much better as he got in the first shot.

"Mr. Peterson, the Pedace police department will not allow any slurs or impediments made against our consultant. While his powers might not mean much to a *human like you*," Brad's emphasis turned the words into an insult, "Among paranormals, the Necromancer is one of the most highly regarded beings in the country. Any further insults about him, or his methods of finding out what happened to your stepson will result in you spending time in jail."

"Jail?" Lloyd's glower increased. "I'm the victim here. My stepson is lying in your morgue after being missing twelve fucking years. You lay a hand on me and I'll see your ass in court so fast your feet won't touch the ground."

Ooh, you are a cocky bastard. "And how will you pay the legal fees for that case, Lloyd?" Dakar used his first name deliberately. "Are you planning to finally cash in on the insurance policy you took out on Warren a month before he went missing?"

Lloyd flinched. "There is no money. The insurance company never paid out."

"Because you couldn't produce a body." Brad nodded, flicking through his note book. "Was it coincidence then, that you made a call to the insurance company at nine forty-five last night, twelve minutes after our officers left your home after advising you of his death?"

"I was simply following instructions they gave me to update them if anything on the case changed as quickly as possible."

"At almost ten o'clock at night?" Dakar leaned forward clasping his hands together so his biceps flexed. Lloyd gulped. "The fact still remains that if Warren's mother hadn't married you, then there is a good chance Warren would still be alive. Now, I'm not the type to believe in coincidences and while I know you haven't specifically lied in this session, your scent still disgusts me. Is it any wonder your wife is so upset? Instead of consoling her over the death of her only son, you spent your time haranguing the insurance company within minutes of learning Warren's body had been found."

"You've got nothing on me." Lloyd stuck out his chin. "The law clearly states that scent evidence from a shifter can't be used in cases involving humans. I'm human." He slapped his chest.

"Which doesn't say much for the human race," Dakar snapped, his growl evident. "We're well aware of the law, Lloyd, but make no mistake, scent evidence might not be admissible but anything else we find is. You reek of guilt, anger and anxiety. We intend to find out why."

"I had nothing to do with Warren's disappearance."

"Phew," Dakar waved his hand in front of his face. "That right there was a blatant lie." He would have said more, but he caught sight of Sy coming back into the room, being heavily supported by Brock. Sy's eyes were closed and he couldn't seem to stay upright. "What the hell happened?"

"Someone used magic suppressors in Warren's room." There was smoke streaming from Brock's nostrils. "I want him arrested for harming the official consultant of the Pedace Police Department." He pointed at Lloyd. "You'll have my supporting statement and evidence as soon as I've taken care of my employer."

"I didn't do anything!" Lloyd yelled as Brad pulled out the human cuffs and slapped them on him.

"I'll call a car to pick this up," Brad said, jerking on the bound wrists.

"I never want to see your ugly mug again," Nancy stalked over to where Brad was holding her husband and slapped Lloyd hard across the face. "Your interference with his room violated the memory of my son."

"Will someone tell me what the fuck's going on?" Dakar muttered as he followed Brock who was carrying Sy by this stage, out to the limo. Nancy came with them, alternating between anger and concern.

Depositing Sy in the back of the Limo, Brock turned to Nancy and gave a half-bow. "Ma'am, on behalf of the Necromancer, I offer my sincere apologies your session was so rudely interrupted. Please, take my card and as soon as you feel well enough, call me and I'll ensure you get a priority appointment with my Master." He held out a thick creamy card.

"Thank you." Sliding the card down the front of her dress, Nancy peered into the limo. "Will he be all right? He reminds me of what my Warren might have looked like if he had the chance to grow up."

Dakar couldn't see the resemblance, but he wasn't going to fault the mother for thinking her son would look like an angel as an adult. Brock seemed to be thinking along the same lines. "The Necromancer is older than he looks." He even managed a small smile. "I promise with rest, and time with his mate, he'll be fine. Don't hesitate to call."

Mate. That's me. Damn it, I should be in there. Pushing past Brock, Dakar climbed into the back seat of the limo. Gathering the slender man in his arms, he brushed away an errant lock of hair from Sy's face, barely noticing Brock was in the driving seat and the car was moving.

"What the fuck happened to him?" Dakar met Brock's eyes in the rear vision mirror. "Why didn't you tell me this Necromancing stuff is dangerous to him?"

"Sir has always been aware of the dangers of his profession and protects himself against it every day. It's one of the reasons he has me. As to what happened, Detective, let's just say someone really doesn't want to be found." Brock refused to say anything more. Holding his mate close, Dakar wondered, even with all his strength and enhanced senses, how he would be able to protect his mate who worked in things he didn't understand. There was no question he was going to try, he just wasn't sure how to go about it.

Chapter Eleven

Sy tried to swallow but his mouth felt like he'd ingested the contents of a fire pit. He blinked and then blinked again; conscious of two things. Firstly, he was in his bedroom, on his bed. Secondly, there was a big-assed wolf, bigger than any Sy had ever seen, cuddled up to him and taking up well over half the space.

"The Detective got overly protective when I told him it could be a few hours before you woke up. He was all for going down to the local jail and ripping Lloyd's head off. We decided letting him shift and guard you, was an equable compromise." Sy turned his head to see Brock holding out a glass of water for him. Sitting up was going to be a problem, with Dakar's head resting on his hip, but with a bit of a wiggle, he managed it. Dakar's eyes opened and a large paw landed over his legs.

Sy sipped the water gratefully. "I thought you said he was only allowed to shift in non-carpeted areas of the house?"

"Don't remind me," Brock glared at the unrepentant wolf. "Your detective's got a head harder than concrete and stubbornness to match."

Sipping more water, Sy hid his grin. If ever there was a case of the pot calling the kettle black....

"How's your magic levels?" Brock continued although Sy knew his friend had picked up his thoughts. "Any lingering after effects?"

Stretching as best he could around his wolf companion, Sy juggled a few energy balls in the air before catching them and letting them disappear into his skin. "No, my magic seems perfectly functional. I've got one hell of a headache, though."

"Your blood sugar is low and you're dehydrated," Brock sniffed. "Keep sipping your water while you tell me and your impatient Detective what happened in that room."

"You don't know already?" Sy looked at Brock in complete shock. In all the years they'd been together, Brock always seemed to know what was happening with him before he did.

"I couldn't enter the room, if you remember. It was warded against my kind. I couldn't even see into it and our link was blocked the moment you stepped over the threshold. I tried to say something, but you couldn't hear me."

Sy's face heated. He hadn't noticed, but then the room was really small. He just thought at the time, Brock was giving him space to spend time with Nancy. "I'll show you," he said as his memories flooded back. Holding out one hand to Brock, he laid the other on Dakar's fur as the big wolf started to growl. "Hush," he said, not sure if human speak worked with wolves. "I'll show you, too." Dakar's head nudged under his hand and he stroked the soft fur between two very alert ears.

Closing his eyes, Sy sank into his memories. Warren's bedroom was small and not overly tidy. There was a layer of dust coating the crammed bookcase and an old sweater, child size, was slung over the back of the chair by the bed. At the time, Sy was besieged with memories of his own room; spartan in comparison and always spotlessly clean. Yet, even after so many years, Warren's essence, his feelings and emotions embedded in the walls and soft furnishings were happy ones.

"He was such a loved child," Sy had murmured quietly. Nancy picked up on it, sniffling into a handful of tissues.

"For so long it had been just him and I," she said. "I had a bit of money left to me by Mr. Jenkins, but we never had much in the way of things. But every day off I'd get, him and me would walk around the shops, dreaming of when we had lots of money and what we would buy. He loved books. Whenever the library had a sale of their old copies, he would badger me for weeks asking to go. He'd save his pocket money, never much you understand, but we could spend the whole day at one of those sales. His little face would light up so, especially if he found one of his favorite authors among the books available for sale. I had to pull him out of those bins many a time."

Sy felt a pang of something; he wasn't sure what. "Did he have a favorite book?" He asked, moving over to the bookcase. All at once he became aware of something slimy and dark, emanating from behind the books on the middle shelf. It hadn't been obvious before, but now he couldn't see anything else.

"Heavens yes," Nancy said. "It was this one." She reached for a battered paperback. Sy hadn't heard of the author or title, but he yelled as the book came away from the shelf in her hand.

"Spiderwebs and cottontails." Sy threw a shield over Nancy as a black fog oozed from the space where the book had been. "Get out of the room, now." Snatching the book from Nancy's hand, Sy pushed her away and faced the bookshelf. His bag was on the bed, but Sy reasoned the book was a key. Actually, in this case more like a cork in a magical bottle.

Simple blocking spell. First grade stuff. Muttering the words needed, Sy corralled the smoke between his hands, then with a sharp push of his innate magic, he shoved his hands towards the gap between the books, followed quickly by the paperback. The smoke went willingly enough and Sy turned to check on Nancy, confident his spell would work. But as he turned there was a loud crack and Sy found himself on the floor; the musty smell of the old paperback filling his nose as it landed on the carpet beside him.

"And that's pretty much it," Sy said shaking his head as his thoughts returned to his own room. He was still finding it hard to believe he'd fallen for something so basic. His father would've smacked his ears if he'd have known about it.

Brock withdrew his hand, his lips thinned into a flat line. "A magical flashback. Whatever gets thrown at it comes back thrice fold on the practitioner. You could've been severely hurt, sir."

"Only my pride." Dakar's fur was so soft beneath his fingers. He saw no reason why he shouldn't keep touching. Dakar's body language was relaxed enough, belied only by the sharpness of his bright eyes and the way his ears were trained in his direction. "Brock, who would be most likely to create such a spell? I picked up no other presence than me and Nancy. The spell had clearly been there for some time...."

"Are you sure of that, sir?" Brock interrupted. "The young man had been missing for twelve years. It would seem foolhardy for one such as Mr. Peterson to lay such a trap at the time. There'd be no reason to do such a thing. Everyone at the time considered the young man a runaway, even the police."

"You think the trap was laid since the body was found? That was only two days ago."

"I can't say with any certainty, sir, not without gaining access to the room myself. Whatever the wards were that kept me out, also blocked any smells or magical signatures. I'm just annoyed with myself no one thought to ask Nancy if they'd had any visitors apart from the police since they were notified of young Warren's death."

Sy realized he had a fuzzy spot in his memories. "How did I get out of the room, if you couldn't get in, and why would someone ward Warren's room against you when you had no problems accessing the rest of the house?"

"Nancy managed to drag you free of the room. She must have realized I couldn't enter." Brock looked pained and Sy realized his stoic butler thought he'd failed him. "She had numerous questions as to why there was magic sullying her boy's room when Mr. Peterson is a known magicaphobe."

"Is that even a word?"

"It's the only one that fits, sir. Mr. Peterson apparently moved to Pedace because there wasn't a recorded coven in the area. He hates magic users at least according to the thoughts I could pick up from him. As for why I was restrained by the wards, one can only suggest they knew you would be investigating and wanted to do you harm."

Rubbing his head with his free hand, Sy looked at Dakar. "Which suggests corruption at a police level or someone was watching the house very closely. Do you have an opinion? Because you should know, I don't speak wolf."

"I shall take my leave, if the Detective is returning to his human form," Brock said stiffly. "I will arrange some sweet tea and cookies for you and something more...substantial for the Detective. I understand shifting from one form to another uses a considerable number of calories."

Sy huffed out a long breath as Brock marched out of his room. There was a tiny part of him that'd been curious, even a little excited about the dinner date Dakar had talked about. But as he had been injured, Brock was likely to spontaneously combust if he suggested taking the night off now. Then there was the worrying thought that Dakar might get the wrong idea about his work. Admittedly, his magic and body had taken a bit of a battering since taking this case, but Sy hoped Dakar didn't think getting hurt was a daily event for him. Necromancy was only dangerous to someone who didn't know what he was doing.

The huge wolf moved his head from under Sy's fingers. A tingle ran down Sy's spine as the air around the wolf shimmered and then the sleek, highly muscled, and naked human form of Dakar came into view. *Broomsticks and dragon eggs, look at that. I've never seen one that big.* Unfortunately, a more in-depth inspection of Dakar's steadily growing cock was forestalled by the first thing that came out of Dakar's mouth.

"Why didn't you tell me being a Necromancer is dangerous?"

/~/~/~/~/

Dakar was sure that even if he lived to be over a thousand years old, he would never get used to seeing his precious mate on the ground. In a matter of days, just days, he'd seen Sy felled twice as the result of his position and what he could do. Admittedly, one of those times was his fault, but seeing through Sy's vision, his mate's petite form flung to the floor by something he couldn't see was, well he wasn't keen on admitting it out loud, but damn it, it was scary. Which was why his tone was sharper than his mate deserved.

And he immediately knew he'd made a mistake. Sy went from being a wide-eyed innocent, catching glimpses of his first naked cock, to the frosty Necromancer most people saw. His cock jumped, hoping to gain some attention. *Hard cock, soft bed, willing mate,* it would be so easy to go down that path, but no, Dakar had to open his mouth and shit fell out. Now, he'd be lucky if he would be allowed to stay long enough to enjoy the food Brock promised.

"Do I presume to inform you how to conduct yourself in your position, Detective?"

Do Necromancers take classes in how to freeze a man's balls in one sentence? Dakar tried another approach. Sitting up, he moved closer, making sure Sy's enigmatic gray eyes were focused only on him.

"From my limited experience your profession seems to take a lot out of you. It's in my nature to worry about you." Oh yeah, lowered tone, bedroom eyes and a half smile. *My charm has never failed. You know you want me, sweet one. How can you be angry at me when you know my cock hardens for you?* Sy's lips twitched and Dakar's cock throbbed. *I'd settle for a blow job,* he thought hoping the thought translated in his heated expression.

"According to the latest statistics released by the Police Association, law enforcement are ten times more likely to be shot than the average citizen. Stress, drug and alcohol abuse, and depression are common among thirty percent of all serving officers. Homosexual officers, while more widely accepted than they were ten years ago, are five percent more likely to be left without back up from fellow officers during a call out. While drug and alcohol abuse are less likely among paranormal staff, other concerns have been noted including...."

"I get your point." Dakar grabbed a pillow and smashed it over his groin, seriously hoping some of his blood supply would return to where it would do most good, like his brain for example. "I admit working in law enforcement is a dangerous job, but all of the Pedace Officers are paranormal, at least those out in the field. I've over twenty years' experience as a detective and only been shot once."

"Did it leave a scar?" Sy's white teeth made a fetching contrast with his plump pink bottom lip.

"I was in wolf form at the time," Dakar was prepared to take even the tiniest hint of concern. "I was healed by the time I shifted."

"Hmm," Sy frowned. "Wards tattooed onto your skin might work. That would be more effective than an amulet with you shifting. I'll have to check my books." He scooted off the bed.

"Where are you going?" *Can't you see I'm naked and needy here?*

"You need protection – against magic attacks, physical harm, gunshot wounds, knife attacks, fire," Sy ticked the items off his fingers. "Runes would be most effective, but I have to check my books to see which ones could be etched onto your skin."

"Wait!" Somewhere along the line, Dakar had lost control of the conversation. Sy stopped by the door.

"Sy, babe, please, come back and sit down."

Warily Sy came back and perched on the edge of the bed. "Sweet one, I know this mating pull is new for both of us. But do you remember the stories I read you, the night I came here for dinner."

"Yesterday." Sy nodded.

My gods, I feel as though I've known him a lifetime already. "That's right, yesterday. Remember me explaining about how protective wolf shifters were about their pack, family and mates; especially mates."

Sy nodded again.

Taking in a long breath, Dakar verbalized his greatest fear. "How do I protect you? Okay, I know I was the one who fucked up by touching you when you were talking to Warren at the crime scene, but this thing today. When you shared what happened at the Peterson's home, I watched you fall as though punched."

"That's what it felt like."

"But I couldn't see what hit you," Dakar wasn't sure he was making sense. "How can I protect you against attacks like that when I don't even know they're coming?"

Sy's face was blank for a moment, but then it was like watching someone connect the dots. "Your wolf feels the need to protect me, because I'm your mate?"

"Yes." Dakar wanted to punch the air. "It's part of who we are."

Sy chewed his bottom lip and Dakar reached over, freeing the abused flesh. The pink on Sy's cheeks intensified. "I didn't even see what hit me today," Sy said at last. "It's not as though I can die from anything like that. I'd be more in danger from someone seeking to drain my magic, rather than hit me with theirs. And draining isn't easy," he added. Dakar probably should have kept his growl to himself. "It a long, extremely difficult and complex process and with someone as powerful as I am, can take days to complete, so there's not a lot of danger to that. Not even my father is strong enough to do me harm that way."

"Is he likely to try?" The more Dakar heard about Sy's life, the more he understood Brock's faithful shadow stance.

"No, he's more likely to try and marry me off by proxy than take my power. Even if he tried, it wouldn't do any good."

Unable to resist, Dakar asked, "Why? If he drained your power, or even part of it, wouldn't that make him more powerful magically than you are?"

Sy covered a yawn and shook his head. "He'd go insane," he said, surprising Dakar by laying a hand on his bare knee. "None of us can handle more power than we are given. Humans may resent us at times;

increased strength, fast reflexes, and super senses, but among paranormals, there are checks and balances. I might have the ability to strip someone of their power, but unless I have a vessel to put it into, the increase in my own magic levels would short out my organs. My body can only handle so much. Likewise, I could raise a dead man, not that there'd be any point, but that individual wouldn't have any power of his own because his would be lost at the moment of death. A corpse can't even be a useful vessel for someone else's power."

"Because in accordance with the laws of nature, magic, life, or whatever you want to call it, no one can have more than they've naturally been given or develop for themselves."

"Exactly." Sy smiled. "Magic users are usually only drained to fuel an experiment or spell. No person can take the magic from another and use it to make themselves stronger." He reached up and Dakar felt the brief brush of lips against his cheek. "Brock is lurking outside the door with food. Are you still angry with me? I only ask because one, I am never really sure about these things, and two, Brock is likely to know, and he won't be happy with you."

"I'm not angry with you," Dakar leaned over and mirrored Sy's hesitant kiss. "A little scared; more than a bit worried I can't keep you safe, but I would never be truly angry with you."

"We'll work on these protective aspects," Sy smiled and the warmth in Dakar's heart spread. "For now, let's eat. Are you too disappointed we didn't get to go out for the meal you promised me?"

"Tomorrow is another day and we have millions of tomorrows." It was only the strong smell of roast venison creeping under the door that stopped Dakar taking another kiss.

Chapter Twelve

"There are only three people registered in town with magical ability. They are all listed as lone lower level magic users," Brad said around a mouthful of breakfast croissant. Dakar decided, during their meal the night before, that the key to solving the murders would be in finding who left the magical trap for Sy. Unfortunately, with no ruling coven in the area that wasn't as clear cut as it sounded. After hearing about Warren's death, Nancy had taken a sleeping pill and gone to bed. If there had been any visitors to the house, she wasn't aware of it. Lloyd, still in lockup refused to talk at all. Brock, when hearing Brad was researching specifically to find the person who hurt his employer, insisted the bear shifter be invited to breakfast. He even provided a wide range of different honeys that had Brad drooling as he sat down.

"The flashback spell is a lower level spell," Sy said thoughtfully. He'd decided, seeing as Brad was visiting, to have his toast and tea at the kitchen table. Dakar spent the night in his wolf form, guarding his bed and while Sy appreciated the unnecessary gesture, he'd slept better than he ever did, leaving his mind sharp and clear. "However, the wards that kept you out, Brock, are a lot more complicated."

"Agreed," Brock handed over another plate of food to Dakar and poured Brad some coffee. "What concerns me, is that whoever did this, didn't aim their spells and wards at just any magic user. We, or rather you, sir, were the one who was specifically targeted."

"By shutting you out." Sy nodded. "That in itself is a major clue."

"How do you mean?" Dakar pushed his plate to one side and pulled out his notebook. "How is that a clue?"

Sy looked at Brock, who gave him an imperceptible nod. "Brock is an extremely rare and unusual being," Sy said slowly. "Every ward is different in its construction. Some, created by someone with lesser magical skills, resemble a concrete wall. They keep everyone out except the person who created it."

"But the ward at the Peterson's house only kept out your hunky butler." Brad winked, and Brock quickly picked up Dakar's empty plate and headed for the sink. "How is that relevant?"

"To create a ward designed specifically for one person, or one type of being is more complex," Sy explained, amused at the interaction between Brad and Brock. "To keep Brock out, they'd either have to have something personal from him, such as a hair, finger nails, blood or other bodily fluid..."

"Or," Dakar prompted and Sy noticed he already had half a page of notes.

"Or the person knows what I am and that's not possible." Brock left the sink, returning to stand behind Sy's chair, his arms crossed.

"You smell like our Captain," Brad inhaled deeply. "Brimstone and…and…."

"Sulphur," Dakar added.

"Your captain is a full demon," Brock said stiffly. "We are not related."

"Brock is unique. To my knowledge he is the only one of his kind," Sy dipped his head, shame flooding his system. As happy as Brock insisted he was in his position, Sy could never forget his grandfather was responsible for Brock's creation. "He's a unique blend of dragon, fae, demon, and Necromancer bloods. The formula for his existence was destroyed along with my Grandfather's grimoire three centuries ago."

There are many types of silences. This one ranked under the heading 'stunned.' Lifting his head, Sy continued. "Brock was created by my grandfather using a golem as a base. I assume you both know what a golem is?"

"A being created in mud, usually resembling a humanoid shape, that can be briefly brought to life, usually for nefarious purposes." Brock's tone gave nothing away. Sy noticed Dakar and Brad exchanging shocked looks.

"You're not real?" Brad seemed disappointed.

"I am over three hundred years old," Brock said sharply. Then he reached over Sy's shoulder and ran a finger down Brad's cheek. "I'm as real as you are."

Brad shivered and even Sy could recognize the lust lurking over the bear's face. "Brock is right," he said quickly wanting to forestall any kind of intimacy over the kitchen table. "He's a living, breathing creation with the same rights as any other paranormal. My grandfather animated a golem, using an infusion of voluntarily donated bloods from the different species I listed before. Then, in a ceremony I was told took three days and two nights, my grandfather infused Brock with a part of his soul and a wisp from the veil between the living and the dead."

"No disrespect to you, Brock," Dakar said, "but didn't you tell me last night, Sy, that no being could assume the power of another? A golem is as devoid of power as a corpse, surely?"

"That is what makes Brock truly unique," Sy smiled at his butler. "Power cannot be taken and then used by another, that is true. But my grandfather, through the course of his spell, willingly agreed to give up part of his very existence by shredding a portion of his soul, in return for giving Brock life."

"Your grandfather drained a great deal of his power to give me life," Brock said. "He only lasted another ten years before his power gave out completely and he faded."

"I'm not trying to be insulting here, but gave you life? What does that make you?" Brad spluttered. "His servant, his slave, or his son?"

"Brock has always been a free and independent man. He could leave me anytime he chooses," Sy knew his eyes were flashing, but he was pissed. This is what happens when you tried to explain magic to people whose only claim to fame was sprouting fur and fangs. "My grandfather had prophetic visions. He knew his future generations would need protection. Brock can read minds, is impervious to fire, can pick up emotions, and travel through the veil. His strength is unrivaled by any form of shifter and if injured he heals in mere seconds. He is able to recall anything he's ever read or heard years later, and not only that, but he is my dearest friend. If anything were to happen to him, I would raise every corpse in a hundred-mile area and level this town until no one was left alive."

"It is not advisable to verbalize threats against the town in front of two of the town's finest detectives," Brock said quietly. "Especially, when one of them is your mate."

"I don't care," Sy said stubbornly. "Should my mate ever get his head out of his furry ass, then I'd do the same for him and his friends. But look at them," he waved at Dakar and Brad who both had their mouths open. "They don't understand. I consider you my father, my family, and my only friend. You bleed, you cry, you're capable of the same gamut of emotions as any other being. Your heart beats as solidly as mine and I won't have them or anyone else treat you like a freak of nature."

"I rarely cry."

"You know what I mean." Sy got the impression he'd said too much and probably upset his mate and his butler in the process. Yorks did not express intense emotions especially in public. It had to be the mating pull, Sy decided, messing about with his emotions. "What you Detectives need to know for the purposes of your investigation, is that someone must have been aware of Brock's genetic makeup, otherwise the wards in Warren's room would not have held him. As part demon, Brock can go anywhere in any realm. Unless, is there a possibility that bodily fluids of yours were shared indiscreetly? If they were, it might help us to narrow down this magic user, provided you can recall where you left said fluids?"

He arched his eyebrow at Brock, unable to even look at Dakar or Brad. He was sure Brad was ready to have him committed to some insane asylum somewhere, and Dakar was probably regretting the day they met.

Brock swallowed hard and then reached for a chair, sitting down with none of the grace or precision Sy was used to. "May I see the names of the magic users you claim live in town," he asked. "It would be helpful if you have photos."

"I swiped these from the magic users register," Brad handed Brock a thin file. "For the record, you're still the hottest being I've ever seen."

"I may also prove to be one of the silliest." Brock opened the file; Sy leaned over his shoulder. He recognized one of the faces.

"Isn't that Harmon Gowitch?" He tapped the photo of a middle-aged man, with a bad combover and rounded face.

"Yes, Sir. He came to see you, claiming his mother's diamond necklace was missing."

"You told me his mother didn't have a necklace like that. You threw him out of the house, I believe."

"You don't need to waste your time with users and charlatans," Brock said, flicking through the file. "He stunk of lust and B.O. and his only intention for his appointment was to ask you out." Brock looked up at him. "He's one of the ones your father warned you about."

Dakar growled, but Sy was more interested in Brock's face which had gone uncommonly pale. "Who is it? Do you know this one?"

The man in the photo Brock was staring at in horror, was handsome enough if you liked big hairy men with full beards. The photo looked a lot like Brad, actually. Brock straightened, meeting Sy's eyes. "I'm sorry, sir, it appears my unruly sexual organs have put your life in danger."

"You'd better rephrase that in words we all understand," Dakar growled but Sy had to stay focused on Brock. His inscrutable mask was firmly in place, but his eyes. *Brock looks broken,* and for some reason, Sy's heart ached at the very idea.

"What happened, Brock?"

"You will recall, when you informed me last week that you intended to spend your social engagement time at the club you went to. You'd heard about it from one of your appointments, am I correct?"

"Yes. I was there the night Warren's body was found."

"Precisely. When you informed me of your plans, I went and investigated the club for myself. Our agreement is, you spend your social engagement hours alone, to give you the chance to interact with others."

"That was the purpose of the contract, yes," Sy agreed. "But I know you never go far."

"Nevertheless, I still ensure that all places you go are…," Brock paused, "Suitable," he said at last.

"No biker bars for me then," Sy smiled, nodding to encourage Brock to continue.

"I went out after you'd gone to bed. I was only out for an hour. I visited the club. It seemed convivial enough for the type of establishment it was. I hadn't desired any sexual relief for some time, but this man," Brock tapped the photo, "invited me to dance and when I was sufficiently horny, took me to the bathrooms to take care of the problem. I left a deposit of my sperm in his oral cavity."

Sy wasn't sure where to look. The urge to giggle was overwhelming, but that sort of reaction wasn't considered adult behavior for a Necromancer. "You didn't think to ensure he swallowed?" He asked, and it was as if a switch had gone off. Brad and Dakar laughed and laughed. Sy let it go on for a while; Dakar in particular had a beautiful laugh. Brock's back was as straight as a

Grecian pillar, staring at something only he could see on the kitchen wall.

When Dakar and Brad finally pulled themselves together, Sy said firmly, "Detectives, this is a serious matter. Brock's body fluids were stolen for the purpose of creating the wards in the Peterson house. Every magic user worth his salt knows who Brock is. This is a crime among our kind."

"It'd be a little difficult to prove theft occurred," Dakar said kindly. "Brock donated his sample willingly, I assume."

"I was led to believe he swallowed the fluids provided."

"Is that the only time in the last month you can think of where you've been with someone intimately?" Sy asked.

"That was hardly an intimate situation," Brock replied. "He was willing, I was horny."

"But there wasn't anyone else in the last month that might have had the opportunity to steal a hair perhaps, or a scraping of skin?" The last thing Sy wanted to do was think about Brock naked.

"No."

"Then I think our next steps are clear, don't you Detectives?" Sy managed to appear to look at Brad and Dakar without catching their eye. "This issue of obtaining fluids to create the ward is a serious matter among magic users. Accordingly, Brock and I will pay this," Sy peered at the file, "Michael Forth a visit. Until we can determine the man is directly responsible for the wards in the Peterson home, your presence would be seen as unnecessary and heavy handed, wouldn't you agree?"

"He could be in cahoots with the killer, Sy. He could even be the killer." Dakar's voice held a hint of what? Warning? Concern? Sy wished he knew more about social cues.

"As the resident Necromancer and in the absence of a formal coven, issues with local magic users come under my purview. It's the law," Sy said. "At the very least, an unexpected visit to his premises would mean he won't have a chance to mask his scent."

"How do you know he masked his scent?" Brad asked.

"Because if he hadn't done, Brock would have recognized him as a magic user and sought relief for his dick somewhere else. No magic user shares his body, mind or magic with another unless he knows that exchange can be trusted."

"Even during celebrations?"

"I am not sure when you've had a chance to view a coven celebration, Brad," Sy said, standing and clicking his fingers. His shoulders sagged under the sudden weight of his leather coat and his fingers curled around his staff. "But if you have participated, I do hope you used condoms and disposed of them yourself afterwards. Brock, shall we?"

"I'll get the car." Brock disappeared.

"Sy," Dakar stood and was standing in his way. "I'm not comfortable with you visiting this man alone."

"I wasn't comfortable with the way you and your partner treated the highly secret information regarding Brock's origins." Innocent he might be, but Sy was no pushover. "No one outside of the family has been trusted with that information before."

Dakar nodded. "You have my word no one will ever hear about it from me."

"Or me," Brad added. He was the only one still sitting at the table, another croissant on his plate.

Sy looked back at Dakar. "Thank you." He struggled to know what to say. "I realize protecting me is in your nature. But dealing with magic is in mine. Until you are adequately warded I don't want you near any magic user but me. I will meet you back at the precinct when we're done. And Dakar," he added as his heart lurched at the sight of his mate turning away. "I do value your concern. Perhaps we could share that meal out tonight? The one you'd promised me yesterday? That is, unless you want more time to consider our relationship before it goes any further?"

"My mind's already made up." Sy could see the wolf lurking in Dakar's eyes. "I will claim you in a heartbeat as soon as you give the word."

There was a simple elegance and dignity in Dakar's confession that reached deep inside of Sy's soul. Lifting his chin, he said softly, "I have reached the same decision as you have. Unfortunately, at the moment, time is our enemy. Till later?"

Sy swirled around and left before he did something stupid. Like falling to his knees and finding out what the fuss was about oral deposits.

/~/~/~/~/

"Did he say what I think he said?" Dakar leaned on the table as his knees went weak.

"Sounded like he was ready to be claimed to me," Brad said cheerfully, taking another bite of his croissant. Dakar noticed he'd dipped the end of it in honey.

"That's what I thought. But what about my job, my house? I don't know anything about magic."

"It'll all work out." Brad swiped his finger over his plate to catch the crumbs then stuck it in his mouth. "First rule of mating?"

"Mates come before all else?"

"Well, that too. But the first rule of mating is the Fates are always right. You two are perfect for each other and if you stopped worrying about mundane things like making a living and where you'll live, you'd see that for yourself."

Stacking the plates, Brad put them in the large sink before collecting his files. "We might not be useful in terms of the magic side of this mystery, but let's see what we can find out about Mr. Forth. Friends, acquaintances, things like that. Maybe we'll find a provable link between Forth and Lloyd Peterson."

"That other guy too," Dakar agreed, pulling his jacket off the back of the chair he'd been using. He needed to get home and change his clothes first. "What was his name? Gowitch? Odd sort of name, don't you think?"

"Got a gut feeling about that one, do you?"

"Never hurts to do our homework." But as they left the house, Dakar's mind was more on Sy's words rather than their case. He had a feeling his upcoming date was going to change his life in way's he'd barely considered. He glanced at his watch. It was only half past nine. *Gods, it's going to be a long day.*

Chapter Thirteen

Sy shivered as he stepped out of the car parked in front of Michael Forth's shop. Like most apothecaries, it appeared small from the outside and the windows looked as though they hadn't been washed in months. The streets were quiet, but with the plummeting temperatures and high risk of snow, that wasn't surprising.

"Did you glamor your appearance when you met this guy?" He asked as he studied the surroundings, letting his senses flair. Apart from a few restless ghosts there was nothing in the shop exterior to suggest an issue for him.

"There was no point," Brock said roughly. "I didn't pick up any indications of magic users in the air and I rarely have the need to hide who I am."

That's a fair comment, Sy thought as Brock moved in front of him and opened the shop door. An annoying little bell let the occupants know they had visitors. As soon as he stepped over the threshold, Sy's skin prickled as it reacted to the magic inside. It wasn't much, he realized as he scanned the room. A few protection wards, some low level spelled items likely sold as magic love potions or health tonics, and the presence of a familiar.

It was likely the familiar who greeted them now. The tall, slender young man with a haunted expression around his eyes, bowed low. "Welcome to my Master's humble place of business, Necromancer. How might I serve you this chilly morning?"

"You can tell your thieving boss who's cowering out the back to present his ass and show his respect when the Necromancer calls." Brock loomed over the hapless familiar. Sy was always happy to let Brock take care of the rough end of their business. When he'd first taken over from his father, Pedace was suddenly flooded with magic users, all keen to be the one who could wrest his authority away from him. They were never successful, of course, but Sy never interfered with Brock's handling of things.

"My Master sends his apologies," The familiar's hair was brushing the floor. "He's indisposed. If you could leave your card, I'll be sure my Master will contact you as soon as he's well."

"Unless you wish for your Master to be indisposed permanently," Sy said quietly, in contrast to Brock's angry presence, "I suggest you comply with my companion's orders."

"Permanently?" The familiar's shock was enough to have him looking up. "This isn't just a random inspection of our premises?"

"Have I ever done that?" Sy caught the familiar's eyes, knowing Brock was already scanning the young man's thoughts. Brock's slight shake of his head was barely noticeable, but it was enough for Sy. The familiar was innocent. "Your Master is through there, am I right?" He pointed with his staff to the curtained area at the back. "You stay here. That wasn't a suggestion."

"No, you can't." The familiar leapt forward to intercept him as Sy moved. "I mean, my Master, he gave me orders; no one can see him right now."

"Brock." Years of working together combined with their enhanced abilities, meant Brock knew exactly what Sy wanted. Grasping the familiar by both arms, Brock forced the young man to meet his eyes.

"Sleep," Brock ordered, catching the young man as he crumpled to the floor. Stepping over the now sleeping familiar carefully, Sy crossed the floor, pushing back the curtain leading through to the back with his staff.

The stench in the small sitting area was impossible to ignore. Dried sweat, semen and old blood battled with lavender, sage and basil. Sy already knew what to expect as he made his way to the shivering figure, huddled under a mound of blankets.

"Mr. Forth? Michael Forth?" he asked.

"Go away. I told that wretch no visitors." The voice quivered, but the figure made no move to get up.

"I don't believe we've met before," Sy said, prodding the blankets with the end of his staff. "My name is Prince Sebastian York, the Necromancer of Pedace. Perhaps you've heard of me?"

"The Necromancer?" Rasping laughter billowed from the blankets before Forth was wracked with coughs. "If you want to talk to me," the voice continued once the hacking stopped, "you'd have more luck beyond the veil. My time on this side is limited to mere hours."

"And yet you are still on this side for now, and you will answer my questions." With a sweep of his hand, Sy magically removed the blankets, barely remembering to mask his shock. In the photo Michael Forth was a big burly bear of a man. Now his skull bones were evident through his skin and his thick black hair was nothing more than wisps of gray.

"From your appearance, it would appear you've dabbled in magic beyond your capabilities," Sy said once he managed to find his voice again. "You're fading."

"Tell me something I don't know." Forth doubled over as he coughed. Sy waited, his mind still trying to process what he was seeing. Brock interacted with this man no more than two weeks before and he'd been hail and hearty enough to attract his butler then. There was nothing healthy about the magic user now.

"All this for the sake of a few wards?" Sy asked quietly, dropping into a crouch. There was no way he'd sit on any of the furniture tucked into the corners of the room. "You gave your life just to stop my companion from entering the room of a dead innocent. Why?"

"There are forces at work you have no comprehension of," Forth muttered and Sy could see the madness in his eyes. "He who lurks in the shadows is just biding his time. You'll see. One day real soon, it'll be you crossing the veil for the last time and when you do, I'll be there to spit on you."

The naked hatred in Forth's voice sent a shiver down Sy's spine and he straightened, tugging his coat around him. Brock's silent presence behind him was a welcome support.

"What did I ever do to you?" He asked. "I've never met you before."

"You exist," Forth tried to spit but his saliva just dribbled down his skin.

"You and your kind don't belong among the living."

There really isn't an answer to that. If there was anything worth gleaning from the fading magic user's mind, Brock would have already done so. As unpleasant as it was, Sy had to do his job. Tapping his staff on the dirty tiled floor, Sy caught Forth's eyes and said formally, "For the crime of stealing another's essence for the purposes of harmful magic, you are hereby sentenced to death. How do you plead?"

"Do your worst," Forth cackled opening out his skinny arms to reveal decidedly unclean long johns that were clearly made for a larger man. "Just remember there are stronger forces at work than you in this piddly town, boy, and when they come for you, I'll be there laughing in the front row."

Sy had only passed judgement a dozen times since he took over from his father ten years before. One of the more onerous jobs in his position, he liked to believe he conducted himself fairly and never took a salvageable life. Forth was drained beyond repair, the force of his spell evident in the lack of power he held now. Killing him would be a mercy, rather than punishment.

Holding his staff firmly, Sy muttered familiar Latin phrases, watching as tiny threads of power left Forth's ravaged body, weaving their way to the skull on his staff. It wasn't a long process. Barely a minute passed before Forth slumped into the dirty cushions, his eyes glazing as he took his last breath. In true magic user fashion, within seconds Forth's body disappeared, his physical mass, what was left of it, returning to dust; ensuring no others could use his body for archaic practices.

"Did you get anything from his mind before he passed?" Sy asked as he handed his staff to Brock. The skull shimmered with the magic it stored and Sy knew he wouldn't be allowed to touch it again until Brock followed the rituals necessary to cleanse the staff and skull of Forth's essence.

"His mind was a dark and twisted place," Brock said curtly, holding the staff away from his body as he indicated Sy should go in front of him. "I did find out the bond with his familiar was forced, however. The young man will now be free to choose his own witch."

"We'll have to set him up in the guest wing then, I suppose," Sy looked at the sleeping familiar. "We'll discuss his future with him when he's had time to adjust to the loss of his bond with Forth." Another one of his duties, as Necromancer, was to ensure all and any familiars in his jurisdiction were cared for. Familiars were human born as a rule, with no magical power of their own. Instead they were a conduit for magic power, often enhancing a magic user's spells. Fortunately, due to the lack of coven in the area, Sy didn't come across familiars very often. He never intended on taking one of his own. But helping the young man wasn't a duty he would shirk.

"I'm not sure your detective will approve," Brock said, scooping up the familiar with his free arm and nudging Sy towards the door. "Until he's claimed you, the wolf will be hellishly protective."

"And after he's claimed me as well, so you told me," Sy replied, opening the Limo trunk for Brock to put the staff in, before slamming it shut. "The familiar is innocent of any crime. This young man is my responsibility until we find another place for him. Dakar will get used to it."

"You can inform him of your plans when I drop you off at the precinct," Brock opened the passenger door and laid the young man on the seat behind the driver. "I'll take this young man home and get him settled and then come back for you."

"You're not coming with me?" Brock never allowed Sy to go anywhere alone and Sy was used to his stalwart presence.

Closing the doors, Brock got into the driver's seat but turned and leaned on the back of the seat before starting the car. "This mating is going to be an adjustment for all of us, as I've said before. I'm sure your detective can protect you among his colleagues, but please advise me if he takes you anywhere else. I was planning to be back for you within the hour."

Sy nodded, his mind still whirling from the events of the morning. Forth's comments suggested someone was out for him personally. At any other time, Sy would dismiss the ideas as fantasy and nothing more. Enough magic users had tried, one way or the other over the years. *But if this threat is tied to the killings...a sacrifice to some long dead deity perhaps?*

There was a part of Sy that longed to be home among his books; he was sure he was missing something in this case. His other half's needs surprised even him – he wanted to see Dakar even if it'd only been a few hours since they shared breakfast. *I need to talk to him about the case anyway,* Sy justified to himself. It had nothing to do with the way his dick perked up and his skin flushed under his clothes, just thinking about the hunky detective. Nothing at all.

Chapter Fourteen

"We have three unidentified victims left. Forty-seven possible files of missing kids, always assuming that both our current victims and the ones still being held were reported as missing," Dakar sighed as he slapped his hand on the files in question. "How the hell are we going to match anything up?"

"Searching for ties between the magic users and Peterson isn't getting us anywhere either." Brad chucked his pen across the desk. "You know we're going to have another body within the next day or so and we're no closer to preventing it happening than we were when the first victim's body was found."

"What would happen," Dakar leaned back in his chair and eyed his partner, "or rather what does happen in Pedace when a magic user moves into town? Is it possible we've got someone else working behind the scenes, who isn't in your files? That

Gowitch might be a letch but he's more the type to molest our missing youngsters than kill them."

"We can't rule anyone out at the moment," Brad stood up and strode across to the giant whiteboard that covered one wall of the office they shared. "We have three known magic users in town, four if you include your Sy, but we already know he was at a club when the last killing went down. Hey, don't shoot the messenger, buddy, I'm just writing out the facts." He scribbled on the white board.

"We can rule out Lorna, the third magic user," he continued, marking an asterisk by her name.

"I thought you said we can't rule out anybody," Dakar was still pissed Brad thought for a second Sy could be a suspect.

"She's the Captain's niece." Dakar's expression didn't change, and Brad rubbed out the asterisk. "Gowitch is still a possibility," he said continuing to write, "and then there's Forth."

"Forth's dead." Dakar spun in his chair to see Sy standing hesitantly by the door still clad in his Necromancer garb. "Is it okay if I come in?"

"Dead? What do you mean dead? Who...what...?" Dakar jumped up, unsure what to do first.

"Here, Sy, take a seat," Brad said sweeping a pile of files off a chair and dumping them on the floor. "We're just going over what we know so far."

"Well, you can cross Forth off your list," Sy said as he made his way to the chair. Every cell in Dakar's body came alive as his gentle scent swamped the room. "Forth was responsible for the wards in Warren's room, but he expended too much power to do it. When Brock and I found him, he was hours from death. I hastened his departure." Flicking out the tails of his coat, he sat down, his back straight.

"We could've questioned him," Dakar growled, searching Sy's body for signs of a fight. The Necromancer looked as unruffled as he had done at breakfast.

"Brock searched his mind," Sy said calmly. "Not that there was much left to find in it. Over use of magic drains everything from a person and I mean everything. He was quite mad when we confronted him."

"This is still a police investigation," Dakar was frustrated, and it showed in his tone. "We needed to question him."

"Really? Question him, how? For one thing, he would've refused to see you," Sy held up a finger. "Second, he was incapable of leaving his bed," he held up another finger. "Thirdly, the stuff he spouted had nothing to do with your investigation and everything to do with a threat to me. Four...."

"A threat to you?" Dakar interrupted his mate rudely, his hard cock draining any commonsense from his brain. "What do you mean and if you're in danger, where the hell is Brock?"

"Brock is taking care of Forth's familiar. The unfortunate man was force bonded to Forth and will need time to recover." Sy gave nothing away in his expression. "The threat to me relates to a black magic user who is using the shadows to hide. I imagine it's the same person responsible for the killing of your young men, but Forth would never be able to divulge the name of that person because he didn't know it."

"Forth worked with the man, he could've told us something about him," Brad said while Dakar tried to get his thoughts in order. *Sy's in danger* flashing like a neon sign in his head wasn't helping the matter.

"Brock has all the information Forth ever had on the matter, and it's not much. I told you Forth was borderline insane when we spoke to him. Names have power," Sy refused to look at Dakar and focused on Brad instead which did nothing to help Dakar's instincts. "None of the dead could tell me who killed them except that they'd seen him beyond the veil. They also told me this man changes form, looks differently when he's on the other side."

"But that narrows it down, right? The identity of the killer?" Brad scribbled 'veil traveler' and 'changes form' under the heading 'suspects'. "How many types of paranormals can travel backwards and forwards between the living and the dead."

"Demons, halflings, dark fae, djinn, ghouls, ghosts, and hell hounds." Sy ticked them off his fingers as Brad wrote them all down. "Necromancers too, of course, but we don't change forms when we cross over to the other side. The others all reveal their true form when they walk among the dead."

"It's unlikely to be a ghost," Sy continued, "unless it's being manipulated by someone else, as they don't have a solid form on this side of the veil and you can probably cross hell hounds off your list as their interactions on this side are strictly monitored and they can't hold a human form for long unless they're mated. Whoever took these boys lived with them, interacted with them and kept them confined for years. It would be impossible for a hell hound to maintain a human façade for that long even if he was working for someone else."

"A ghoul would be more likely to eat his victims rather than leave them for us to find," Brad muttered, still writing quickly. "A djinn," Brad hesitated a moment, "not impossible, but unlikely. They don't have a long enough attention span."

"Hang on a minute," Dakar interrupted angrily. "Are we forgetting the bit about you being in danger?"

"And so are eight more boys who are all slated to die," Sy jumped to his feet. "I can handle myself. They can't and besides, there's a good chance this person, whoever he is, is killing them to raise the power to take me out."

That last statement was too much for Dakar and he let his instincts take over. Leaping over the desk, he crowded Sy up against the wall, using his bulk to shield Sy from everyone and anyone. His wolf rippled under his skin and only the intensity of Sy's gray eyes stopped him shifting. "I can't let anything happen to you," Dakar growled softly.

"You can't fight magic until you're warded against it," Sy reminded him. "Until that happens, being seen with me is too dangerous for you. We must find those missing boys."

"We've got no clues," Dakar insisted, frustrated that his mate was right. "We're just running around in circles. I'm not leaving you alone in the meantime."

"But you do have clues," Sy didn't back down and Dakar allowed himself to be pushed back, but immediately wrapped Sy's body in his arms, as Sy waved at the board. "Missing clues. The boys mentioned living in a concrete structure. Victim one had never seen grass before he was killed. That tells us two things. One, the structure is private, concrete, and likely remote but it will be handy to Pedace as all the victims were left here. Secondly, victim one was probably a toddler when he was taken. That will help you find out who he was."

"This is good," Brad said, writing it all down.

"You need to go through property records," Sy continued. "Find structures that would be large enough, see if there's any reference to a Sanctuary. Necromancers have lived in this town for centuries, but I've only been in my position for ten years. This guy has been here longer because Warren had been missing twelve years and he was the fifth victim. From what I could surmise from the victims they are being killed in the order they were taken."

"That's not strictly true," Dakar was doing his best to follow all Sy was saying. "The Johnson boys were taken at the same time, but you said the living brother is Peter number eight."

"Damn, I did to." Sy leaned back in Dakar's arms as he thought. "It can't be age, although all of the victims…. No. Swizzle sticks." Wrenching himself out of Dakar's hold, Sy started to pace. "Age. Age *is* the key here. He's had the boys for years; raised them as his disciples. Peter is older than Warren and Peter's brother is younger than him by four years.

The killer is taking them out, one a week, from oldest to youngest. There's a good chance the youngest will be no more than a year old. That's why he's doing this now."

"Why someone so young?" Dakar threw up his hands and then pointed at the dusty files. "We've spent two days going through files of missing men who would be aged eighteen to twenty today. Now, you're telling us a baby's been taken?"

"Or created," Sy met his eyes. "Created just for this purpose. Check your current records, but I'll bet a steak dinner there's no missing person's report on a baby in the last year. That would cause too much hue and outcry. He's not going to want that. Not yet."

He looked across at the pile of files Dakar and Brad had spent hours going through. "Are these your possible victim files?"

"Forty-seven missing kids." At least thoughts about the victims had pushed Dakar's lust to the back of his mind.

"Do you have a private room I can use?" Sy asked.

Dakar looked at Brad and then back at his mate. "One of the interview rooms should be free."

"Take me to it and bring the files, please." Sy exhaled long and slow. "They should've brought me in on this years ago. Dakar, if you don't mind, I am going to need you with me. You'll be my tether to this world. Brad, please guard the interview room door. No one can be allowed to come in until I give the okay. Also, please text Brock and let him know I'll be busy. If he comes, just get him to guard the door with you."

"You can find missing kids?" Brad's mouth dropped open.

"I can trace anyone if I have knowledge of them," Sy's voice was sharp. "Its part of my damn contract. This," he said, pointing at the files, "none of this was necessary. These should all be closed cases."

"Brad told me your contract with the police included an hourly rate so high, the local council rarely allow for the additional expenditure, claiming they didn't have the budget for your services." Dakar wasn't sure why he was defending his employers over his mate, but Sy's disgust was more than he could handle.

"Add that to your clue board, Detective," Sy hissed and the anger on his face was so strong, Dakar almost took a step back. "My father might have demanded a high price for his services, but when I took over, I renegotiated the contract with this department. I might have hated that the damn contract existed in the first place, but I know my duty. My services for police, fire and medical personnel are and always have been free of charge. The same for any family who comes to me worried about a missing loved one. These poor souls could have all been found years ago if someone had thought for a second to let me know what was happening."

"Everyone knows it costs the earth to get in to see you," Brad protested. "It's common knowledge in the department."

"Common knowledge, or back room gossip?" Sy produced a long scroll from thin air and spread it on the nearest desk. From what Dakar could see, it was an ornate document, covered in fancy cursive script containing a lot of legalese Dakar couldn't begin to understand. "Clearly you think I'm lying. Look there," Sy pointed to one of the lower paragraphs.

Looking over Sy's shoulder, Dakar read, *And so in accordance recognizing the position of Necromancer is now being filled by Prince Sebastian York, son of the former Necromancer, it is agreed that any fees, payments, or disbursements previously required for magic services are now to be considered null and void and the said current Necromancer hereby named, will waive all rights to payments for any and all of his work and expenses from this date forward.*

"That is a fancy way of saying I work for free." Sy's scowl was fierce and Dakar's wolf immediately wanted to do something, anything to make things right again. Unfortunately, this time he and Brad were responsible. "I always have. That means that any of these men who were taken in the last ten years, could've been found within a day of going missing, if someone had told me they were gone. The person you can blame for that, has signed right here." He stabbed to a florid signature Dakar recognized. The Captain. "Believe me now?"

Dakar gulped.

Chapter Fifteen

Sy was so angry he could spit and considering he believed that sort of behavior only fit for people raised in a pig pen, he obviously wasn't going to do it. But he was mad – boiling mad and the pile of missing person files was just the tip of the iceberg. *How could the person who calls himself my mate suggest these missing children are my fault, when I never knew it was an issue? And trust? No, clearly not in his agenda either. I don't know why I even bothered thinking there could be something between us. Led by my broken cock...stupid, stupid, stupid.*

"Sy, I didn't mean...." Dakar opened a door into a small room with cream walls and nothing but a table and two chairs inside.

"I haven't got time for this now." Sy focused on the files Dakar put on the table. It was going to take him all afternoon to get through the pile. "I need you to sit there," he pointed to the chair furthest from him. "You'll need your notebook," he continued as he sat in the chair opposite the scowling detective.

"I need to say something first."

"No." Sy should've been daunted by the intensity of Dakar's eyes, but he was more worried about the victims. This was what he was trained for – what he'd spent a lifetime honing his skills for. "Our only hope right now is that one of these files relates to one of the eight men currently sitting on this killer's version of death row. If he is, if I can find just one, then we can find the others. Anything personal between us can wait, do you understand?" He met Dakar's worried gaze. "It can wait until I've found at least one of those poor men. And then, and only then mind, you can explain why you saw fit to distrust me when you claim to be my mate."

Dakar wanted to respond, Sy could see it in his eyes, but pulling his power around him like a cloak, he ignored it. When Dakar did speak, he simply said, "What do you need me to do?"

"Take notes. I will speak as I am able to, just copy down what I say. Whatever you do, don't talk to me." Sy took a deep cleansing breath. Not easy to do when Dakar's shifter essence filled the room. "If I thump the table with my hand, then touch it. Just touch my hand."

"What will that do?" Dakar's resolve reflected in his tone.

"Pull me back from the veil. I'll pass out, but if I thump the table it's necessary."

A thousand questions crossed Dakar's face, but Sy gave him credit that all the detective did was nod.

Opening the first file, Sy touched the photo attached and read out the name, "Peter John Matthews." Sending his power soaring, Sy set out to find the first of the missing men. How many of them related to the case at hand was impossible to tell, but Sy vowed by the end of the afternoon he would know exactly what happened to every one of the forty-seven missing men.

/~/~/~/~/

Dakar flexed his fingers, he was getting cramp. Sy had been doing whatever it was he did for over an hour. One file after another. There were long periods of silence when Dakar wasn't even sure if Sy was awake, but he guessed it couldn't be easy locating a soul when Sy wasn't sure which side of the veil they were on. Just from the notes he'd taken, Dakar had enough information to keep a dozen officers busy for a week.

Fortunately, some of the boys were alive, although of course, they were boys no longer. In some cases, Sy provided details on why they hadn't been found, or wanted to be found. In other, more upsetting cases, the missing boys were already dead. Sy's tone didn't change as he reported where bodies could be found and who was responsible for the crime.

As the session continued, Dakar's respect for his mate grew alongside his anger at a department who didn't consider using such a valuable resource. However, his wolf had a different concern. Sy's voice was hoarse and he wavered slightly in his chair although he didn't stop. *Our mate needs food. Drink. Rest.* His wolf insisted, and Dakar knew his animal half was right. But Sy insisted he not be allowed to speak and after his balls-up in the other office Dakar was struck with indecision.

He didn't say I couldn't text, and as much as it galled him to have to rely on Sy's butler, in this case he didn't know enough about what Sy was doing to make his own decisions. As Sy pulled another file towards him, Dakar fished his phone out of his pocket and sent Brad a hurried message.

Is Brock here?

Yep, furious and pacing the corridor. Apparently, this shit, his words, is dangerous over long periods of time.

I'm in enough shit of my own, tell Brock to get in here and stop him. He needs food, rest and something to drink.

On it.

Dakar slipped his phone back in his pocket and picked up a pen as Sy recited yet another name. These cases were all over five years old, occurring well before Dakar had even come to Pedace. But he was still angry that so much could've been done and wasn't. *What does the Captain have against the Necromancer? Does this have anything to do with his niece?*

"Deceased." Sy closed his eyes, his back slumped against his chair. "Petrov says he was killed by his uncle on a fishing trip. His body, in his words, has gone. Fish food in the

Pedace harbor. The uncle used a fishing knife, black bone handle with serrated edges. That will be found as the boy claims his uncle never went anywhere without it." He slowly pushed the file to the deceased pile and reached for another one just as the door to the interview room opened.

"Sir, don't you dare," Brock warned, striding over and snatching the file from Sy's reach. "By the Fates, detective, how could you let your mate deplete himself like this? Do you want him to fade?"

"Don't blame him. I told Dakar not to interrupt me while I was working," Sy's eyes fluttered open and Dakar was shocked to see them filled with tears. "Forty-seven young people missing, and these are just the ones with Peter in their name. Decades worth. No one called me, Brock, not once. Why?"

"Because many people, paranormals included, are pig-ignorant and stupid about things they don't understand," Brock said fiercely as Brad laid out a picnic hamper and passed Sy a bottle of water. "This is not your fault. You are contracted to this department, but you have no idea if there are cases you could solve unless they come to you and tell you."

"I should've asked. I should've pushed more. These poor people. So many needless deaths." Sy swallowed the water in large gulps. Dakar was torn between watching the delightful bob of his Adam's Apple and assuaging Sy's pain.

"Sy," he said gently, reaching over and lightly touching his mate's free hand. "Brad and I saw how you were treated when you visited here last time. I imagine this time was no different. They just don't know you."

"They don't want to know me," Sy said bitterly as he pushed back his chair, a surge of power filling the air. He picked up the deceased files from the table and headed for the door, pushing through before Dakar could stop him. When Dakar caught up with his mate, they were in the main bull pen, the dozen or so people in the room frozen as Sy stood among them. Dakar knew they were all shifters and they could feel Sy's power which ebbed like a storm cloud around the room. But their fear was completely unfounded. *What the hell is going on?*

"I am the Necromancer." Sy's voice boomed around the room. "I am contracted to help this department. Ten years ago, I agreed to work for free for all of you, so this," he held up the sheaf of files, "didn't happen. Unnecessary deaths, every one of them. They are on your heads." He threw the files on the floor.

"What's the meaning of this?" The Captain's office door slammed open and the man himself strode out looking every inch the demon he was. "How dare you cause a menace in my department?"

"Menace?" Sy's feet left the floor and he floated, he damn well floated until he could meet the Captain eye for eye. "You call unnecessary deaths a menace? Are you calling your discrimination towards me a menace? You signed my contract. Why wasn't I told about the countless missing person cases you have unsolved, some of them years old? How many murders are unsolved? How many people died, human and paranormal alike, that I could've saved if I'd have known about them?"

Dakar could see some of the officers looking at their Captain in askance. Being shifters meant they knew Sy was telling the truth. He moved closer as the Captain's face turned an ugly red. "I can't stand magic users," the Captain snarled. "Shifters are tied to their animal spirits, they do as they're told like good little pets. But you, you are a menace. Throwing your power around like you're some kind of god. Well, let me tell you, you're not. You can be killed just like the rest of us and I'll prove it." His hand reached out and Dakar had just enough time to register giant black claws, before that hand wrapped itself around Sy's slender neck. He made to dash forward, his wolf already surging through when he found his four feet glued to the floor.

"Don't," Brock said quietly appearing by his side. "I've waited seventy years for this moment. For the Necromancer to finally realize his true worth. Trust him detective. Trust your mate and see with your own eyes what a magnificent partner the Fates have blessed you with."

Struggling to get his feet free, Dakar couldn't see anything but Sy's face turning a bright red as he fought for breath. But then, just as Dakar was ready to chew Brock's arm off, a strong wind ripped around the room and the sound of thunder rumbled overhead. Sy's hands came up and he easily brushed the Captain's hand from his throat. Hovering in the air like a black-clad angel, Sy widened his arms his palms facing upwards. "There is a reason why Necromancer's are respected around the world, Demon. Do you know why that is?"

The Captain couldn't speak. He was struggling, that much was obvious, but it was as though he was bound by some invisible force and couldn't get free. His only movement was the narrowing of his eyes and the throbbing bulge of a vein in his forehead.

"Necromancers can see the true intent of a person's heart." His arms still outstretched, Sy floated in a circle, acknowledging every person in the room. "People fear us because they don't understand the nature of death, but death is simply another doorway we must pass through during the many phases of our existence. However, we have our designated life threads for a reason known only to the Fates, and when someone deliberately allows those life threads to be cut before their time, it causes a ripple through the very fabric of life itself. Those files on the floor are just a few examples of ripples your Captain is responsible for by the very nature of his position and his failure to utilize all resources at his command."

Turning back to the Captain, Sy arched his eyebrow. "Did you want to speak? Did you want to explain to these fine upstanding officers that you demean as pets under your control why you furthered the rumor my services were never used because the local council wouldn't allow the increase in budget required? You can speak." Sy waved his hand. "I love how shifters can smell a lie."

"Your days are numbered, Necromancer," the Captain rumbled. "You might get rid of me, but there are others out there who will gladly spit on your grave."

"That's the second time I've been told that today – maybe you guys should form a club," Sy said airily. "But, as a Necromancer, demon punishments fall under my jurisdiction, don't you agree? Therefore, in accordance with my position, and with full agreement of the local council and the higher governing councils concerning magic, Demon, Bal...."

His words were cut off as a shot rang out. Dakar snarled at Roger, the Captain's assistant, standing behind the Captain with a smoking gun in his hand. "I won't allow it," Roger's voice trembled as badly as his hands around the gun. "I won't allow anyone to kill or punish him. The Captain's a good man...honest...he...he...." Roger's eyes widened so far, Dakar thought they were going to fall out. "Why aren't you dead?"

Shit. Sy! Dakar was so wrapped up in trying to get to Roger he didn't give a thought to where the bullet had gone.

His mate still floated above the floor, but now there was a growing blood stain only noticeable with shifter eyes blossoming on the black of his shirt.

"I really wish you hadn't done that," Sy sighed as he held his hand above his chest and a spent bullet appeared in his hand. "Now I have a hole in my best work shirt." He didn't seem to notice the blood, but Dakar could smell it and his wolf snarled and curled his lips up showing his teeth. "It's all right, Dakar, it would take more than a bullet to take me down. I could pass through a hail of bullets and the only inconvenience would be when Brock has to buy my new clothes."

Turning back to the Captain and his sidekick, Sy smiled. "Now, where was I? Oh, yes. Roger. I know you thought you were doing the right thing, but you weren't. It's an offence to shoot at a Necromancer, especially one under contract with the department. Brad will take you into custody shortly."

"As for you Captain, because you managed to inspire loyalty in one person, even if that person was misguided, you shall live for now. However, as Necromancer, I sentence you to a full demon lifetime in the pits, sentence to be carried out once the detectives here have questioned you with regards to your knowledge of the serial killer currently working among us. Oh yes," Sy continued as gasps rang around the room, "don't think I missed that little comment you made about my meeting a bitter end. It's the same thing Forth said to me this morning before he died." Lightening zapped from Sy's fingers to the Captain's arms, leaving him with solid silver cuffs engraved with runes. "No amount of magic or force will enable these to be removed before I say so. And remember, Captain, I know your true name and there isn't anywhere in heaven, earth or hell that I can't find you."

Floating down until his feet were flat on the tiles again, Sy nodded to Brock. "Please let the detective go, Brock, and see to it these two fools are secured somewhere safe. I really need to eat something."

"Yes, sir," Brock bowed but that was all Dakar saw because in the next breath his feet were free, and he raced to his mate who welcomed his furry form with open arms. This close, Dakar could tell his mate's strength was completely spent. Unwilling to let anyone see him in that condition, Dakar shifted. Ignoring his nudity, he swept Sy into his arms as though in a passionate embrace and hurried out of the room.

Behind him, the bull pen was in chaos, officers wanting to know what the hell was going on as Brad and Brock subdued their captives. But Dakar's only thought was for Sy and as he closed the door to the small interview room and arranged Sy on his lap and assembled a sandwich from the food Brad and Brock provided, he realized his focus was exactly as it should be between mates. He was an idiot for not realizing that before.

Chapter Sixteen

Sy lolled against Dakar's broad chest, too tired to care that his detective was naked. His mouth moved automatically, chewing the bite sized pieces Dakar was feeding him without tasting anything. Nothing in his father's training prepared him for the blatant discrimination shown by the Captain but then he'd only met the demon once before and that was at his contract signing. At the time, he put the malice stemming from the man down to disrespect because he looked so young. But it appeared the Captain's feelings ran far deeper than that.

"Do you think we could focus on us for just one minute," Dakar asked quietly as Sy found another morsel of food tucked into his mouth. "I know…I mean…you were wonderful out there."

"Powerful you mean. The joys of being a Necromancer from an ancient family line." Sy pushed away Dakar's next offering. He was too tired to eat. He could feel the heat of Dakar's body through his leather coat and he put his hand up to stifle a yawn. "The people you work with still hate me. I wish they didn't, because there's so much I could offer a place like this, but if I'd pushed harder, earlier, then maybe lives could've been saved."

That was what upset Sy the most. Yes, he'd chaffed being under any form of contract at all, but that was just part of his nature. He could never hold down a full-time job because he liked the freedom to get up when he pleased, go to bed when he pleased and work when he wanted to. But what the Captain had done was criminally negligent. Sy had the power to help in so many cases, and maybe if he had, then he wouldn't have just faced down a room full of suspicious shifters.

"Whatever it is you're thinking, don't," Dakar said gently and Sy's eyes closed as a rough finger traced along his jaw. "You and me, we seem the have the same ideas and want to follow the same path together, but somehow life and attitude get in the way and it's not as though we know each other very well yet. I didn't mean for you to think I didn't trust you when we were having that hassle over your pay. I've only been in this department three months as it is. If I can't show loyalty to the people who sign my paycheck, then that goes against my animal nature."

Sy was almost asleep, his eyes lulled shut from Dakar's soft tones, but they flew open again at that comment. But it seemed Dakar hadn't finished explaining himself as a thick finger pressed against his lips. "But I should've shown my loyalty to you above everything else and my only excuse for why I didn't was we were here in my place of work and it's like my brain was in work mode. Sy, I haven't even claimed you yet and I'm already thinking of how I can change my life so that we can be together all the time."

"All the time?" Sy studied Dakar's strong face. "I warn you now, you'll get hellishly bored. I spend most of my days with my nose buried in ancient books."

"But that's not going to continue, is it?" Dakar didn't seem the least bit worried about how Sy spent his lonely days. "You want to work more with this department. There's a mountain of cold cases that need clearing. You have your appointments that you see at home too, and my family will want to meet you at some point after we've mated. With all that and the rampant sex we'll have, I doubt we'll be bored."

"Rampant sex?" Sy was sure his voice squeaked. All at once his tiredness disappeared as he was suddenly aware of where he was, and the fact Dakar still hadn't put any clothes on. *I'm sitting on a naked lap and Dakar's not carrying a gun, which means that lump pressing into my hip....*

"I know you're not ready today," Dakar said softly. "You've used a lot of energy and I don't want you to fall asleep during our first time together."

"I doubt that's even possible," Sy said, swallowing hard. He thought for a long minute and realized Dakar was right. They didn't know each other very well yet, and he was just as prone to over reacting as Dakar seemed to be. "I don't have experience with relationships. I mean, I'm sitting on your naked lap, your dick is digging holes in my pants, or trying to, and while my own dick is...is...is in the same state," he rushed that last part but damn it, if he was going to use said body part he needed to be able to talk about it. "I've still got files to go through. We must find more clues to where these missing men are being held. But when you mention rampant sex, I...er...I want to know about that too, but at the moment we can't. Because of those missing men. Not because I don't want you, I mean. Do you get what I mean?"

"I understand what you mean." There were flecks of green in Dakar's eyes, Sy never noticed before. They seemed more pronounced when Dakar was horny. And the big wolf shifter was definitely horny. Even Sy, with most of his virgin boxes still fully checked, could see it. "Work first, then our dinner date and after that I'm going to take you home and stay with you." Dakar wriggled his eyebrows. "All night. In my human form this time. In your bed, with you. Just in case you were in any doubt about it."

"No doubts." Sy tried to press down on his own length to stop it leaking into his pants but it didn't help. If anything, it made matters worse. "You should be dressed." A click of the fingers took care of that.

Dakar chuckled and ran a finger down Sy's flushed cheek. "I love that I can make you blush. I'm going to kiss you now, before you get back to what you were doing, and Sy, this time when I think you've done enough and need a break, I'm going to stop you, okay?"

Sy's response was swallowed by the heat and passion behind Dakar's kiss. Curling his toes, Sy hung onto Dakar's arms; for once his mind was blissfully silent.

/~/~/~/~/

It was getting on for five in the evening. In between writing notes and making Sy take a break every half an hour or so, Dakar made reservations at his favorite restaurant for them both for seven thirty. He was eagerly anticipating a quiet romantic evening where he could woo his sheltered mate with fine wines, succulent steaks and sexy touches under the tablecloth. His mind was dwelling on all the different ways he was planning to use to reduce Sy to nothing more than a trembling mess when Brock slapped him on the arm. Dakar immediately looked at Sy, who was still in what he'd named a trance state, purely because he wasn't sure how else to describe it.

"Roy Peters," Brock hissed against his ear, stabbing his finger at Dakar's notepad. "Sir thinks there's a link to the killer."

Sy was deathly still, his eyes closed, his mouth twitching as though he was mentally talking, but then the words became audible. "You were taken... five years old... concrete rooms... barred windows... spikes on walls... meetings... what? How? Can you smell him? Sour... lemons... something old... can you take me back? ... show me... it's okay... I'll... okay, all right ... hold tight... here we go."

He's spirit walking, Brock scribbled on Dakar's note pad. *I'm not getting much, they're moving too fast. Hang on, hang on, I know that area.* "Touch him now."

"He'll fall asleep. We've got a dinner planned in two hours," Dakar hissed.

"You won't have time for your date. You'll be too busy arresting people," Brock snarled as he reached over and touched Sy's hand. Immediately, Sy slumped on the table, his head resting on his arm.

"Why couldn't he come back on his own," Dakar growled as he pushed past Brock and pulled Sy into his arms. "If he'd come back on his own, then we'd have known what he'd seen."

"I could see where it is," Brock scribbled an address on Dakar's notepad, tore the page off and thrust it at him. "Let me take the Necromancer home while you do your job. Detective, I know how patient you've been. I'm sick of the smell of your arousal. But there's going to be another killing. The victim is being prepared for a ritual sacrifice as we speak. He only has a few hours of life left. Because the ritual was magic in nature, it threatened to pull sir in and he needed to be brought back before his presence was detected."

"I do not have a fucking clue what you are talking about when you go on about this magic stuff." Dakar looked at his sleeping mate, then at the scrap of paper in his hand. Heaving a sigh, he carefully handed Sy over to Brock. "Take him home. I'll be there as soon as this business is over."

"I'll keep dinner for you and your bear friend," Brock gave a half smile. "You know you're doing the right thing."

"I know my balls are going to burst and my wolf's going to make an appearance if I don't get to claim my mate soon." Dakar tugged his pants from around his swollen cock.

"The Necromancer will be fully rested by the time you get back."

Rested. He'll be ready to...oh, my gods, soon wolf. Soon. But first, my friend, we hunt. With his wolf howling in his head, Dakar brushed a kiss on Sy's forehead and ran from the room. "Brad! Gather the troops. Everyone we can spare. I want surveillance, pictures, maps, plans, anything you can get on this address. We're heading out in thirty minutes, so move it, people. We've finally got a fucking lead."

Chapter Seventeen

"I remember this place," Brad whispered as he crept up beside Dakar and peered through the foliage. The winter sun was long gone, and the forbidding structure looked all the more impenetrable thanks to harsh spotlights that flooded every corner of it. "It used to be a school."

"A school for who? Demons?" Dakar shook his head. There was nothing welcoming about the solid concrete walls, complete with twelve-inch iron spikes that fanned out from the top of the walls at an angle making them impossible to climb over. "I'm more worried about how the hell we can get in there."

"There's a supply entrance, sir." The young cat shifter who'd been so scared of speaking to a Necromancer, crept over and pointed to the left of where Dakar was crouching. "According to control, it's the least guarded entrance although they warned of possible wards. There's a lot of static showing on the camera feed."

"And I suppose the only magic users we had capable of breaking the wards was the Captain, or the Necromancer, both of whom are out of commission." Dakar scratched his forehead.

"Can't Brock do it?" Brad asked, holding up his phone. "I could at least text him and ask."

"He's not going to want to leave Sy." *I don't want him to leave Sy, but if we don't get through these wards then another innocent man is going to die.* "Do it. He knows how damned important this is."

While Brad busied himself with his phone, Dakar scanned the building. If it wasn't for the lights, the place would look deserted. Overgrown grass reached at least a foot up the walls. There were cobwebs blowing between the metal spikes and the driveway leading up to the main gate was so overgrown with weeds it was barely visible. But it was more than just the visual aspects that made Dakar pause. There was no noise in the crisp cool air. Not the twitch of a bird, insect or rodent. It was as if every living creature knew better than to approach. Even the cobwebs looked old and long abandoned.

"Well?" Dakar asked as Brad put away his phone.

Brad pointed over his shoulder and Dakar turned to see the man materialize in front of him. "Yes, this is the place," Brock said in a deep voice as he spread his arms, his neck tilted as he sniffed the air. "This is where you will find the missing victims, and I will destroy the one who seeks to harm my Master."

"You get all that from one sniff?" Brad asked.

Brock looked at Brad and Dakar would swear the man's lips twitched, but anything that was going to be said was forgotten as the young cat shifter sprinted over, his eyes white with fear. "I heard a scream, around the back."

"We must hurry," Brock said, running in the direction the cat pointed, his feet making no sound on the ground debris. Dakar followed, with Brad coming up behind. "Shift, detectives," Brock said quickly. "Shift, all of you who can. You'll be less susceptible to magic in your furry forms."

There was a flurry of clothing as a dozen men and women of various shapes and sizes flung off their clothes and initiated their shifts. There was a lot of nervous energy spiking the air. Since the Captain's imprisonment, many of the officers felt lost and betrayed. More than one of them had come up to him and offered a muttered apology and congratulations on finding his mate while they'd prepared for this mission. Never had Dakar been so thankful for a shifter's innate sense of duty than he was in this moment.

"On my mark." Brock held up his hands, pushing at something that Dakar couldn't see. But he could feel it; like an invisible steel wall. As Brock worked to break through, the magic made Dakar's fur stand up on end. A sole drop of sweat ran down the side of Brock's face, the muscles under his shirt straining the seams with his efforts. Just when Dakar thought there was no way he would get through, there was a loud pop and it was as if suddenly everyone could breathe again.

"Quickly," Brock warned, lifting his leg and kicking at the solid door, which flew open under his boot. "The devil knows you're here."

Shaking his fur, Dakar dashed inside, followed closely by Brad's bear form. The air inside the building was surprisingly clean; the doorway opening midway in a long corridor. To one side, Dakar could scent the faintest traces of blood. To the other…Dakar flickered his ears in amazement. Children. He could hear young children singing. He nudged Brock's leg with his nose and flicked his head in the direction of the singing.

"Oh yes, they must be taken out of here tonight," Brock agreed. "You, you, you, and you," he pointed out to four different cat breeds. "Move quickly and quietly but get those children to safety. Brad, you can cover them."

The huge grizzly planted his feet firmly on the tile and shook his head, lifting his snout in the direction of the blood. Brock threw up his hands in exasperation. "You then," he said pointing to a wolf Dakar knew only as Steven. He was one of the uniforms and his human form was as solid as his wolf. "Cover them, don't worry about anything else, just get those kids out of here and to safety immediately." Steven nodded and ran after the cats in the direction of the singing.

"This way," Brock said, sprinting in the opposite direction. The smell of blood got stronger the further down the hall they went. Towards the end of the corridor was a large double wooden door, covered in runes and exotic designs. Brock didn't stop. He just planted his foot into it and ran inside. Dakar was hard on his heels, his claws slipping on the polished tiles as the butler came to a stop.

The room was the stuff of nightmares. Stainless steel marred with blood smears ran up the walls. The floor tiles were originally white, but they too were splattered with blood, some old, some fresh. Across the back wall was a solitary shelf containing thirteen glass jars. Five of them contained human hearts.

The hair on the back of Dakar's neck rose as he spotted a black robed figure bending over the slender form of another teenager; a blood covered knife in his hands.

"Don't move, you freak of nature or the boy gets this knife right through his heart." The voice was harsh, as if dull through lack of use.

"You're the reason I was created," Brock roared, throwing himself at the hooded man. The two men fell to the floor in a flurry of limbs and punches. Dakar needed thumbs and with a single thought, shifted to his human form. Hurrying to the steel table, he checked the young man's faint pulse; Brad still furry by his side.

"Carry him out of here," Dakar said, one eye on the fighting pair and the other on the young man. "I'll stay to help Brock."

The scents coming from Brad were mixed and Dakar wondered if his partner was more emotionally invested in Brock than he'd thought. But with minimal hesitation, Brad sidled up to the steel table. Dakar draped the body over the bear's back, but the boy was unconscious and couldn't hold on.

"You have to shift, he'll fall off." Dakar didn't want to hurt the young man any further, but when the fighting duo got perilously close to the table, he had no choice but to swing the injured man into his arms. Grunts and muttered curses filled the air along with the buzz of magic. Rather than shift, Brad stood up on his back legs, his furry head lightly grazing the ceiling, holding out his arms. Dakar barely had time to get the young man settled before the steel table went flying into the air.

"Go. Go," he yelled, letting his wolf take control again. He wasn't sure how much help he would be for Brock, especially with the magic in the air. But he could distract the robed man, keep him off balance. Crouching low, his ears flicking madly, Dakar waited for his chance, lunging in and taking a bite whenever the evil doer got close. The stench was nothing he'd ever smelled before – rancid almost, definitely more in tune with rotting meat than a human or magic user smell. Whoever the man was though, he was strong and not prepared to give up. Brock's cheek was smeared with blood, his hair a mess. His black shirt was ripped along the shoulder seam and his pants were torn in two places Dakar could see.

A boot to his ribs made Dakar snarl. *This is the man who's trying to kill our mate.* His wolf wasn't the giving up type either. Rather than sit in the shadows, Dakar leapt forward as a cloud of black smoke rose from where Brock and the killer were fighting. He staggered back as the smoke filled his lungs. He heard a warning yell from Brock, but it was too late. The last thing Dakar remembered was his head hitting the unforgiving tiles.

/~/~/~/~/

Sy woke with a start, his heart pounding, his breath ragged. Using their bond, he tried to get in touch with Brock, but all he got was static. That in itself was a warning signal. As he jumped off the bed, he tried to remember the last thing he'd been doing. *At the precinct. I got a link. Flea-bitten Hellhounds, they've gone without me.* Sy's heart ached. Brock had been his rock for decades and Dakar...*He cares about me* and for Sy that was a rare and precious gift he wasn't prepared to lose.

Now is not the time to sit around like a wilting daisy, he told himself firmly as he sent out his powers looking for Brock's last known whereabouts. The link he got was faint, as though it was blocked by magic. But it was enough for Sy to act on. Pulling on his finely honed magic skills, Sy disappeared from his bedroom.

/~/~/~/~/

Brock's fury grew as he saw Dakar's beautiful wolf form slumped on the floor. Baring his teeth, he shook his head at the killer who was staring at him aghast. "Magic doesn't work on me, idiot."

The killer regained his senses quickly and laughed. "But your pet's not immune. How sad. Too bad. Tell me how to kill you, golem and I'll make it quick."

"What makes you think I can be killed?" Brock snarled as he reached for the killer's robes. "I was created with you in mind." Tugging the man to his feet, Brock grabbed the side of the killer's neck. "You, however are nothing more than flesh and blood."

"Magic beast, your deed is done, return to dust from where you come," the killer babbled, his fingers tugging at Brock's hand.

Brock stood firm, his grip never wavering. "Not while I have a master to protect."

"The Necromancer must be stopped. He threatens us all." The killer coughed.

"And killing innocent young men is your way of doing it?"

"I'm just the tool." The killer smiled showing a mouthful of missing teeth. "Collecting the ingredients needed for my master's spell. You can't stop him. He sees all, he knows what you are doing."

"Then he can watch this." With one quick twist of his hand, the killer's neck was broken. But the things Brock saw in his mind lingered and a shiver ran down his spine. Dropping the killer's body, Brock turned to see Sy hovering over Dakar's body as if unsure of what to do. *Tears do not belong on that young man's face,* he thought as he hurried over and picked Dakar up from the floor.

"Ingested magic," he said quickly. "He will need your powers to counter the spell, but not here. Don't use your magic here."

"But Dakar... and you. What happened to you?"

"I'm fine. Nothing a bath won't cure. And Dakar will be fine after you've cleared the spell and he's had a good night's sleep," Brock promised. "It is your turn to look after him for a change."

Chapter Eighteen

Rolling over, Dakar rubbed his head. "Did you get the number of the truck that hit me?" He asked as he opened his bleary eyes. The first thing he noticed was that he was in Sy's bed and he inhaled sharply, letting his mate's scent work its magic on his tired body. Turning slightly, he saw Sy was sitting in a large chair, the skin under his eyes bruised, his curls a mess and his eyes were dull as though he hadn't slept for a week. "You look tired, sweetness. Come over here. I don't bite." He patted the covers beside him.

"Brock told me you'd need food as soon as you woke up." Sy's elegant fingers were twisting on his lap. "Shifter metabolism is faster than other paranormals and humans, requiring large amounts of food to keep the animal side strong. You've been hurt…you…." Sy's voice broke.

Shaking the last dregs of sleep from his system, Dakar sat up and swung his legs over the bed.

"You can't get up until you've fed." Sy jumped up from his chair. "I'll get Brock. He can...he can...."

"I need to hold you," Dakar said firmly. "My wolf doesn't like you being so far away from us, especially after last night."

"Last night? Last night? It's been three days. You've been here three days, just lying there...," Sy mumbled as he took a step closer and all at once Dakar understood why his mate was upset.

"Come here, please," he begged softly. "All I want to do is hold you. I want to hold you in my arms while you tell me what I missed."

"I've never been so frightened for another person before," Sy admitted, his voice nothing more than a whisper as he stepped into Dakar's embrace. "Brock said, he told me the magic was meant for him. If you'd been a smaller man, or in your human form you would've died. You didn't shift back until last night. I don't understand what I'm feeling but I don't like it and I don't know how to handle it."

"Oh Sy," Dakar knew exactly what Sy was feeling; the same way he'd felt since he knew the young Necromancer was his mate. "You care about me and that's exactly the way it should be between mates. You were scared for me and you've no idea how good that makes me feel." Raising Sy's face gently with his hands, up close Dakar could see how stressed his mate had been and something in his heart unfurled. "We have a connection, you and I. Once claimed, you will always know where I am or if I'm in any danger. You've promised me wards on my skin to help protect me from something like this ever happening again and if for some reason, the Fates felt it was time for me to pass, I would never leave the edge of the veil, no matter what forces compelled me to. I will always, in this life and the next, want you close to me."

"You won't die!" Sy said fiercely, his fingers curled around Dakar's shoulders like a vice. "I won't allow it. What use is it you having a Necromancer for a mate if I can't save you? You have to claim me, I must claim you. You need those wards, but no, Brock said you needed to eat first. Please, let me get him and then…."

Not likely. Dakar gave into his instincts. His mate was bordering on hysterical, albeit quietly and while he could understand the maelstrom of feelings swirling around Sy's body, the Necromancer didn't. With no concept of mates, Sy had no idea what is was like to crave being so close one man couldn't tell where he finished, and his mate started; where breaths were shared along with every heartbeat. Dakar understood it and without giving it a second thought, he fused his lips over Sy's, exhaling gently from his nose.

Sy froze for just one second, and Dakar had to remind himself it wasn't a rejection. Something that was made clear in the very next blink. Pressing closer, Sy's hot hands flew across Dakar's back muscles while his lips twitched under Dakar's own. Teeth and tongue were involved, and Dakar recognized that for what it was. But what Sy lacked in technique, he made up for with enthusiasm.

Taking a chance, one his cock would never forgive him for if he didn't try, Dakar tugged at and then slipped his hands under Sy's shirt. He was sure Sy could feel his heartfelt groan right down to his toes. Sy's skin was smooth as velvet with not a blemish Dakar could feel. He felt the rumblings of his own stomach, no doubt complaining about the lack of food, but Dakar needed his connection with his mate so much more.

Falling back on the bed, he brought Sy with him, finally wrenching his mouth free when breathing became paramount. "Tell me you want this," he growled around his fangs.

"I do," Sy panted. His flushed lips were puffy and slick with Dakar's saliva and his nostrils flared as though he struggled to breathe. "I don't want to be apart from you anymore. These last three days have played hell with every part of my being. You have to help me, I don't know what to do, but I want to be your mate, I promise I do."

Thank you. Thank you. Thank you. Wasting no time, Dakar rolled them over, pushing Sy's shirt up to his chin as he nuzzled the soft skin of his mate's belly. Sy wasn't ripped like most of the partners he went for, but Dakar hadn't realized what he'd been missing. The softness, the smell that permeated Sy's skin, the leaking hardness in Sy's pants all filled Dakar with emotions he wasn't used to either. So, he focused on the one he knew best – lust.

The smell of precome assaulted his nose as Dakar tugged at Sy's zipper. From the damp spot on Sy's boxers, his mate wasn't going to last long enough for Dakar to do what he had to do. *I hope he's got a good recovery period.* But of course, all of that was moot. This was their claiming. In a matter of mere minutes, they would be as one no matter when Sy got his orgasm. Dragging the pants and boxers down lean legs Dakar buried his nose in the dark curls that framed Sy's dick.

"Yum," he grinned up at Sy's shocked expression before licking along the length he'd exposed. "I love a good-sized cock in my mouth."

"Yeah, well, get used to that one, because you're not having anyone else's." Sy's voice turned into a wail as Dakar sucked the mushroomed head, his mouth filling with spunk almost instantly. He wanted to chuckle; not an easy thing to do with his mouth full, but he sensed Sy's embarrassment and just swallowed before licking his mate's length clean.

"Delicious," he said, sitting up and licking his lips. "Please tell me you have lube."

Sy muttered something into the pillow he was clinging to.

"What was that?"

"I'm already ready, you know, down there." Sy waved his hands at his hips.

This I've got to see for myself. Torn between the needs of his gut that thought his throat had been cut and the pressure in his balls, Dakar flipped Sy's legs over his shoulders, his hands running down lightly furred thighs until his hands cupped Sy's butt cheeks. Keeping a close eye on Sy's serious but flushed face, he gently pushed a questing finger in the deep grove, closing his eyes as he felt dampness on his first swipe.

"You, my sweet, have hidden depths," Dakar said as he forced his eyes open. "I plan on spending the rest of my life learning all there is to know about you."

"I read a lot while you were sleeping. I found…." Sy's cheeks got impossibly redder and he had difficulty meeting Dakar's eyes. Dakar reminded himself, that to the buttoned-up Necromancer, with his legs in the air and his shirt still wrapped about his neck, his current situation was very new and possibly difficult for him. "Brock found a book of spells he thought might be useful."

"I'm glad to hear Brock didn't suffer from his run in with the serial killer," Dakar smiled. His heart was racing and there was a flutter in his guts that had nothing to do with his empty stomach. His wolf lurked under his skin, ready, primed, and waiting for the claiming they'd hankered after for fifty years. Looking down, Dakar noted his cock was already dripping and as he caught a glimpse of Sy's loosened hole, he swallowed hard and tilted his head back up to catch Sy's eyes. "Prince Sebastian York, Sy, will you be my mate? Will you allow me to claim you, fill you with my seed and bite you in the way of our kind? Will you be mine forever more?"

"I vow to ensure you never regret your decision to take me as a mate." Dakar was momentarily thrown by the formal answer, but he put that down to Sy's nerves. His mate's heated gaze, the way his cock was already hard again told the true story. Gripping the base of his cock, Dakar lined up. *Don't. Fuck. This. Up.* He thought as he pushed forward and immediately groaned.

Dakar expected Sy to feel tight around him. The man was a virgin and even with a spell, he felt incredibly snug. But even if Dakar discounted the virgin status that made him want to beat his chest with some misguided caveman pride knowing he would be the only one who would ever take Sy like this, he still felt a deeper sense of coming home. When the Fates crafted this man, they did it with him in mind and my gods, he fit. He fit too well. So well in fact, his carefully crafted reputation of being able to pound an ass for hours was in serious danger of being shredded.

"Are you okay?" He panted in an effort to divert himself. Speech was difficult. With his fangs grazing his bottom lip it was damn near impossible, but for the first time since he'd learned what it was for, his cock wasn't in the driving seat. His heart and wolf combined to put a rein on his urge to pound, and Dakar tapped into his rarely used caring side.

"Please." Sy gave a full body wiggle. "It's...I feel...aren't you supposed to move or something?"

Gently sliding Sy's legs down his arms and onto the bed, Dakar leaned over. Due to their differences in height, kissing was difficult, but Sy reached up and grabbed him around the neck bringing their chests together. *This is it. I am staring at the rest of my life,* and instead of feeling trapped or anxious as he had in the past when anyone got clingy, Dakar felt nothing but pride...and the overwhelming urge to climax.

Rocking gently, Dakar kept his movements soft and slow, despite the clawing inside of him pushing him to punch forward to the end. Sy would never have another first time. He'd never go through another claiming. On one hand they were having sex and yet the ramifications of their actions would echo through the rest of their lives. Electricity arched between them as Dakar felt Sy's emotions swing from nervous anticipation into passion.

When Dakar angled slightly, Sy yelled; he actually opened his mouth wide and yelled to the ceiling as Dakar's cock grazed the spot he was looking for. This was the man Dakar dreamed of alone in bed at night. Flushed, eager, and completely uninhibited, his straight-laced magical powerhouse was everything Dakar didn't realize he needed. The slap of skin on skin let Dakar know his thrusts had sped up, but Sy was matching him perfectly.

Reduced to grunting, Dakar strove to hang on even as his hips took on a life of their own and his balls tightened. This primal act between them was long overdue. He'd been patient; he'd waited even when his animal half didn't understand why they should. Now the moment was here. Sy arched his graceful neck and any ounce of control Dakar had snapped at his submission. His neck bent, and his teeth were embedded in Sy's skin before he knew what was happening. Sy's body shuddered as he let out a long moan, and as the splash of blood coated Dakar's tongue, his balls unloaded. With his wolf howls bouncing around his head, Dakar's soul reached out and found his mate's; the two of them entwined in a bond that would last for eternity.

Pulling back, Dakar gently licked the large wound gracing Sy's neck. There was no doubt it would scar. As he panted through the afterglow, unwilling to move even though his arms were trembling with his weight, Dakar became aware of Sy muttering in a language he didn't understand. Sy's hand heated, almost like a brand on his neck, but as Sy's voice rose to a crescendo, Dakar howled out loud; his wolf taking over his throat as he felt something snap inside. Sy slumped back on the bed, his breathing heavy and for the first time Dakar realized his abs were coated in spunk and Sy's face was bright red.

"Sweet one, mate, are you all right?"

"I hope you like tattoos," Sy chuckled as he waved his hand in front of his face, fanning himself. "Just hot, and I'm not sure my heart has worked out how to slow down yet." Sy glanced at him, his expression suddenly shy. "Was it okay? Was I okay?"

"Fucking amazing." Dakar bent down for a brief kiss before trailing his lips over Sy's jaw. "Next time though, let me show you the manual prep side of things. I think you'll like it."

Dakar expected blushes, smiles or even a quick nod, but Sy's mouth dropped open and he laughed. "Next time," Sy said, once he could speak again, "Next time, I'll be topping you."

Waiting for his wolf's growl, which always appeared when anyone suggested that sort of thing in the past, Dakar was surprised yet again. It seemed he and Sy were perfect together as his wolf barely blinked. He was too busy mentally strutting at claiming his mate. It was in that moment Dakar missed his pack; people who would appreciate his wolf's understandable pride. But then his stomach rumbled loud enough for anyone to hear and Sy was all business.

"Shower," he said, pushing at Dakar's shoulder. "You go and shower or bathe, or whatever you want to do, and I'll get Brock to serve us some food in the small sitting room where we shared our first dinner."

"Stay there my sweet," Dakar said, wincing as his cock left Sy's warmth. "I'll get a cloth to clean you up. Don't move." Going in for one last kiss, Dakar got up and padded to the well-appointed bathroom. Catching sight of himself in the mirror, he stopped long enough to admire his new artwork. Sy's mating mark was of his staff, complete with skull, but the eyes of the skull shined as if jeweled and Dakar recognized his own wolf form curled around the skull. The tattoo was bigger than Dakar expected, *but then this has been the day for surprises,* he thought. Nothing could stop his smile as he hunted for a washcloth in the many cupboards under the bathroom counter. No one would ever be able to doubt who he was mated to and Dakar couldn't be happier.

Chapter Nineteen

Sy seriously needed some alone time; not that that was going to happen anytime soon. His first experiences with sex shocked and thrilled him, making him feel more alive than he'd ever been. The urge to claim, the words that fell from his lips automatically as he branded Dakar as his own; it was all wonderful and exciting, not to mention slightly scary, but he needed time to process everything. Unfortunately, Dakar and Brock conspired against him.

"Sirs, I must speak with you both." Brock was back to his unflappable self, immaculate in his suit and not a hair out of place. He'd been a lifesaver during Dakar's unconscious state, ensuring Sy ate and slept. His congratulations on their mating was just as Sy anticipated – calm, measured, but with the degree of warmth only Sy would notice. The food prepared for Dakar was nothing short of a feast and while Sy still wasn't hungry, he picked enough food off his plate to please his lifelong companion. But now Sy's appetite was ruined completely and he put down his fork and gave up any pretense at eating.

"Please tell me you're not leaving now I'm mated, Brock? My life wouldn't be the same without you."

Brock swallowed. "I have no intention of leaving and I never will. Please put that out of your mind immediately. But what I have to say, in part, has to do with the current threat against you and I apologize for doing this on your mating day, but it honestly can't wait."

"Why don't you sit down, Brock," Dakar suggested, putting aside his napkin and pushing his plate away. "Has this got something to do with the serial killer you did away with? I thought he was the threat."

"He was, at least to those young people and indirectly to you because of what he was doing." Brock perched uneasily on the nearest chair. "However, what I gleaned from his mind before he died has me in a quandary. He told me quite clearly that he was a tool for someone else and what I saw in his mind confirms that."

"Were you able to tell who was behind this?" Sy asked, already knowing the answer before Brock shook his head.

"The killer's mind was like swiss cheese; full of holes, as though any thought he might have had for the one he called master was simply plucked from his head with no thought of the consequences for any of his other memories."

"But he does know who's behind this." Sy was starting to see what was bothering Brock, but before he could put it into words, Dakar interrupted.

"What is the threat, exactly? What can kill a Necromancer? What is this guy trying to do?"

And isn't that the sixty-four-thousand-dollar question? Sy listened with half an ear as Brock explained.

"Necromancers don't die. By extension, now you're mated, neither will you nor I although we still can't travel beyond the veil without extensive preparations," Brock said. "However, a necromancer can be weakened or cut off from his body while he is on the other side of the veil, making it virtually impossible to return. If something were to happen to Sir's body while he's on the other side; if someone cut his throat or something on this side, then he wouldn't be able to return until his body healed, leaving him susceptible to attack beyond the veil. Not a death as such, more like a living hell, if you can understand my meaning."

"What does that have to do with the hearts we found?" Dakar asked. "Why thirteen deaths and not five, ten, or twenty? What's this guy trying to achieve?"

"That's a different part of his objective," Sy said quietly as various random puzzle pieces fell into place. "Whoever this is, is in one respect trying to be me; he wants to wield the power I have beyond the veil. Many have tried before, usually because they want to bring tortured or evil souls back from the dead. True Necromancers understand how impossible something like that is. You can bring back a soul, but there is no way to house that soul in a workable body. Like all paranormals and magic users there are checks and balances for what I do, but as our lore is steeped in secrecy others presume we are more powerful than we are. However, we are the only beings who can wield magical power beyond the veil although the uses for it, beyond basic protections is limited."

"Your power keeps you safe beyond the veil." Dakar nodded. "That makes sense if you visit there frequently. But what's the significance of the number thirteen? How does that fit with this?"

"The ancient Egyptians believed the number thirteen symbolized immortality and that there were thirteen stairs on the ladder to eternity. If this person used thirteen hearts, thirteen innocent deaths to symbolically take his place on each step on that ladder, then it's likely he believes he'll become immortal. If this is what he's trying to do, and if he'd asked, I would have told him it wouldn't work, there is still one thing that puzzles me." Sy warmed to his theme. "When I spoke to the victims they'd said they'd seen the Master on the other side of the veil and he didn't look human. Yet his victims were all human."

"The man I killed was definitely human. There's no way he could have set the wards that protected his so-called sanctuary and the magic spells he used against me were all in vials rather than his power or natural talent," Brock said.

"Hang on a minute," Dakar rubbed his head. Sy could understand his frustration. Shifters lived far simpler lives than their magical counterparts. "Did we get the serial killer?"

"Did we dispose of the man who took those innocent lives?" Brock nodded. "We did. Justice, sparse comfort that it is for those young men who died, has been done. However, that was only part of the puzzle and the serial killer's death now serves another purpose."

"He holds the name of the man who wants me disposed of," Sy explained when Dakar still looked confused. "His master expects me to try and speak to the serial killer now he's dead."

"Because he knows, I know and therefore you know, that he knows who that person is," Brock agreed. "And now you can see where my quandary lies."

"Well, that's simple," Dakar said firmly. "If the serial killer is a trap set for you in a place where I can't save you, you won't go beyond the veil until this being is caught."

Sy couldn't believe the audacity of what he was hearing. To think he'd entertained warm and fuzzy feelings for the detective. "Going beyond the veil to find answers is my job, my duty, and my calling. There are still over twenty missing person files I need to find answers for and that's without the countless ones you passed over because the names didn't have a reference to Peter. It's not possible to do any of that without slipping through the veil."

"Wait, wait." Brock held up his hand, forestalling what would be an epic argument. Determination was etched over Dakar's face but Sy was just as adamant. No one was going to stop him doing his job. "The name Peter. That must be another clue. Maybe there is a deceased someone connected to the one they call the Master with that name. Maybe he wants the power of necromancy to bring this person back to life."

"The name Peter was more likely a reference to you, Brock," Sy said, breaking his glare with his new mate and looking at his companion instead. "I've often said, in the company of others, you are my rock. That is what the name Peter means. Jesus spoke in the bible about how Peter felt as though he was nothing more than a pebble tossed about by the sea, yet Jesus claimed he would become the rock the Christian church was founded on. Whoever this person is tried to separate us with the wards in Warren's home and you said yourself, the serial killer expressed amazement when you couldn't die. Whoever is doing this, clearly believes that without you, I'll lose my powers or at least be considerably weaker. Maybe he believes our powers are tied together in some way, given how I am rarely seen out without you."

"Our mystery man is well-read then," Dakar observed coolly. "We have references to ancient Egypt and the bible, but none of that tells us who this person is."

"And we need to know because there's no telling what this person will do next. Which leaves us two choices," Sy stood and eyed both men. They were equally protective in their own way but Sy knew his duty. One thing his father had done for him, was ensure he didn't raise a quitter. "We can either wait until the matter escalates and more innocent people are killed, which I will not live with. Or I can do what I was born to do and go and speak to our dead serial killer on the other side of the veil."

"Wait. Maybe there is another way," Dakar said quickly. "Are the tales about Necromancers true? Can you reanimate a corpse without going through the veil?"

"For a short while, yes." Sy wanted to slap himself. Clearly having sex limited his brain power. "Of course."

"And," Brock added, also standing, "the distasteful man's brain isn't going to be full of holes this time. If he won't speak verbally, then perhaps I can glean more from his soul. Good work, Detective. I'll go and bring the car around."

"Fancy a trip to the morgue?" Dakar winked at Sy and despite his earlier anger, Sy couldn't help but smile.

"I can see you're going to be taking me to the most romantic of places," he chuckled.

"It won't be as private as I'd like. I'll call Brad and let him know to meet us there. He can fill us in on what happened to the rescued youngsters."

Dakar was there, by his side, filling his senses with his larger than life personality. The big hand resting on his lower back gave Sy a sense of permanence he didn't know he was missing. "I didn't mean to boss you about regarding your job. That was wrong of me," the big alpha said quietly.

Compromise, Sy thought, because Dakar had been bossy but from all Sy had read and learned about shifters over the years, Alpha types didn't apologize often which meant Dakar was seriously trying to make amends. "I'll try not to jump down your throat next time you do it," he promised, lifting his face for a kiss. Dakar didn't disappoint and Sy was well on the way to scratching table sex off his sexual bucket list when Brock's overly loud cough sounded at the door and broke them apart.

"There are reporters at the gate, sirs. It appears someone tipped them off that Detective Rhodes is responsible for taking out the serial killer and they want a statement."

"You killed the serial killer, Brock," Dakar said, a deep furrow developing above his eyes. "You took out the wards as well, otherwise we'd never have gained access to where the victims were. Sy was the one who found their hiding place in the first place. All I did was get myself gassed from some shit-tasting magic puff. I'm hardly going to discuss that with any reporters."

"You need to take responsibility for the killing," Sy said with an urgency that caught Dakar's attention. "It was a righteous kill. The man was evil, and you caught him in the act of trying to take the life of a sixth young innocent. You won't get into any trouble for it. You'll probably be labeled a hero. You have to say you did it."

"But I didn't do it. There's no way I'm taking credit for something I didn't do," Dakar insisted and while Sy hated how confused his mate was, he had to think about Brock as well.

"No one knows Brock's origins," he said. Taking a chance, Sy reached up and palmed his mate's face, forcing their eyes to meet. "Brock has to stay out of the limelight and you can bet your detective's badge that if they think the Necromancer and his bodyguard had anything to do with this case then any credit for all the wonderful work the police department has done would be lost in the furor."

"We wouldn't have had a case without you two."

Suppressing his impatience, because Dakar was new to his and Brock's life and unquestionably honest, Sy tried a different tact. "No one ever says anything nice about Necromancers in the popular press," he said. "If the papers catch wind of me and Brock having anything to do with this, then within a week the tabloids would be claiming we only knew about the serial killings because we were connected to them in some way. The headlines would scream, 'Serial Killer and Necromancer in Weird Heart Exchange Pact,' or something equally sordid. People fear things they don't understand, and necromancy ranks right up there with things that scare them."

"But if I explained, if I told them about all the good things you do…."

"Your career would be over in a heartbeat, Detective," Brock said gravely. "Sir is right about this. I know it's not in your nature to lie, but this time I must insist."

"You can make some spiel about the hard work of the police department and how it was a team effort, which it was," Sy tried one last time. "Please, mate, for me. If journalists start investigating Brock's origins too closely there's no telling what they'll print when they can't find anything. You'd be protecting him and I by doing this."

Invoking the concept of protection was clearly the right thing to say, and while Sy hated manipulating his relationship with Dakar so early on, he had a duty to them both. Dakar was exactly the type of man humans and paranormals alike wanted to see on the front pages of their papers in the morning. Handsome, strong, and ready to protect the innocent at a moment's notice. It would be better for all concerned, if he and Brock stayed in the shadows. Sy shivered as if someone walked over his grave. They weren't the only ones who stuck to the shadows.

Chapter Twenty

Dakar was no stranger to fronting before the press. In his previous department, he was often called upon when questions got too difficult for his Captain to answer especially in relation to cases he worked on personally. News of the Pedace Captain's arrest was still under wraps and there was a good chance the story would never make the papers. All that would be reported was the appointment of a new Captain when one was assigned.

But standing in front of Sy's limousine now at the gates of the mansion, with cameras flashing and microphones shoved in his face, Dakar was struggling to keep his temper. Once he'd delivered the news that the serial killer had been taken out during a raid involving the entire department, as far as he was concerned that was the end of the matter. The press had other ideas.

"Detective Rhodes," a pushy ass by the name of Clive shoved his microphone in Dakar's face. "What's the reason you're here at the home of the Necromancer this morning? Does he have ties to the killer? Can we expect more arrests?"

"Prince Sebastian York has nothing to do with the killings. It's public knowledge he's contracted as the only consultant the Pedace police department has. Where do you get your inane ideas?"

"Informed sources, Detective." Clive tapped the side of his nose. "Got to protect my informants just like you do. Tell us, what links does the Necromancer have with this case. Did he know the serial killer?"

"Do you know the serial killer?" Dakar prodded Clive in the chest, pushing him back, causing his colleagues to scramble. "You claim to have a lot of sources and an unhealthy interest in the most powerful magic user in

Pedace. What do you know about this case?"

"Nothing," Clive protested, looking around at the other journalists for support. "I'm human."

"So was the serial killer. So were the five poor young men who'd been taken from their homes years before and who ended up murdered all for some deviant's amusement. The eight young men we rescued during the killer's take down were also human. This is a human crime against humans."

"There're bad apples among every species," Clive tried to stand upright which wasn't easy when some of his brasher colleagues were busy filming the interaction. "That doesn't explain why you're here at the Necromancer's mansion first thing in the morning. My readers have a right to know. What's the magic user's connection with this?"

He's my mate! Dakar wanted to scream the words to the sky; he wanted to tell everyone that he, a lowly detective was true mated to the one man who had more power in his little finger than any of the beings in front of him. But commonsense prevailed along with imagined headlines. 'Detective and Necromancer in Collusion.' 'Corruption among police ranks as Detective stays silent on serial killer case.' Articles filled with innuendo with no basis of fact but the damage to Sy's reputation would increase.

Standing tall, Dakar met the eyes of every reporter present, making sure each one of them noted the presence of his wolf in his eyes. "Prince Sebastian York has been the trusted consultant of the Pedace police department for ten years. His work with our department is invaluable. In his private practice he has spent his life consoling families and providing answers to those inevitable questions that occur then a loved one dies suddenly. His unique ability to talk with the dead is one that is accessed by people from all walks of life in our fair town and the police department hope their long association with him continues. As to specifics about his assistance in this case, I regret that while our investigations continue I can say nothing more. Now, if there is nothing else, we all have somewhere else we have to be."

"Don't think I'm not onto your lies, Detective," Clive hissed as Dakar turned and opened the passenger door to the car. "I've been on the police beat for five years and this is the first time the Necromancer has ever been involved in a police case. You're a newcomer, so I'll assume you don't know how things work in this town. But choose your friends carefully. Association with the dark ones in this town won't do you or your career any favors."

"Is that a threat?" Dakar's voice was calm, but the claws that shot from the end of his fingers told another story.

"A friendly piece of advice, Detective, nothing more." Clive wisely moved back but held out his card. "I have numerous contacts in this town. Maybe you'll have need of my help one day."

Spearing the card with one of his claws, Dakar slid into the open door of the limousine and slammed the door shut. "Run them over," he snarled as he flicked the card to the floor. Brock immediately turned the ignition key. Seconds later the limo was moving carefully through the crowd.

Reaching down, Sy scooped up the card, a wry smile on his face as he slipped it into a plastic bag and put it in his pocket. "That reporter was very careless; discarding something he's touched and that relates to him personally. As one who travels through the veil, there is a wealth of damage I could do with that sort of information if I was indeed one of the dark ones the reporter mentions."

Shocked from his own anger at Clive and his insidious innuendo, Dakar just stared. Sy was dressed in his Necromancer's garb and yet the smile that graced his face was one of a lover sharing secrets. Dakar's mind flashed back to the night they met; the night when he'd put his giant-sized feet in his mouth. He'd wondered then what Sy's face would look like when he smiled. It was as glorious as he'd imagined.

"I wouldn't actually do anything, of course." Sy clearly misunderstood his silence. "But when one throws shit at others, they shouldn't be surprised if they get an infection from the manure they carry around."

"I wanted to proclaim to the world you're mine." Dakar said the first thing that came into his head. "How do you live with the ignorance around you?"

"I remind myself that one day I will meet them beyond the veil," Sy said simply. "Death is not only a great leveler, it's also a huge learning experience for the uninitiated. You'd be amazed at how many people who slander me in life, can't wait to hold my hand on the other side."

Dakar wasn't quick enough to swallow his growl at the holding hands comment. He covered it up by pulling Sy close and burying his face in his curls. From the stiffness of his body, Dakar realized his mate had been affected by the things he heard more than he'd let on and he vowed at the very next opportunity, the world was going to know Sy was his precious mate. Being a hand in need on the other side of the veil was one of Sy's many duties, but Dakar now had a new purpose. He was going to show the town of Pedace just how important their Necromancer could be on this side of the veil.

Chapter Twenty-One

"You know what would make this easier?" Brock murmured as Sy prepared to call on the spirit of the deceased killer. It wasn't something he made a habit of doing; preferring to leave the dead in peace or visit them on the other side of veil. Spirits torn back through to the living side of things weren't necessarily co-operative, but Dakar's idea had merit in this case. They did need answers. But it wasn't like Brock to interfere while he was going through his preparation ritual. "We should have brought the familiar with us – Connor," Brock added when Sy ignored him.

Sy stopped long enough to rub the middle of his forehead. "I'm not bonded to him; I don't plan on bonding with any familiar especially one who's been force bonded before. What good would come from having him here?"

"Having who here?" Dakar strolled over from where he'd been talking to Brad and Doctor Barker and Sy stepped away from the table. "If you're worried about the last victim, don't be. Brad got him to the hospital and he's making a full recovery. His family is with him, full of praise for him having been found at last. The other victims taken to safety by the officers are with Family Services until their families can be notified. It's all good."

"I'm glad they're safe, but no, Brock wasn't talking about them. We have a familiar staying with us. Connor." Sy sighed. "He was force bonded to Forth; the bond broke when Forth died. Brock seems to think he'd be useful here."

"A cat?" It was Dakar's turn to frown. "I never scented anything like that at your house and yet you say he's living there? How come I didn't know he was there?"

"Familiars are human," Sy explained. "Although some of them can shift into other animals which is probably where you got the idea of the cat from. But Connor is very definitely human – as a familiar, he's a magical conduit and of course he's staying at my house. It's part of my job to look after unbonded familiars until they can support themselves or find themselves a witch they chose to bond with. He's been through a rough time of it lately. You won't have noticed him because he stays in the guest wing, which is totally separate from the main house. Just because familiars are my responsibility doesn't mean I want to share my bathroom with them."

"Sir prefers his privacy," Brock agreed. "It's why the guest wing was created. It's also why, despite employing over twenty domestic staff, you'll never see anyone but myself in Sy's half of the house. However, domestic concerns are not what's important now. I think I should go and get Connor. He would provide a useful earth between the veil and the body."

"Earth?"

Sy could tell Dakar was even more confused and probably a little unhappy someone else was sharing his house. But if he had to explain every nuance of his work, simply because they were mated, it was going to get frustrating very quickly. Maybe he could write a book about it, just for Dakar. Later.

"An earth is what holds the spirit to the body while the questioning takes place. It stops the spirit trying to inhabit anyone else who happens to be in the room." Sy looked at his arrangements around the corpse. "I was planning on doing it myself, but if you think Connor will be a better idea, Brock, then I defer to your judgement. Go and get him. But if I think this will upset Connor in any way, then I'll send him straight back to the house. I'm sure he's too young to have experienced necromancy in any shape or form. He's still recovering from whatever Forth did with him."

"The young familiar is in perfect health. I assure you, he'll be fine," Brock gave a brief nod. "I will be back directly." Brock's body disappeared in a smattering of particles leaving Sy ridiculously aware of Dakar's hovering presence. *How am I meant to focus with him around being all sexy and...and...him?*

"We have a house guest you didn't think to tell me about?" Dakar's breath whispered across his ear.

"Don't you think we've been rather busy to chat about domestic concerns?" Sy wanted to pull away, but it seemed when Dakar came within two feet of him all he wanted to do was touch. He reached behind him and pulled Dakar's arm around his waist, leaning against his broad chest. "I haven't seen you moving your things into the house yet. We've not even talked about if you're going to stay with me. I can't leave my house and I don't have a say in the day-to-day running of it; I leave all that to Brock. But don't you think we should be sharing an address before you start wondering who else lives there?"

"I'm renting an apartment, month to month," Dakar crooned as though he was making love to Sy's ear. At least that's what is sounded like to him. "I can be packed and out of there in an hour. I didn't want to be presumptuous."

A sickening thought felled Sy out of nowhere and he turned in Dakar's arms, ignoring Dr. Barker and Brad completely. "This is real, isn't it? What we have," He whispered, his hands flattening against the heat of Dakar's chest. "We are permanent, aren't we? We're always going to be together, no matter what?"

"Always and forever. No one else, just you and me," Dakar leaned over, his breath brushing over Sy's heated face. "I told you before, I wanted to tell the world we're together this morning. But our mating is far too important and precious to tack onto the end of a news release about a killer, don't you agree? Especially, after what you said about keeping Brock out of the public eye."

"I do. I know." Sy wasn't sure where his unease was coming from, but he'd learned years ago not to ignore it. "It's just…I don't know why I'm feeling this way. Like some giant thundercloud is heading our way, or like someone is waiting around the corner ready to brain me with a baseball bat."

"No one is going to separate us," Dakar growled and Sy tilted his chin to meet stormy eyes. "You might not know a lot about my kind, or maybe you've read a lot about us and just haven't considered what those words mean in real life but know this. When the thunderclouds come, I'll be the one holding the umbrella over your head. No one will be waiting for you around any corner, because I'll smell him first and beat that sucker's brains out with his own bat. You and I are forever and nothing and nobody can tear apart fated mates. If you can't believe in them, then believe in me. Everyone knows a wolf shifter can't lie to their fated mate."

Sy let out the long breath he didn't know he was holding, resting his forehead on Dakar's shirt. "I'm sorry. I'm just being silly. This is all so new to me, you know? I've never had anyone I've cared about before except Brock and I know he can't die."

"And now you're terrified something will happen to me." Dakar's grin was evident in his tone. "You realize I now know how much you care about me. That makes me happier than you could ever imagine."

"Silly puppy," Sy stroked the chest he was leaning on. "How could anyone not care about you."

/~/~/~/~/

Dakar wondered if he would ever get over the dichotomy that was his mate. On the one hand, Sy was cute, shy and seemed so innocent about sex, life, and being in a relationship. But when he swirled his coat, banged his staff on the tiled floor of the morgue and called out for the dead serial killer to come back to his body, the hair on the back of Dakar's neck stood up. Sy's power filled his nostrils, causing his wolf to sit up and howl. It was impressive, it was other-worldly and through it all, all Dakar wanted to do was fall to his knees and beg to suck his mate's cock.

Which was not the way to conduct a police investigation. In a morgue. With his partner Brad throwing him knowing looks, and Doctor Barker sniggering in his chair. Flipping out his notebook, Dakar addressed the animated corpse. The glazed eyes were knowing once more and if it wasn't for the long line of crude stitches running from the man's collar bone to where they disappeared under the sheet, Dakar would swear the man was still alive.

"The wolf shifter," the dead man sneered as Dakar caught his eye. "You lived. What a pity. Did you eat the bottled hearts left for my master, or did you manage to restrain yourself?"

"You're only here to answer the questions." Dakar looked down at his note pad. "Why did you attempt to kill Roy Peters?"

"A man needs a hobby." The killer scratched his nose. "I needed his heart. He wasn't going to live without it."

"We found five hearts belonging to five dead young men in jars in your killing room," Brad said from the other side of the table. "Why were you keeping the hearts?"

"They were to be an offering to the all-powerful necromancer," the dead man sneered. "Thirteen hearts. Thirteen innocents willingly giving up their lives so that he might be immortal."

Necromancer? He can't mean....? Dakar looked at Sy who was standing at the head of the steel table the corpse was on. His face was a mask and not a flicker of emotion was evident in his eyes. Despite his forbidding pose, Dakar knew the dead man had to be lying.

"Our Necromancer has spoken with the young men you killed," he said, turning his focus back to the table. "The one you're working for doesn't have a human form when he moves beyond the veil. He can't be a Necromancer. What is he?"

To Dakar's surprise, the dead man laughed – a hollow sound that rang around the room and sent a chill running down his spine. "You've been taken in by a pretty face, detective. Do you know the significance behind the number six? The sixth victim. They all have a purpose you know. Six is the perfect number. Six days mortal man was meant to labor. Three sixes form the mark of the beast. Six is the power of balance – that sixth heart would have generated chaos. Chaos like the world has never seen."

"You're talking rubbish," Dakar scoffed. "Start saying something useful."

"Oh, I will, detective." The corpse showed his lack of teeth. "Did you know, in tarot, the sixth major arcana card is the lovers, Detective? Is it any wonder you are sniffing around that innocent face now? He's tricked you, bewildered you, ensnared you, hoping to keep you off balance. Yet you were too fast for him, weren't you, wolfy, killing me, when you should've been killing him. If you'd have let me take that heart, then the innocent face you see now would've been unmasked to reveal who he really is. The chaos he craves lurks there under his skin, as readily as your wolf does yours. Did you fuck him, Detective? Did he claim you were mates?" The corpse laughed again. "You've been taken in, you've all been tricked. One day that innocent face will be seen for who he truly is. The devil." Yelling loudly, the dead man pointed straight at Sy, who still gave no sign of even hearing anything.

Dakar couldn't think. He was in shock; the man's words reverberating around his brain like a pinball. Everything in his instincts told him the spirit was lying, but there was no deceit in the air. All he could smell was fucking bleach. He noticed Brad opening his mouth to ask a question, but Connor got their first, struggling to hold the corpse's feet. "I can't hold him. He's too strong. Banish him before he gets loose."

"The interview is over. Be gone, spirit," Sy yelled thumping his staff on the ground. "Be gone and never grace the land of the living again."

The spirit's cackling laugh could still be heard long after the body stilled. For a long moment no one moved or said anything, until Brad pulled out his handcuffs. "What the hell are you doing?" Dakar asked, seeing his partner moving Sy's free hand behind his back. "You can't believe that spirit was serious? Sy's no more the reason behind these killings than I am."

"I'm doing my job," Brad said, clicking one end of the cuffs to Sy's wrist. "I read the manual the Necromancer's father provided, the same as you did. A summoned spirit can't lie. Prince Sebastian York, I'm taking you in on the suspicion of masterminding the killing of five men, the severe wounding of a sixth and the abduction of thirteen children over the past twenty years."

Silently Sy handed Brock his staff and put his other hand behind his back for Brad to cuff. "Take care of Connor," he said softly to Brock. "If we have a lawyer, it might be an idea to call me one although, I doubt it will do any good. Stay and protect the house until I return. Let no one in. No exceptions."

"You're just going to accept this?" Dakar grabbed Sy by the arm as Brad tried to move his mate forward. "Just tell Brad the truth. That is wasn't you."

"It wasn't me," Sy said and as he looked up Dakar could see the wealth of pain in his pale gray eyes. "But that spirit believes it is and I can't prove otherwise. Not yet. Watch yourself please, detective. Someone else is walking around with my face. Trust no one, not even me unless you see the scar on my neck. Brad. Let's go."

"I won't forget you're the one who betrayed our friendship, bear," Brock snarled, holding a shaken Connor under his arm. "Any one with half a brain would know this was a trap and that means you've got bigger problems than you thought. The mastermind behind this works at the police department and can shape shift."

His lips tightening, Brad put a large hand on Sy's shoulder and escorted him out the morgue. Dakar looked to Brock, hoping he would have some answers, but the curled lip told him none were forthcoming. Holding tight to Connor, Brock and the young familiar disappeared leaving Dakar with a corpse and Doctor Barker who touched his shoulder gently.

"You just failed your first test," the old man said, shaking his head. "I'll bet my pension this is the first time your relationship has suffered a hardship, given how new it is, and you failed abysmally."

"What would you have me do?" Confusion didn't sit well with Dakar and he was glad he had an outlet for his anger. "Brad's my partner. I read the same damn manual he did. He's right. A spirit can't lie, no matter what form he takes. Brad is just doing his job, no matter how distasteful it is."

"And yet, you know in your heart of hearts, the young necromancer is innocent and still you let him be led out of here in handcuffs. I'd love to be a fly on the wall when you try and explain that to the mate you promised to protect forever." Barker leaned closer.

"Didn't you hear what Sy's companion said?" He whispered. "There's something else you don't know about spirits, detective. Something I learned from the Prince's father. Spirits have no sense of smell and neither do humans, not like paranormals do." He looked at Dakar expectantly.

"Sense of smell? What the hell does that...." Dakar's eyes widened as the events of the afternoon fell into place. Sy's warning about someone wearing his face...Brock's anger at Brad.... "Someone in the police department can glamor their appearance so they look like Sy?"

"The spirit was damn sure he was working for the prince. But the prince talked to the dead men long before this asshole crossed the veil." Barker poked the serial killer's chest. "You told me about that. Why didn't the spirits of the dead recognize Prince York when he was on the other side of the veil as the one behind their killing? Was your mate lying to you when he told you what poor Warren said?"

Dakar shook his head. He remembered that much at least but everything else was churning around his head like a freaking tornado.

"Damn it all," Barker huffed. "You alphas are all the bloody same. You're blessed with super senses and you don't use them. Think about it. If your necromancer didn't lie about Warren, and this asshole spirit didn't lie about thinking he was working for the necromancer, what does that tell you?"

Finally, Dakar understood the ramifications of what he'd learned. But then he remembered something else. The Captain. "We've already got an employee of the police department in our cells with the capacity to shape shift and it's not Sy." Dakar fumbled for his keys. "Phone the department. Talk to Brad. No one else. Tell him what you told me. I've got to get to my mate before he's booked."

Running like the hounds of hell were after him, Dakar took off out the back door to the morgue. *Shit. I came with Sy,* and there was no sign of the limo or Brad's vehicle in the parking lot. Shoving the useless keys back in his pocket, Dakar sprinted down the road. The police precinct was only four blocks away. *Surely no harm could've come to him yet. He's only been gone fifteen minutes at most. He's got to be safe.* And yet, the huge sinking feeling in Dakar's gut and the edgy growl of his wolf told another story. *Please, let me get there on time.*

Chapter Twenty-Two

"You know I didn't want to cuff you, don't you?" Brad peered at him through the rearview mirror, but Sy ignored him. That 'ugly feeling' of blossoming terror he'd felt earlier was increasing the closer they got to the police department and he knew if he walked through those doors he was in for a power of hurt and a lot of people could get caught in the crossfire.

If he didn't go in, he'd be a fugitive.

Three blocks to go. Sy could see the bright blue sign for the police station getting closer. *Dakar.* Sy's heart ached at how his mate did nothing but make a token protest at him being arrested. Anyone with an ounce of commonsense would know he wasn't responsible for all of this. The threat was against him. The dead serial killer, Forth and even the Captain made that plain.

My alpha might be a hunk, but he's sadly lacking in the brain department and don't get me started about his loyalty. All those lovely words Dakar whispered in his ear not half an hour before. Sy shook his head. He was a fool to believe anyone would care for him. But gods, it galled him that his father was right. Blinking away his tears, Sy weighed up his options as the precinct got closer.

He'd never been a fugitive before. He'd barely had anything to do with the police department before this case. In normal circumstances he'd go along with the arrest. His innocence wouldn't be easy to prove without magic, but he could do it. Eventually. If he got locked up, the evil would find him. From the aura Sy could see around the police building, it was already there waiting. If he went home the evil would track him there.

Realizing that, Sy knew he had no choice. His books, Brock, the very heart of his power stemmed from his family home. Hanging around the cells, hoping to catch a glimpse of the man who stole his freaking heart then stomped on it, wasn't going to do him any favors. If he was going to fight this thing then he needed all the magical ammunition he could get. As Brad pulled up outside the precinct, Sy called on his power.

"I'm sorry, Brad," he whispered as he disappeared from the car, leaving his cuffs on the back seat.

/~/~/~/~/

Dakar's boot sounded like thunder claps as he ran into the bullpen, causing more than one head to turn his way. But that wasn't what caused him to slide to a stop. No. It was the Captain standing large as life, addressing his officers, with Brad standing by his side looking as though he'd eaten a lemon. He was too late.

"The Necromancer will be caught," the Captain's voice boomed around the room. "I was against contracting with him or his family and fought against it for years. But I was overruled and now, after all this time, I've finally been proven right. Find him men and show our beloved community why shifters make the best type of officer."

"Yes, sir." The response from the room was muted, but a glare from the Captain and everyone suddenly looked busy. The Captain caught Dakar's eyes and showed his teeth. "Detective, in my office now."

How? Why? Dakar mouthed at Brad, but the wretched bear wouldn't meet his eye. Crossing the room, Steven, the wolf who'd protected the children and cat shifters back at the Sanctuary, pulled him aside. "Watch yourself," he whispered as Dakar tugged his arm free. "The evil's so bad in here you can taste it."

"How did...." Dakar didn't have the chance to finish the question as the Captain yelled at him from his office door.

"Now, Detective."

Slipping Dakar a piece of paper, Steven moved away. Shoving his hands in his pockets, Dakar headed for the office, his head held high. Brad was already standing by the Captain's desk, staring at a point on the wall only he could see.

"Close the door," the Captain ordered.

Dakar's wolf, which until now had been focused on finding Sy, growled a warning, but Dakar did as he was told. Standing in front of the Captain's desk he stood at parade rest, his eyes focused on the framed Community Award hanging on the wall behind the Captain's head.

"You've been corrupted by an evil force." The Captain didn't waste any time getting down to brass tacks. "You knowingly fornicated with, aided, and abetted a criminal. What do you have to say for yourself?"

"As far as I'm aware, Prince Sebastian York hasn't been charged with any crimes. In fact, he was invaluable in assisting this department in solving the serial killer crimes you ordered him brought in to solve."

"The Necromancer is a fugitive!" The Captain thumped his desk so hard a large crack appeared. "He slipped away when your partner tried to bring him in for questioning. He's evaded arrest. That makes him a criminal."

"What are the charges, sir?" Dakar refused to look at the Captain directly. His wolf was screaming at him to get away, but he kept his feet still.

"Didn't you hear me, man? He evaded arrest. What more do you need?"

"And I want my statement recorded for the record that when Prince Sebastian York was led from the morgue, in cuffs I might add which wasn't necessary, he was being treated as a person of interest. There aren't any grounds for arrest because there were no charges against him in the first place."

"We'll find the evidence we need when we capture him." The smell of sulphur and brimstone increased making Dakar's head woozy. Clenching his fingers behind his back, Dakar stiffened his spine although he was sure he wavered slightly. Just as he thought he was going to fall over, the smell disappeared, and the chair creaked as the Captain leaned back on it.

"You can relax, Dakar. I'm prepared to give you the means to redeem yourself."

This isn't going to be good.

"You will lead a team of the best and strongest officers and break into the Necromancer's stronghold. Bring me the Necromancer in chains, and I'll forget about your indiscretion towards this department."

Like fucking hell! Dakar inhaled sharply, struggling to control his sudden panic at the thought of his beloved Sy in chains. *Think. Damn it. Think.* "Previous visits to the Necromancer's home during the course of this investigation indicate it would be impossible for anyone to enter without magical means," he said with as much calm as he could muster. "The home is strongly warded. The family protect their privacy."

"And yet, you can come and go as often as you like, can't you detective?" The Captain's smile was not pretty. "After all, why would the Necromancer's home be warded against his alleged mate?"

"I...er...I..." Dakar looked across at Brad, but he was getting no help from that quarter. The man could be a statue for all the emotion he was showing. "The spirit we interviewed today said the Necromancer deceived me and that we're not mates at all."

Fuck, the urge to rub the ache in his chest was strong, but Dakar's will was stronger. "The Necromancer heard what the spirit said. He has to know he's been found out. He's not likely to ever want to see me again."

And ain't that the truth. Fuck, Sy, I'm so sorry. Dakar wished with everything he had that he could turn the clock back to before the spirit was summoned. He'd still have to listen to the same cock-and-bull story, but the moment Brad pulled out his cuffs, Dakar would have shot him. In the arm, but enough so that he and Sy could get away. Now Sy was holed up in his huge mansion with no one but Brock and Connor for company.

"Hmm," the Captain's voice might have sounded friendly if it wasn't for the demon's fangs poking out from his top lip and the hint of smoke trailing from his nostrils. "It's just as well I have someone on the inside of that mausoleum the Necromancers call home then, isn't it? Someone who'll make sure the wards are down and the doors unlocked at precisely eight o'clock tonight. You will arrest him then."

Fucking hell. It must be Connor. The lanky familiar who Sy took in out of the goodness of his heart. The one who claimed he couldn't hold the spirit any longer, causing Sy to send him away before any further questions could be asked. "Eight o'clock. Yes, sir. I'll start organizing a team right away," Dakar said, his mind racing. He needed to get in touch with Sy. That's if his mate would ever give him the time of day.

"And Dakar," the Captain warned as he opened the office door. "Don't leave the precinct. I'm not an idiot. The Necromancer might have tricked you into believing you two were mates, but there's no telling what silly ideas your protective wolf might come up with. Like warning the Necromancer you're coming, for example. You can't help it. It's your animal nature. But it can't be allowed to happen. Consider this me doing you a favor; a way for you to keep your job. After all, you wouldn't want to be jailed alongside the Necromancer, would you? Especially, when the man tricked you and your animal half so badly."

The words "You can stick your damn job up your ass," hovered on the tip of Dakar's tongue, but he swallowed them. If he resisted, the Captain would send another team to apprehend Sy and Dakar would probably be staring at steel bars. No, he needed to be free, to ensure Sy's protection. And he might not be able to leave the building, but he was going to have a serious chat with his fucking partner as soon as he could get him alone.

His lips twitching at the way Brad stuck to his ass as Dakar left the office, he headed down the corridor to the locker room. *No cameras in here*, he thought as he pushed open the door with one hand while the other tugged at his zipper. *Nothing to see here. Just a friendly chat over the urinals.*

Chapter Twenty-Three

"I'm glad to see you escaped unharmed, sir. We've got a spy in the house," Brock said as soon as Sy reappeared in his library. "Connor just offered me a blow job."

"That dick of yours must be sending out neon signals to bad guys. Maybe you should start wearing lead underpants," Sy said, slumping in his chair. "What did you pick up from him, apart his desire to eat your dick?"

"It wouldn't have been so bad if he'd actually wanted to go through with the act. I almost felt sorry for the young familiar when I turned him down." Brock waved his hand and a tray with Sy's favorite cup and a pot of tea appeared on his desk. He reached over the desk and started pouring a cup; the scent of chamomile soothing Sy's ragged nerves.

"I don't see anything in that familiar's mind to indicate he's got evil intent," Brock added as he set the teapot down and handed Sy his cup. "But he did plan on attempting to earth our wards, rendering them useless and ensuring the main house doors were unlocked by eight o'clock tonight."

"One would assume we're expecting company then." Taking a couple of sips, Sy set the cup back down on the tray and rubbed his chest. He looked up see Brock watching him with something akin to pity in his eyes. "Why is this happening? Some of those children we rescued had been held for over ten years. I wasn't even the Necromancer then. My father was."

"Your father was a hard man." Brock tapped his fingers on the desk. "The only one I can think who'd hold a grudge that long is that demon in the police department. The Captain."

"But he's in cuffs, in jail. He can't access his magic or persuade anyone to set him free from there. Although, from the vibes I was getting from the precinct building before I left Brad I would be double checking those cuffs under any other circumstances."

"Maybe you should be checking." Brock rubbed his temples with his forefingers for a moment before looking up. "It appears the familiar has been hiding more from me than I thought." Brock straightened and held out his hands, clapping them together hard. "Connor, I summon you. Appear before me immediately."

There was a clap of thunder and a flash of light and then Connor landed with a thump, ending up sprawled across the carpet. "Hey," he said with more spirit that Sy had noticed before. "If you'd changed your mind about the blow job, you could've just asked. You didn't need to drag me from my bed with a demon tug."

"Did you forget the only reason you have a bed at all, is because of the Necromancer's largesse?" Brock's arms were folded across his large chest. "It would behoove you to show a little more respect." He nodded in Sy's direction and Sy realized that with the desk in the way, Connor originally thought he and Brock were alone.

"The Necromancer?" Connor got to his feet in a flurry of long limbs and a few elbow knocks. This was the familiar Sy remembered. Hunched shoulders, a mop of hair over his face, almost trembling and refusing to look at anything but the floor. "My apologies, great magic one, if I've caused any offence."

"Your subservient attitude pleases me." Sy was still in his Necromancer gear and he leaned back in his chair to show off the full effect. "I'm strongly tempted to take you as a familiar, now I'm mated. Would you be willing? You proved very helpful this afternoon at the morgue. I believe if you were trained properly, your powers would definitely increase."

Connor's mouth dropped open and he peered at Sy from under his bangs. Sy didn't hurry him for an answer. Brock would be picking up Connor's every thought. As the silence stretched on, Sy added encouragingly, "I imagine bonding with me would bring you a lot of prestige among your kind. You can't get higher in the magical hierarchy than a Necromancer, can you?"

"No, er, sir. What I mean is I'd never thought about it, before now that is. It would be a huge honor. But what sort of work would I be assisting you with? A familiar can't touch anything to do with black magic."

"Is that what you think I do?" Sy brought his fingers together to form an arch, his index fingers tapping his chin. "You believe I'm a black magic user?"

Connor looked back and forth between him and Brock.

"It's okay," Sy managed a tight smile. "We are completely private here. Speak your mind."

"Yes...er...well." Connor's shoulders heaved. "The de...person who sold me to Forth. He and Forth talked a lot about you and your expertise in black magic. They were talking originally about how you might be persuaded to work with them, that you could be useful to them. But then," he shot a quick look at Brock, who's expression hadn't changed. "They said you had a golem and that was apparently a big problem. All familiars know a golem that lives this long has to be a product of black magic."

"Is that what they teach in familiar school these days?" Sy chuckled. "Brock is not a golem. He's my oldest and dearest friend."

"Not a golem?" Connor swallowed hard. Then his words came out in a rush. "But they said, you were there when the boys were killed. The one's like Warren. They said you laughed and joked and danced around in their blood."

"You think you saw me?" Sy looked across at Brock who shrugged.

"No. I wasn't there, but the de...person who came to Forth, asking for the wards that drained his powers said the wards had to be strong because with every heart you consumed you were getting stronger."

"Seems those Peterson house wards weren't just meant for you Brock." Something was nagging the back of Sy's mind, but he couldn't work out what it was.

"Why don't you call this person what he is," Brock said harshly. "You were consorting with a demon. Something expressly forbidden to familiars everywhere because their powers aren't strong enough to shield themselves from ill intent."

"It wasn't intentional." Connor scuffed the carpet with the edge of his new sneakers. They still had the price tag on the back. "I was sold to a demon by my parents. It's not as though I had a choice in the matter. He kept me a while, then he sold me to Forth."

"But through it all, you're still bonded to that demon, aren't you, Connor?" Sy leaned forward and rested his elbows on his desk. "There's no point in lying. The only reason I didn't sense it before was because of your bond with Forth. The breaking bond when Forth died should have left you laid up in bed for weeks. Even a forced bond break can kill familiars. Yet you were well enough for Brock to suggest you could aid me with the summoning of the serial killer. Why did it take him over ten minutes to zap back here and pick you up?"

"I was in the shower." Sy could barely hear Connor's mumble.

"No, Connor, I think you were in the police cells, providing an earth between the demon Captain and the energies from the shifters who work there, so that he could break the cuffs I slapped on him. Would I be right?"

Connor's body trembled.

"How did you know your demon was in jail, Connor?" Sy's tone hardened.

"My brother, Robert." Connor looked up, his eyes filled with tears. "The demon holds him prisoner; I have to do as he says."

"Save your tears, boy. Robert is one of the Captain's willing concubines, who shot the Necromancer when the Captain was taken into custody. An arrest he deserved because he allowed countless needless deaths over the years, by not using the magic services the Necromancer would willing supply if only he was asked." Brock grabbed Connor's arm and shook him. "The only one practicing black magic is that scurrilous demon. Were you the one who provided him with enough energy to glamor his appearance, so he looked like Prince York?"

"No, I mean, I don't know. Maybe. I spelled a lot of items for him ages ago, before he bonded me to Forth. I didn't know!"

"Let him go, Brock." Sy sighed and leaned back in his chair. He picked up his cup, but the tea was cold. Magical reheats never tasted the same as a fresh pot. "The only thing Connor is guilty of is pure stupidity, lying through omission, oh, and the fact he intends to let a team of police officers storm in here tonight to take me away in spelled chains, so my powers can be drained by the murderous Captain to the point I fade from existence."

Connor gasped. Sy ignored him. "How would my father have handled something like this, Brock? I mean, what are we looking at here?" He held up his fingers. "Assisting in murder, attempted murder of a Necromancer companion, breaking someone out of jail and that's without paying back the hospitality and care he's been shown with nothing but treachery."

"Your father never tolerated any form of disrespect," Brock said firmly, keeping a tight hold on Connor who was probably trying to translocate. He wasn't successful. "But Connor could prove to be useful to us, one last time; given how he has a bond, albeit a weak one, with the problem demon."

Sy smiled. It was always a comforting feeling when he and Brock were on the same page about things. Unfortunately, his heart ache reminded him he couldn't say the same about his mate. Pushing thoughts of the sexy detective aside, he said, "prepare the summoning room, would you, please? I think it's time we had a chat with a certain demon preferably before someone tries to ram-raid their way into our house."

Keeping a tight hold of Connor, Brock headed for the library door. Thinking about what Connor said, Sy called out, "Just for the record, Connor, when the *police* finally killed the man responsible for murdering those five young men, their hearts were still in the jars they'd been stored in. That demon has done nothing but lie to you from day one. Of course, I can't guarantee he hasn't eaten them now; he probably stole them from evidence. But I find heart meat rather stringy, don't you, even when cooked? And there is no way a power transference can occur from eating the remains of a dead person. You really should've paid more attention in school."

Brock's chuckle lifted his mood better than Connor's frightened face, but as soon as the two men left, Sy was left alone with his thoughts once more. Facing a demon didn't bother him. His father started summoning and chucking demons at him from the day he first came into his powers. Each one was stronger than the one before until eventually his father got a missive from the underworld telling him to cease and desist.

But on my very first attempt to let someone else into my life I get my heart stomped on. Letting out a long breath, which did nothing to ease the pain in his chest, Sy resolutely put his negative thoughts aside. Seventy years' experience told him the only person he could rely on was Brock. The past week simply proved it to him. In his head, as Brad cuffed him, Sy imagined Dakar wolfing out, challenging the bear – proving the masterful alpha wouldn't let anyone treat him badly. That he would protect him, despite his job, position or what anyone else thought of him.

And what did I get instead? Sy sniggered. *An alpha who just stood there with his mouth open, preferring to believe his friend and wanting to keep his job, more than he wanted to protect me.*

In one respect, Sy wished the spirit he'd summoned had been right and he had tricked the wolf into claiming him. But the dull ache on the side of his neck that seemed to intensify the longer he was away from the darn wolf, proved otherwise. *Maybe this is for the best,* he tried to tell himself as he made his way slowly out of the room. *Maybe it's better to learn Dakar doesn't mean what he says now, before my heart gets anymore invested and he's actually sharing my house.* Unfortunately, even to his mind, he wasn't very convincing.

Chapter Twenty-Four

"We should've left the precinct a lot earlier than this," Dakar growled as he and Brad studied the forbidding exterior of Sy's house. Over the last hour, dark thunderclouds had rumbled over the town, giving everywhere an eerie air. A crack of lightening lit up the night sky for a split second, before it all went dark again.

"I want to know where the Captain is," Brad grumbled. "He makes all that fuss about you not being allowed out of the office and then shuts himself in his and doesn't even bother to see who we picked for the team to come out here."

"I thought we'd already hashed this out." Dakar snarled at his friend. The bruise on his jaw from Brad's fist still ached slightly, but the cut on Brad's eye was going to scar if the bear didn't shift soon. "The only one in the department who could possibly glamor himself to look like Sy is the damn Captain. You told me the Captain threatened to fire you for not using anti-magic cuffs on Sy when you tried to take him in. It was the Captain Sy humiliated in front of the whole department after he proved just how much of a bigot the Captain is. Now, you're whining about his whereabouts like he's your fucking kid. What the fuck?"

"I'm just saying we should be careful, that's all." Brad looked across at the mansion pensively. "I'm trying to hang onto my job, and you've only been mated five minutes, if you're even mated at all. You don't know how Prince York is going to react with us going in there any more than I do."

"Fuck, I should've chained your ass to the locker room radiator while I had the chance." Dakar turned to the four others who were watching silently. Steven was one of them, as well as the rookie cop who was terrified every time Sy came into the room. If

Dakar had had his way, the rookie would have been left at home, but once the Captain made himself scarce, so did everyone else.

"I'm going in to protect my mate," he said sharply. "Tell me honestly. How many of you believe in the Necromancer's innocence?"

Steven's hand went up in a flash and Dakar appreciated the support from a fellow wolf. The rookie looked at the other two cat shifters and slowly raised his hand. The other two followed suit. Dakar looked at Brad whose arms were stubbornly crossed. "You still think this is a trick?"

Brad shrugged although he didn't look happy. "My job is all I've got. I have to follow orders and my orders are to watch your ass and drag Prince York back to the precinct in chains. His guilt or innocence isn't up to me. That's for a court to decide."

"As if Sy would ever make it to a court." Dakar wrenched open his jacket and pulled the collar of his shirt aside. "What do you see?" he tapped his neck.

"A tattoo?"

Sighing, Dakar arched his neck. "Fucking sniff it but do it quick because I haven't got all night. Sniff the damn thing. It's the mating mark Sy gave me when I fucking claimed him."

Brad leant forward and sniffed then shrugged. "Just because you claimed him doesn't mean he's not a criminal."

"Oh, I fucking give up." Dakar snarled. "If you want to kiss the Captain's ass so bad you can do it by yourself." Dakar ripped the rest of his shirt open and pulled it off along with his jacket. Dragging his detective badge from his pants pocket he slapped it in Brad's hand.

"You can tell your Captain, I quit. I know my mate's innocent. He told me; I believe him. But if that's not enough for you, think of the facts. Sy was at a nightclub the night the fifth victim was found. It was Sy and his companion who were targeted at the Peterson household, not us. It was because of Sy we got the break and killed the guy who murdered five young men." Dakar wisely kept the fact that Brock was the one that did the killing to himself. "Through it all every message Sy receives is focused on a danger more powerful than he will ever be, coming for him. Forth, the serial killer, the Captain. Sy's the one being threatened here, and he's not done one thing wrong. If the Captain had one shred of decency he'd be ordering us to protect Sy himself. For fuck's sake. Sy's contracted to the department. He deserves our protection even if he wasn't my mate."

"Following orders ensures I get a pay packet every month," Brad snapped back. "Right or wrong. Good or bad, no one will ever say I didn't follow orders."

"Even when you know those orders are wrong?" Brad was a good man, a decent detective and a commendable shifter. When Dakar was initially paired with him he relaxed into his new job, confident Brad would have his back. But now? Shivering in the darkness, Dakar knew he had to hurry.

Tugging off his boots and removing his pants while staying crouched wasn't easy, but Dakar did it. As soon as he shifted into his four-footed form, he shook himself and bounded out of the bushes.

As he got closer to the house, his skin prickled. The wards were still working. *Good.* The only problem was, he had no way of getting into the house. Thunder crashed overhead, and a bolt of lightning hit a tree not ten yards from where he was standing; the branch falling with a loud crack. *This is not good,* his wolf warned. *Bad magic in the air.*

There was only one thing left for a wolf to do if he wanted to attract attention. Tipping his head back, Dakar closed his eyes and howled for his mate. The thunder wasn't making it easy for him to be heard, but Dakar kept on howling, pouring his emotions into his vocalizations. *I'm sorry. I believe in you. Let me in.*

/~/~/~/~/

Sy lifted his head and listened. He could barely hear the wolf howl over the noise of the storm, but suddenly his heart beat faster and his cock stirred. "Our company has arrived," he said, turning back to his work. "Have all the wards been strengthened?"

"They have." Brock said calmly. "I believe the howling wolf is your detective, sir. He most likely wishes to gain entrance. The bear, another wolf and three cat shifters are hiding behind the bushes, a distance away from him. It is possible they anticipate rushing the doors once the detective is admitted to the grounds. However, your detective's only intention is to get to you."

"Until I get this right, I don't want any disturbances. We can worry about who thinks what and why later." Contrary to folklore and popular belief, summoning a demon wasn't a case of throwing down a salt circle and calling the demon by his full name. The "demon tug" Brock used on Connor was easy enough for demons themselves to achieve. But for a human like Sy, summoning required skill, precision, and a clear focus.

Sixty candles, hand lit, were placed the exact same distance apart from each other to form a perfect circle. The pentagram inside that ring was already drawn, but Sy made an offering at each point of the symbol to the corresponding spirits of air, earth, water and fire. Each offering was an elaborate ritual in itself, involving ancient Latin phrases where every word had to be pronounced exactly right for them to work.

Connor, bound in a magic circle of his own to the side of the room, wasn't making the job any easier. When kicking out of the circle caused his leg to burn, he curled in on himself physically. But it didn't stop him trying to blow out the candles from a distance. "He won't come," he yelled as Sy attempted to center himself for the final part of the summoning. "That is no ordinary storm out there. He's coming for you, but not because of your pathetic attempts at summoning him."

"For a familiar who enjoyed the benefits of my hospitality, you're inconsiderately noisy," Sy said sharply. "One more word out of you, and I'll turn you into a newt."

Connor's teeth snapped shut. Closing his eyes, Sy tried to slow his breathing. He needed absolute calm. He winced as his cock jumped in time with the wolf he heard howling again.

"Brock, can you whisk that wolf somewhere quieter please? Shove him in the guest wing for now. I'm sure Connor won't mind sharing; that is if he's still staying here after tonight."

Nodding silently, Brock left the basement. Sy knew his butler was simply being considerate. One wave of his companion's large arms and he would have to start lighting his candles all over again. "Anything else you want to get off your chest before I do this?" Sy asked, glancing at Connor.

Lips pressed tightly together, Connor shook his head. From his mutinous expression Sy decided he couldn't take any chances and flicked an invisible gag over the boy's mouth, ignoring the familiar's outraged eyes. Connor's youth excused a lot of his behaviors, but Sy's gut told him he needed to be fully focused on the upcoming confrontation. He could soothe the ruffled feathers of the familiar later if he needed to.

Taking the lock of Connor's hair Brock had cut for him earlier, Sy dropped it in the bowl sitting on the fifth point of the pentagram. He was invoking Spirit. The seat of his power. Pulling his knife from his belt, Sy made a diagonal cut along his left palm, allowing exactly five drops to fall into the bowl before he clenched his fist.

Pointing his right index finger into the bowl, Sy muttered the words passed down to him from his father, his father's father and his father's father's father before him. The hair in the bowl began to glow bright red, the blood droplets expanding into a mass of bubbles that grew and multiplied until they overflowed the sides of the bowl. Sy relaxed. The offering had been accepted and the summons could be made.

"I summon you, Demon Baltoc Gravis Pendamin Selphine; son of Balthazar, spawn of Lucifer. Heed my call. I command you."

There was a sudden rush of wind as the inner pentagram filled with smoke. A loud bang echoed around the concrete block walls as all the candles blew out. Sy stood firm while the smoke began to slowly mold itself into the demon form of the Captain. Bigger than he appeared at the precinct, Baltoc's skin was an earthy red; two large black horns sprouted from the top of his head and muscles bulged over muscles across his bare chest and arms. In comparison, his legs were short and very thin, although his balance was supported by a long tail thicker than Sy's arm. This was how the demon would have appeared to his victims on the other side of the veil; the Captain's true form.

Only he wasn't alone. Sy's eyes narrowed as he noticed the two human forms dangling from the Captain's meaty hands. Brock's uncharacteristic curse behind him gave Sy the courage he needed to continue.

"Baltoc, you have exceeded the parameters of your position and broken a dozen laws by bringing your pets with you. Send the humans back from where you got them."

"It's you!" One of the humans opened his eyes and Sy recognized that face. It was Lloyd Peterson although he was missing his customary scowl. In fact, he looked terrified. "You're the magic boss. Get me out of here. I didn't sign up for this shit."

"Oh yes you did," the Captain let out a malicious laugh as Lloyd was shaken like a rat. "You gave up your eternal soul and that of your step-son for a pile of riches and pussy on tap." He had the audacity to wink in Sy's direction. "Twelve years, this pathetic excuse for a being has been waiting for me to deliver on my promises and now I have. It's almost a shame he won't last long enough to enjoy his side of the bargain. His soul is mine. The deed is already signed and there's nothing you can do, Necromancer."

"He's a foolish man. He should have been content with the life he could have had with Warren's mother." Sy nodded to show he agreed. "The other one you're holding. The familiar's brother, I deduce?"

"Yes, Robert. He can't bear to be apart from me. He begged to come along. He loves me." Baltoc showed off jagged teeth as he licked along Robert's unresponsive face. "Of course, he prefers my human form, but love is such a wasted emotion on a demon, don't you think?"

"Agreed," Sy did his best to ignore the anguish he could see on Connor's face from the corner of his eye. The outcome for Robert wasn't looking good. "Is he human? Does he still hold the rights to his soul?"

"Yes, and yes," Baltoc huffed as though insulted. "You can try and take him but he's not going to appreciate being kept away from me. He and I have covered a lot of miles together and from the murky state of his soul, he won't be seeing any pearly gates in his future."

"He's young. He has time to change his life around. How about you put them both aside for a minute, so you and I can talk?"

"We've got nothing to discuss, Necromancer." Baltoc's mocking laugh bounced around the room. "Three hundred years I've been waiting for this day. Twenty years ago, I saw my chance and I've schemed and skulked in the shadows, building my powers, waiting, waiting, until now. Everything I've done has led to this moment. The day I can take you down."

A shiver ran down Sy's spine. He crossed his arms, and in the most bored voice he could muster he said,

"I know I'm going to regret asking this, but can you tell me what I did to incite such fanatical devotion to my demise? I wasn't even born three hundred years ago, and my father was the Pedace Necromancer twenty years ago."

"You're paying for the sins of your grandfather," Baltoc's eyes were almost closed, as though lost in his memories. Sy didn't let his guard down. The demon's grip on the two humans hadn't wavered. "The old man was an evil bastard. He faded far too quickly for me to get my revenge and as for your father, he wasn't worth spitting on. He was a weak-kneed, selfish, and greedy cur. But then you came into your powers and made your first visit to the other side of the veil. That attracted my attention."

"What did my grandfather do?" Sy racked his memory trying desperately to think of anything his relative might of done. It's not as though he'd ever met him and the only story his father told about his grandfather related to Brock's creation. "Brock, is this to do with you?" He whispered.

"Your grandfather foresaw a great evil that would arise well into his future, threatening the whole city, nay, the whole country with its influence." Brock's calm voice over his shoulder, as though discussing what they'd be having for dinner, helped soothe Sy's confusion. "That vision was the reason I was created. My sole purpose was to protect first your father and when he retired, I took care of you. Maybe the demon is jealous he wasn't consulted or even invited to donate to your grandfather's cause. Baltoc is related to the blood in my veins. I could sense it the first time we met."

"He created you by taking the life force from others," Baltoc shouted, his face contorted in anger; his hands shaking as Lloyd and Robert dangled helplessly, their feet unable to touch the floor. "The demon part of the blood cocktail running through your veins came directly from my brother, Petrov. I would've stopped him if I'd have known about the Necromancer's experiments, but by the time I learned what happened, it was too late. The deed was done. My brother never recovered. For three hundred years he's spent his existence tormented by trolls, ghouls and evil spirits too weak to fight off even the most insignificant of demon. He's trapped. He can't die and my pleas to the lord of the underworld go unanswered. Your grandfather broke every law on every realm the day your golem started to breathe."

"No." Sy shook his head, his teachings of a lifetime pounding through his brain. "It's not possible to take the life force from one being to power another. Grandfather knew that. It's a core part of our teachings. Your brother donated two pints of blood for the spell. I remember my father telling me. Four magical beings; eight pints of blood. All four beings donated in exchange for a gift and left this house in the same state they arrived."

"Then how do you explain what happened to my brother?" Baltoc's lips curled back, and Sy smelled the singe of burned flesh as Robert's leg swung over the lines of the pentagram. "He told me it was your ancestor."

"Your brother lied, and you can't tell me that's not possible." Sy's confidence lifted at Baltoc's grimace. "My grandfather was the one who faded giving Brock life. He gave his power levels to Brock; a transition only possible because he went beyond the veil and tore away a piece of his soul, mixing it with the mud of the golem. That was the only reason his power could be channeled into and used in Brock's body and endures to this day. My grandfather sacrificed his life gladly, because of the threat to his future generations, and absolutely no one else was harmed because of it. The spell wouldn't have worked if harm had been done to anyone else."

"Your grandfather *caused* the threat to his future generations! He took the essence of my brother's life leaving him a shell of his former self." Spittle flew from Baltoc's mouth. "For centuries I've watched my brother's feeble attempts at living. I buried his wife. I raised his kids while he does nothing but hide in the shadows too weak and disfigured to show his face."

Sy's confidence wavered in the sheer conviction of Baltoc's arguments. He turned around, needing to see Brock's face. "Is it possible any of this is true?"

"No sir." Sy let out a long breath at the firm conviction in Brock's voice and the honesty in his dark eyes. "Admittedly, I never met or knew the beings who gave up their blood for me, but one of the first things your grandfather did when I came into existence, was explain the magic that allows me to live. No one was harmed by this except your grandfather. Trust in your teachings. The power drain this demon claims, isn't possible under any law of magic."

"You lie, and now you'll die." Baltoc's voice sounded a lot closer. Sy whirled around just in time to see the demon step on Robert's body that had been used to create a bridge from inside the pentagram. Tears streamed down Connor's face and suddenly the hole in Robert's chest and the blood smears around Baltoc's mouth made horrific sense. Swallowing down his nausea, Sy looked around for Peterson who was cowering in the opposite corner of the room, his arms covering his head.

"I was really looking forward to the sixth heart you deprived me of." Baltoc grinned showing blood stained teeth. "Roger was no innocent, but his would do at a pinch. All along, you've thought you had the answers. There was so much you got wrong; playing about with your little number schemes trying to work out my plan. Immortality was never my plan; rendering your soul non-existent was closer to the truth. But you were right about the number six. It really was significant. The antithesis of balance is chaos and it begins with your death."

Faster than the eye could track Baltoc raised his hands and Sy was thrown back against the wall, the impact hard enough to rattle his teeth. As Sy struggled to rise, he saw Brock caught in mid leap. His convulsing body was suspended in mid-air; his hands clawed, reaching for Baltoc. "Blood calls to blood, golem." Baltoc laughed. "I'll drain yours and give it back to my brother." A black chalice appeared in his hand. "Let's see how well you can protect your Necromancer when you're nothing more than a dust heap on the floor."

"Let him go!" Pushing himself to his feet, Sy called on his power; pulling on everything he was and everything he could ever be. The lure of the veil tugged at his veins, threatening to pull him under, but Sy fought to stay in the here and now. Brock was in danger. His only friend. The closest thing to family he cared about. Nothing else penetrated his thoughts. Holding his arms out in front of him, Sy flung his power through his shaking fingers tips; shards of light rivaling the lightening that flashed outside.

His aim was true. The light struck Baltoc right through the heart. Baltoc jolted and then continued to jerk as though hit by an electric current. Sy didn't stop, not even as his knees failed him. Baltoc stumbled and Brock crashed to the floor as the demon's power over him failed, knocking over a dozen candles in the process. But Baltoc wasn't done. Throwing his head back he started chanting to the ceiling and Sy's spine almost cracked under the feeling of dread that filled the room. Baltoc was calling the underworld. All hell was about to let loose, quite literally, in his basement.

"You need your mate," Brock groaned as he crawled towards him. "You can't fight this alone. You'll fade."

"Keep my mate safe." Reaching deep down into his soul, Sy tore open a hole in the veil. It was the one thing his father told him never to do. The power behind the veil was more enticing than a siren to sailors at sea and harder to break free from. But with dark ghouls seeping through the basement blocks and the power he was pouring into Baltoc fading fast, he had no choice. If he lost, Baltoc would send his ghouls into the city and Pedace would become a sub-station of hell. He was the Necromancer. He had a duty to uphold. Hated and feared, misunderstood and reviled by most, it was still up to him to save the town and everyone in it.

Blocking his ears to Baltoc's chants, Sy called upon the spirits; tapping into the well of energy that existed beyond the veil. As the added power poured through him, Sy screamed. Every cell in his body was overwhelmed at the sudden surge of power. His heart was beating incredibly fast and his lungs caught; he could barely breathe. He was dimly aware of Brock's hand on his ankle, lending him his support and trying to soften the blow the added energies were having on his body.

Arms trembling, Sy gave a final push, filling the room with all that he was, pushing the darkness and dread aside. Thick glops of sludge dropped from the ceiling as the ghouls dissipated. Baltoc was writhing on the floor; his earthen red skin peppered with black cracks that were spreading across his features. *It's working. He's going. He's going. I've just got to hang on two minutes more....* Reaching inwards down to the tips of his toes, Sy pushed one more time.

Black spots hampered his vision. He couldn't hear anything for the roar of his blood in his ears. The light emanating from his fingers started to stutter and Sy flicked his hands in frustration. *One last push, just one last push, just one more....*

And then, like the clouds under the heat of the sun after a storm, all the tension and strain in Sy's body disappeared. He blinked away the black spots in front of his eyes; his heart and lungs returned to their familiar rhythm. He was still a conduit for the veil, the connection was still open, but the stuttered magic he was suffering from before got a renewed lease of life. Plucked from the floor, Sy felt the heat at his back as he was encased in familiar strong arms.

"You can do this," Dakar whispered in his ear.

"One last push should do it, sir," Brock wavered against his side, his hand a welcome comfort on his shoulder.

Looking down Sy saw Baltoc was clawing at the concrete floor. Skin was peeling off his face as though burned and yet his eyes still carried the flames of hatred. "You haven't won yet," Baltoc groaned as Sy sent the lethal blast, scattering Baltoc's body into miniscule dust particles nothing could come back from. There was a loud clang as the portal Baltoc opened to the underworld slammed shut and all that was left was the black sludge from the dissipated ghouls dripping from the walls and Robert's poor dead body.

And the sound of angry clapping. Sy looked over to where Connor had been saved by his own magic circle. The familiar hadn't been touched but he was furiously clapping his hands and then pointing to his mouth. "Did you gag the familiar, sir?" Sy noticed Brock was leaning on Dakar heavily and marveled at the strength the wolf shifter had to support them both.

"Yes, and Peterson," Sy couldn't see the man anywhere among the wreckage. "What happened to Peterson?"

"It appears Mr. Peterson caught a lucky break, sir." Brock said slowly. "One can imagine with the demon's demise, his contract with the beast for his soul is now null and void. I assume he's been returned to his home or wherever Baltoc picked him up from. One would hope he hasn't been permanently traumatized by the incident."

"It might make him think twice about dabbling in magic again." Sy slumped against Dakar's chest. He was surprised the detective hadn't said anything, but maybe he was traumatized, too? Maybe Dakar was just lending his body strength to him and Brock out of common courtesy, or maybe it's a police officer's job.

If this is the last time he holds me, I'll enjoy it while I can. Surely the fates will give me that much. In the meantime, Connor is one mess I do know how to cope with. Addressing the weeping familiar, Sy put as much strength into his voice as he could and said, "I'm going to remove your gag. You will not yell at me. I only wish to confirm you are well now you are not bonded to anyone else. Agreed?"

Lip's pursed in what was probably an attractive fashion, although Sy would never be sure, Connor nodded his head madly. With a thought the gag was gone. "What can be done for my brother?" Connor asked quietly.

This was the part of the job Sy hated the most. Some people had unrealistic expectations when it came to Necromancy. He could bring someone back from the dead, but the spell never lasted more than half an hour at most, and once a person had passed through the veil, they were never the same. "Nothing," he said shaking his head. "Dead is dead, at least for Robert's kind. Brock and I both require rest and something substantial to eat. After that...."

"I'll take care of it, Sir," Brock wobbled as he leaned away from Dakar, but with an effort he straightened his spine and tried to smooth the wrinkles and crud from his jacket.

"You will not," Dakar said, his voice quiet but firm. "If you can loan me something to wear, Connor and I will take care of this mess, his brother's body and anything else that needs doing. All you need to do, Brock, is make sure your master gets to his room safely and find me a pair of sweat pants."

Sy wanted to protest. He wasn't sure where he even stood with Dakar anymore. He also had the nagging sensation he'd forgotten something, but his mind was too foggy to focus. Dakar's arms tightened around him momentarily, and he felt the slightest brush of lips in his hair, but then Brock was there, sliding his arm around his waist, his jaw tight as he forced his spine to cooperate. Sy decided he'd done enough. Anything he'd forgotten could wait until morning.

Chapter Twenty-Five

"The Necromancer has more power than I've ever seen in my limited lifetime, and I spent two months in the underworld," Connor said quietly as he and Dakar respectfully wrapped Robert's body in clean linens and stowed his body on a table Brock provided before attempting to clean the mess of sludge, candles, bowls, and chalk dust strewn about the basement floor. Dakar wasn't in the mood to talk to anyone. He was too busy processing all he'd been through, which admittedly wasn't much in comparison to Connor. But seeing Sy at what had to have been the height of his power, was both awe inspiring and terrifying. *How could I ever compete?* Yet he recognized Connor's tactics for what they were. The boy was scared. He likely watched his brother die and thanks to the gag, was unable to do anything about it.

"Were you close to your brother?" Dakar used a shovel he'd found in a hall cupboard to scoop black tar-like substances into the bucket Connor was holding.

"Yes and no. He was my half-brother." Connor blinked rapidly and rubbed a dirty finger under his eye. "Our parents weren't the best. Dad whored my mother out in the hopes of magical offspring he could make use of. They were both human. Life got better for me when I identified as a familiar, but Robert was nothing in their eyes."

"Is that how you became bonded with the Captain? Because you were a familiar?"

"It was illegal for the demon to bond with me." Connor screwed his nose up at the now full bucket. Setting it down by the door, he reached for another one and Dakar kept his head down, scooping more goop. "Familiars are like catnip to demons. Dad tried finding me a witch to bond with, but

Dad wanted money for the deal. There was this one guy, just after I turned eighteen," Connor sighed. "His name was Kirk. I think he really liked me, but he was an honorable witch. Familiars and witches bond on trust, you know, or at least they are supposed to."

Dakar stayed silent but nodded encouragingly. What he knew about familiars would fit on the head of a pin. Connor was the first one he'd met.

"When Kirk wouldn't pay the money dad wanted, Dad was furious; ranting and raving about how we were eating him out of house and home and he'd never get a decent return on what he called his investment. The very next day the demon knocked at the door and Dad handed me over. Robert was thrown in as a bonus."

Dakar looked up to see Connor biting his lip, tears pouring down his face. "Robert just wanted to be loved," Connor said, dropping his bucket, covering his face with his hands. "I told him there was no point in giving your heart to a demon, and now he has, permanently."

Shit. Comforting others wasn't something that came easily to Dakar, but he set down his shovel and hugged Connor close, letting the young man vent his tears. When Connor finally reached the hiccupping stage and wiped his face with his hands, Dakar took that as the hint it was and backed away, giving the familiar his space. He stacked the buckets filled with muck by the door. He'd ask Brock what to do with them when the butler had rested.

"Is it true, you've claimed the Necromancer?" Connor asked. He was looking anywhere rather than at Dakar. He picked up a mop from the floor, sloshed it in a bucket of hot water before starting to splash water all over the dusty flagstones. "It can't be easy for an alpha wolf to be physically bigger but know that your mate will always be stronger than you."

"One of the things you will have to learn if you want to attract a decent witch," Dakar said sharply, "is that not everything is your business. Prince York and I are only newly mated. We barely had time to exchange marks before the shit hit the fan. I've fucked up with him twice already and I'm finally starting to realize why I think that is."

"Why?" Dakar wasn't sure if Connor was genuinely curious or simply wanted to hear the sound of someone's voice. But now Dakar was thinking about it, the words just spewed out of him.

"Because I'm in fucking awe of him. Because when I look at him I see my future and I still can't believe the fates ever believed someone like me could be worthy of someone so...so...fuck, I can't even think of the right word because my brain turns to mush and that's what just thinking about him does to me. When he's here, or in the same room as me, I seem to revert to pup behavior. I can't think straight; my mouth doesn't work. It's like my brain is so busy thinking just how fucking awesome my mate is, I lose track of what's going on around me and when I do work out what's going on, by then I've usually fucked things up."

"By being silent? It's better than putting your foot in it all the time." Connor didn't seem to be making much progress with washing the floor, but at least he wasn't crying.

"Look what happened at the morgue." Dakar knew he was onto something and Connor made the perfect sounding board. "Brad arrested Sy; put him in cuffs and took him away from me. I did nothing. My wolf was all about coming out, tearing strips off Brad, standing there and growling at anyone who'd dare touch my precious mate. But, dying as I was from the biggest case of blue balls I'd ever had just from being in the room with Sy, I'd suppressed my wolf, so we didn't go jumping him in his fancy necromancer duds. By the time my brain caught up, it was like…duh…the cuffs were already on and Sy was gone, and then he was gone and oh, fucking hell." Dakar slapped his head.

"Something else you'd forgotten?"

"There are five police officers staking out the house. They've been there since seven thirty. I guess we were waiting for you, was it, to drop the wards and unlock the doors?"

"Yeah, well at the time I didn't think I had any choice." Connor stabbed the mop back in the bucket. "I haven't got a clue what's going to happen to me now."

Dakar upturned an empty bucket and sat on it. "In my ideal world, Brock or preferably Sy would've overheard my confession to you just before and realized that I'm actually a worthy partner for Sy. That I will protect him, and I'll come to love him if we could spend more than five minutes alone for a change. My wolf would've let me know he was watching me. I'd look up and he'd be standing there in the doorway like a pocket-angel in black." Dakar waved his arm to indicate the empty doorway.

"Our eyes would zero in on each other instantly. There'd be that long, poignant pause. I'd be holding my breath, watching his gorgeous face; mesmerized and struggling to believe he actually came looking for me. We'd both move at the same time, slamming our bodies together in the middle of the room. I'd smother his face in kisses, licking away any tears. He'd be half laughing, half crying and oh my god, our hands wouldn't be able to touch each other quick enough."

"He'd be all understanding. I'd be all alpha and horny," Dakar sighed. "It's one thing I am good at. And then, when we finally had to breathe, we'd swear undying love to each other. But this time, when the movie or the page faded to black, for us the adventure would just be beginning. We'd spend at least a week never getting out of bed. Hot sexy mating times for both of us and by the time we finally faced the world again, misunderstandings would be a thing of the past because we'd be so in tune with each other."

Dakar shook his head at the empty doorway. "At least that's what happens in the movies and romance novels. No chance of that here." Glancing up at the ceiling, Dakar imagined Sy in his bed two floors above him. "With the poor showing I've been giving Sy and Brock since we met, I'll be freaking lucky if they allow me an hour appointment once a week to see him."

"You're mated." Dakar had forgotten for a moment Connor was even there. "At least you have the chance of being with someone for the rest of your life. You need to grovel, lots. Buy him things, hug him a lot and most of all talk to him. Tell him what you told me. It all sounded like pretty powerful stuff to me; the sort of thing any significant other would want to hear."

"Well, it's not as though I won't have the time to do all these things," Dakar sighed. "I quit my job before I shifted and started howling for Sy's attention this evening. I didn't realize he was trying to summon the Captain at the time and needed to focus on what he was doing. Brock wasn't impressed with me. I've got a lot to learn about magic."

"I'd be happy to answer your questions," Connor grimaced. "However, from what I've learned over the past few days, I think my schooling in the magic department was a little skewed. I'm hoping the necromancer might take pity on me and let me stick around for a while."

"After you were going to let him get captured?"

"You let him get arrested, after you'd claimed him as a mate," Connor shot back.

"Yeah, yes, I did. And hopefully my mistakes can be forgiven once I've explained to Sy how much he means to me." Dakar stood in one fluid movement, his fingers hooked on the waistband of his sweats.

"I'm not giving you a blow job." Connor leaned away.

"I'm shifting, you nit-wit. I've finally worked out where I'm going wrong with the mating."

"I thought you already explained all that in your overly dramatic monologue I just listened to."

"I meant every word I told you, but sometimes life is simpler than that. We need to be together, Sy and I. We're going to be glued at the hip; I don't want him to ever be out of my sight again. That way, I'll stop being such a klutz around him. Me and my wolf will get used to his power and we will be the best alpha wolf mate he could ever have. And we'll get a chance to really get to know each other."

"Once he's woken up," Connor reminded him. "That could take a few days. I've never seen anyone wield that much power and not fade away. If you hadn't been around, Baltoc would have pushed the necromancer over the other side of the veil and made sure he had no way back. That's been his plan all along, I'm sure. If the necromancer was blocked from contacting Brock, then the demon planned to use Brock to heal his brother and he would've planned to take the necromancer's power for himself."

"Which he couldn't do because it goes against the laws of magic, nature, life, the Fates, or whatever." Dakar was learning, and he did listen to Sy.

"No matter who you believe the demon couldn't use Sy's power for his own purposes."

"He can't now," Connor agreed. "He's dead and that's not a common thing for a demon to be. The Necromancer had the veil wide open when he zapped the demon for that last time. The demon's soul is trapped behind the veil and with nothing but dust left of him on this side, the demon is officially as dead as someone who can't die can be."

"Gods, this is all so confusing." Dakar dragged his toe through some dust left on the floor. *Demon debris?* "Give me the mop," he ordered, determined to give the floor another wash. "Go and find us something to eat from the kitchen."

"I thought you were going to shift and spend time with your mate?"

"I was, but now I'm worried freaking sick that some of these dust modules will somehow find a way to meld back together to give Baltoc's soul something to come back from the veil too."

"I'll grab another mop," Connor sprinted to the hall cupboard that contained all the cleaning supplies.

"I told you to get food," Dakar called out swinging the mop head from side to side across the floor.

"We both need to learn more about this sort of stuff. I've got visions now of Baltoc's body coming back together in tiny globs that get bigger as more balls come together, and then more and then more, like a type of revenge of the dust bunnies' scenario."

"That's why you should always clean under the bed. The more dust bunnies there are, the more chance you have of it happening."

Connor came back in with a dry mop and started moving behind Dakar as he washed over the whole floor, using plenty of water. It was probably five minutes before Connor asked, "do you think the Necromancer will give us both a chance?"

"If he doesn't, we can probably start our own commercial cleaning company." Dakar surveyed the floor. Not one speck of dust could be seen. "Come on, young one; food and bed for you; food and cuddling with my mate for me. First one awake makes breakfast. Deal?"

"How do you like your eggs?" It was tiny, Connor's smile, but it gave Dakar hope for some reason.

As they climbed the stairs from the basement to the living areas, Dakar accepted he'd fucked things up pretty much from day one. He'd actually done the one thing Sy used to complain about. Dakar had treated Sy like a necromancer instead of a man who was his mate. That's why his wolf was in a tizzy all the time. That's why he could never get his brain to work. As a Necromancer, Sy was just that powerful.

But Sy was also a man. A man who stood in front of a rampaging demon, while denizens from hell threatened the whole town's existence. *No, damn it. Don't think like that. That's what stuffs you up every time.*

Think cute little mate Sy, who's had a rough day at work and deserves a hot bath, a warm bed and a strong cuddle. Yeah, Dakar could see that line of thinking working. *Maybe a foot rub, a bit of a blow job...I could get my dick....*

"You can cut out that line of thinking; those sweats don't hide anything," Connor pointed to where the lump of Dakar's erection was growing down his leg behind the material. "I think I preferred it when you were worrying about Baltoc's body reforming."

Thanks a lot for ruining my buzz, kid, Dakar scowled.

Chapter Twenty-Six

Sy was woken by whispering voices. Brock and Dakar. *I'm in bed – that's a positive.* He wiggled his hands and toes slightly. *I can still feel my extremities, so they are all there.* His stomach gurgled. *And I'm hungry.* He pinched his thigh, hidden by the blankets. *I'm not skin and bone so I haven't faded. Score one for me.*

It was unusual for Brock not to have noticed he was awake, although this wasn't the first time Sy had crawled into awareness since his battle royal with Baltoc. Each time he'd come to, he felt the heat of a wolf laying against his back. It was a comforting sensation Sy knew he could get used to. At one point he had fur up his nose and realized he'd buried his face between Dakar's shoulders. A sneeze and a roll, and Sy was asleep again with a fur free nose.

Dakar's voice got louder. "I really don't care how many times that bear leaves me a message to call him. I quit the police department. That's why I was howling outside your wards making a fool of myself. Because I believe in Sy and maybe I haven't been quick enough to show it at times, but I don't see the point in listening to anything Brad has to say."

"Detective Summerfield has his reasons for the way he behaved."

"And I'm glad those reasons make sense to you. You can give him a shoulder to cry on. Lord knows they are big enough. But my first focus is Sy. And then it's Sy and after that it's Sy again."

"That is as it should be."

Sy grinned into the pillows. Brock was warming up to his mate.

"Nevertheless," Brock went on, "all the Pedace Police department knows at this stage, is that the Captain disappeared along with his PA in the middle of a ferocious storm that sprung up out of nowhere. You were magicked through our wards. Brad and the others froze their tails off until daylight hoping you'd reappear. I realize you find it difficult to believe, but Detective Summerfield is concerned for your well-being."

"I'm not leaving Sy." Sy felt the mattress move and then a large weight settled against his back. "I will discuss how he wants to handle this situation with him, when he wakes up."

"Sir is already awake." *Damn it.* Sy heard Brock's measured steps along the floor. "Eavesdropping is not polite, sir. Did you want a meal in bed, or shall I serve food for both of you in the small dining hall?"

Pulling his face out of the pillows, Sy brushed back his curls with his hand as he yawned. "How long was I out this time?" His throat was rough with lack of use.

"Four days, sir, and there have been developments you should be aware of," Brock replied. "Most notable is that annoying journalist, Clive is calling repeatedly for an interview. He's investigating the disappearance of the Pedace Police Captain. Likewise, Detective Summerfield also wishes to take a statement from you and your mate. I explained to both men you were indisposed however they are equally persistent."

"Sy needs to eat," Dakar growled, "and then he and I will require time alone to work on our bond. It's about time our mating took some precedence here. I plan on taking him out to dinner this evening and I'll shoot anyone who tries to stop me this time." A heated hand rested heavily on Sy's thigh.

"What time is it?" Brock hadn't opened the curtains and Sy had no idea what time of day it was.

"Seven forty-five in the morning, Sir."

"We're having breakfast then. That's good. It's decidedly disorientating if I wake in the middle of the day." Sy thought quickly. He felt a lot better than he had a right to, but his stomach was empty, and his bladder was full. "Dakar and I will get up for our meal and have it in the small sitting room where we had our first date. I haven't finished," he added as Dakar whined in protest. "Please inform Detective Summerfield he can meet us for breakfast *tomorrow* morning and conduct his interviews with us then. Contact the paper this journalist is affiliated with and find out what he's angling for. No media organizations have been interested in me before. Find out what changed if you please."

"Yes sir. Shall I run you a bath?"

"Not right now, no, thank you. I do need to use the facilities, and I doubt I'll hear anything my mate has to say over the rumbling of my stomach. We'll take care of that first. Dakar, please put some clothes on. I assure you, after breakfast Brock will leave us in peace unless something urgent comes up. We have a lot of catching up to do, in bed and out of it." Peeking over his shoulder, Sy's eyes widened at the heat in his mate's expression. Suddenly daring, he winked; something he'd never done to another person before.

Dakar's lust filled growl had him scrambling out of bed. "I need the bathroom first," he called back over his shoulder. "You try going four days without peeing."

Slamming the bathroom door shut, Sy leaned on it and chuckled quietly. Hearing what Dakar said to Brock about him being his mate's new focus, gave Sy renewed hope that they could make things work. Admittedly, the detective had said similar things in the past but maybe what they both needed was to get to know each other better and spend time together. As he wandered over to the toilet and did what he had to do, Sy hoped Dakar didn't plan on talking too much about their last two weeks. By his recollection, it was Friday; his regularly scheduled masturbation day, although his dick had no idea how to tell time. From Dakar's expression, Sy felt it was safe to assume his hardening dick would get all the attention it needed and with any luck, before the regularly scheduled ten pm.

/~/~/~/~/

"Are you allergic to anything?" Sy looked up from the sheet of paper he was reading from and frowned. "I don't know why you're laughing. Brock printed this out as a guide to help us get to know each other. The answers could be important."

"It sounds like he's copied it from a random magazine site online." Dakar wiped the grin off his face. Leaning his elbows on the table, he rested his chin on them. "I'm a shifter, Sy, I'm not allergic to anything but silver and wolfsbane."

"Handy to know." Sy had an endearing habit of biting the tip of his tongue when he was writing. "Next question. What's your favorite movie?"

"Hang on," Dakar said quickly, shaking his head. "This is *us* getting to know each other; not just you learning things about me. Are you allergic to anything?"

"I doubt it. Necromancers don't ever get sick." Sy frowned. "I won't eat asparagus, tinned meat, or sour hard-boiled sweets. Does that count?"

"Great." Dakar beamed. As much as he'd far rather be doing sexy things with his mate, he had to admit this was fun. His breakfast, that included steak and strong coffee was digesting nicely. The cool winter sun was streaming across the table illuminating his necromancer's smile. And best of all, he had Sy's attention. His wolf was preening. "My favorite movie is Lethal Weapon. Any one of them would count as an answer."

"There's more than one?" Sy wrote the answer down, then scratched his nose with the end of his pen. "I can't remember the last time I watched a movie. Can I ask Brock and get back to you on that one?"

Leaning over the table, Dakar squeezed Sy's hand. "Babe, if you have to ask someone else, then it's not your favorite. Mark that down as something we can explore together."

"Good idea. Okay," Sy scanned his piece of paper and Dakar got the impression his mate was skipping some of the questions.

"You know you can ask me anything, right?" He prodded gently. "Mate's don't have secrets from each other."

Sy's cheeks turned a delightful shade of pink that contrasted beautifully with the gray of his eyes. "I'm just not sure I feel right about asking some of these things. Like what's your go-to Karaoke song?" He looked up from the piece of paper. "What on earth is Karaoke? Is it a kind of special cult, club or musical genre I don't know about? And then there's this other one; how do you feel about PDA? I'm not sure what PDA stands for either. It sounds like something associated with an accounting firm and I know some people don't like talking about money. I could be insulting you by even asking the question."

"Let's make a mutual decision that neither one of us answer the karaoke question." Dakar shivered dramatically and Sy laughed. "Karaoke is where you go to a club and random people get up on stage and sing along to covers from music they like. From my experience, the more drunk the singer gets the more they think they can really sound just like the artist they're pretending to be. Admittedly, some of them have amazing voices, but I'm not one of them. I won't go to places like that because I hate being dragged up on the stage by well-meaning friends who think I should just 'try it'."

"No karaoke. Right. PDA? Is this to do with money? Do you need a copy of my bank statements? I assure you I'm financially well situated. I have extensive investments and...."

Dakar put his finger over Sy's lips. "I think to appreciate the meaning of PDA you'll need a demonstration. It has nothing to do with money." Getting up, Dakar motioned to Sy to stand as well. "Okay, let's move away from the table. Now...." He stopped Sy moving to far toward the door and in a deliberate move invaded his personal space; cupping Sy's face with one hand. The skin under his fingers was like warm silk and his body trembled with the urge to go a lot further than standard PDA allowed.

"PDA refers to public displays of affection," he said, his voice dropping an octave thanks to Sy's proximity. "For example, when we are out on our date tonight, I will want to hold your hand where others might see us. Some people don't like to do things like that, but I do."

"I liked holding your arm when we were at the precinct that time." Sy's smile was shy.

"Holding my arm is another form of PDA, yes. It shows others that we're together – a couple. Another thing I might do could be stroking your face while we're waiting for a course to be served at dinner." Sy leaned into the brush of his fingers and Dakar swallowed hard before he could speak again. "Some people consider that an intimate act but for me it's a way of showing my focus is on you, rather than what's going on around us. That should be important between mates, I think and something I've neglected up until now."

"What else is considered PDA?" Sy's husky voice, lowered eyelids and the way he was blatantly swaying his hips towards the bulge in Dakar's pants sent his pulse into overdrive.

"Kissing," he said quickly. Sliding his hand around the back of Sy's head, Dakar fisted his mate's curls and tilted Sy's head up. "Light kissing is acceptable in some public situations," he whispered as he bent down.

He honestly meant to take just a quick taste but when Dakar felt Sy's arms snake around his middle, tugging their bodies closer, his lust exploded. His free hand slid under Sy's untucked shirt, seeking the warmth of his back. But that wasn't enough. Their height difference meant he wasn't getting the full impact of his mate's lithe form against his and he wanted it. He needed to feel the evidence of Sy's excitement; to soak up every tremble of his mate's body against his as he sucked and nibbled on lips more succulent than the ripest cherries.

"There was another question," Sy whispered when Dakar finally came up for air. His mate's lips were puffy, and his eyes sparkled. Sy leaned closer. "The question was what do you like in bed?"

"Oh babe," Dakar groaned as he slid his hands down Sy's back to cradle his butt. His mind was already providing the images of possible answers. "I'm glad you didn't ask me that first. I'd have never found out you don't like asparagus if you'd started with that one."

"Is it the type of question you can answer during your PDA demonstration?"

"What I like to do in bed requires me showing you things I don't want us doing in public." Dakar growled at the very idea someone would ever see his beautiful and sexy mate in the throes of passion. Hell, if he had his way, no one would ever see Sy naked except him. In fact, he was going to insist on it. But his attraction to Sy went a lot further than appreciating the way his sweet body leaned into his. The teasing eyes, the shy smile – Dakar didn't know what it was about his mate, but his balls ached, his cock was beating a tattoo with his heart and he just wanted. So, he said so. "I want you. That's the answer, plain and simple. What I like in bed is you. What I love in bed is you. What I want in my bed for the rest of my life is you. Just you. Does that answer your question?"

"Hmm," Sy's teeth worried his bottom lip. "I thought the question related to sexual positions and whether or not you want to use toys, gags, or restraints. Did you prefer top or bottom; how do you like oral sex and if you were a fan of piercings. I didn't want to ask the question because I didn't know how I would answer it." Beaming up at him Sy said, "I really like your answer though. Are you ready for some magic? I've been inspired by your PDA demonstration; I want to show you what I like in bed if you don't mind."

I'd get off on you just standing there biting your bottom lip. Hell, why would you think I'd mind? Dakar barely had time to nod and hold tight before they materialized in Sy's room.

Chapter Twenty-Seven

After the magic he'd expended, plus tearing through the veil and his subsequent closure of it, Sy expected to feel like death warmed over. Instead, he felt renewed, invigorated, and yes, he was prepared to admit it, damn horny too.

There's so much of him, Sy thought as Dakar sprawled out on the bed, crossing his arms behind his head. *Where the hell would anyone start with a buffet like this?* Sy wasn't the type to jump into things. He was more a savor small amounts type of person. But there wasn't any small amount of anything on Dakar. *Diving in it is then.*

Crawling up the bed, Sy decided to start with what he'd learned so far. Kissing was fun. Kissing Dakar sent Sy's insides fluttering and made his balls tingle. Although, he had a problem with what to do with his hands. Grasping at shoulders and stroking up biceps was one thing, but

Dakar's shirt was in the way. *He has to learn to take me as I am,* he thought as the shirt disappeared.

Sy swallowed the sudden excess of drool threatening to escape his lips. He'd forgotten how much there was of Dakar – everywhere. Unable to face the teasing glint he was sure Dakar was sporting, Sy buried his face in the dip between two well-formed pecs instead. The smell of a shifter's skin wasn't something a necromancer usually noticed; becoming used to the smell of death from an early age tended to diminish the ability to pick up anything except the sharpest of scents. Yet, Sy nuzzled instinctively, his tongue moving past his lips in an effort to catch more.

His fingers caught the tip of Dakar's nipple and the bigger man moaned. *Wow.* Unsure of the response he'd get, Sy cautiously licked the hardened nub and then gave into his urge to nibble it. He jolted as a hard hand grabbed the back of his head; making it impossible for him to do anything but lick, nibble and suck on the skin beneath his lips.

Eyes closed, Sy analyzed his new persona. *This is fun,* he realized. *Dakar's writhing and moaning and it's all because of me.* Sy watched the porn Brock found for him years before. It was churlish not to when his butler was trying to encourage him to have a life. But as he swung his head over to Dakar's other nipple, Sy remembered how he thought the porn responses couldn't be real. No one moaned or groaned or threw their bodies about the way he'd seen in the movies he'd watched.

And yet Dakar was doing exactly that. What was more, Sy could feel Dakar's hips jerking beneath him as he rubbed his cloth covered bulge against anything he could touch. Pushing aside the butterflies in his stomach, Sy ducked out from Dakar's hands and licked his way down his mate's torso. *Who knew eau de abs could taste and smell so good?* Licking along the deep indents that outlined every muscle, Sy gave into another urge and sucked up a lurid red mark. Pulling back slightly he couldn't get over his cocky sense of pride at seeing what he'd done. *Another ab, another mark. Dakar has eight of them.*

Bending to his task, Sy was thwarted by Dakar's hands guiding his head towards the cloth covered lump in his pants. Sy knew what a blow job looked like – something that would involve him undoing those pants. But giving into the urge to tease, he curved his lips where the bulge was most pronounced and blew.

/~/~/~/~/

Damn it, when did my necromancer become such a tease? Dakar knew his mate had no experience. It was why he was prepared to lay there and let Sy do a spot of exploring. But he was a simple guy when it came to sex. He wasn't into body worshipping; he'd never spent a long lazy afternoon sensually entangling his limbs with another while they stroked and teased each other to a completion that could take hours to achieve. His cock was cramped in his pants; his balls were threatening to blow. Dakar's entire body was primed for an orgasm and his mate hadn't even lowered his zipper.

Thrusting up with his hips, Dakar was torn between being fair and being pushy. He always took control in his previous sexual encounters; his wolf wouldn't allow anything else. Yet, his wolf was surprisingly, dare he even think it? *Submissive.* The release of his pants button and the sound of his zipper had him groaning in relief. But once Sy had freed his cock from the material, he stopped. Yes, there were soft hands loosely clasped around the base of his dick, but where were the firm twists, teasing tongue and sucking mouth movements?

Arching his neck, Dakar saw Sy sitting between his legs, looking down at his cock. Not doing anything. Just looking. As if conscious of his gaze, Sy looked up at him and then almost immediately looked back down at the cock in his hand. "I want to top you."

Question? Statement of intent? From Sy's tone it was hard to tell. "Are you asking me or telling me?" Blunt worked best as far as Dakar was concerned. Especially, when he was horny.

"Telling, asking." Sy chased a pre-come drip with the tip of his finger and Dakar felt a shiver through his balls. "I'm not sure what to do. You said something about how you preferred prep when you penetrated me, but I don't want to hurt you through lack of experience."

"Babe, I'm a wolf shifter. It'd take an awful lot to hurt me." Dakar wasn't about to mention it was his first time on the receiving end. His mate was nervous enough as it is. Besides, a pinch of pain might let him last longer than five minutes because even though Sy's hands were loose around his cock, it was still enough to cause him to blow with a hint of imagination.

"Why don't you use your magic on me?" He suggested. "I can always show you the prep side of things next time." Or the next or the next because Dakar's insides were screaming for an orgasm and he figured it might take two or three rounds before he could do the gentlemanly thing and take his freaking time.

But Sy frowned. "No. You mentioned the importance of prep and I don't want to disappoint you." He tapped Dakar's thigh. "Can you roll over?"

"Let's get these pants off first, shall we?" Dakar sat up, pushing his pants down his thighs. *Roll over, rub off on the sheets.* At this point Dakar was beyond caring. Grabbing a pillow, he shoved it under his hips as he rolled over. *Friction. Glorious friction.* He humped the pillow a couple of times and then stilled as Sy's hand landed on his ass.

I can do this. Couple of deep breaths. Relax. Let my mate get off and then I'll fuck him into the mattress. Oh yeah. Pleased with his plan Dakar didn't flinch when Sy's finger rubbed around his outer sphincter. There was a sensation of warm stickiness and Dakar figured his mate had magicked the lube. He wished he could see his mate's face, but he could imagine it. Sy would be wearing a studious frown; his mate was so serious especially when focused.

Picturing the tip of Sy's tongue peeking from his lips, the steely focus of those stunning gray eyes, Dakar moaned as a slender finger pierced his rim. He knew to huff out as the finger slid forward and encountered his inner muscles. There wasn't any discomfort, but as the finger slid in further, Dakar became aware of a growing warmth that stemmed from his rectum and seemed to be spreading along every sexual nerve he had. His balls throbbed, his cock pulsed; even his nipples were tingling as they did when Sy was sucking them.

"What?" Dakar swallowed and tried again. "What's that?"

"I know a bit about lubrication. This is my own creation," Sy's voice sounded huskier than usual and Dakar spared a passing thought to how things looked from his mate's end. It was his ass in the air, and his legs spread wide. Dakar groaned at the mental image. He loved the muscular firmness of a male ass. He'd just never thought of his own that way.

The pressure of a second finger eased past his muscles and the warmth traveling through his body increased. It was radiating from his insides and Dakar rubbed his chest on the linen of the covers. He'd never felt so wanton; hell, he was sure the word had never applied to him before but the linen on his nipples set his nerves on fire and he spread his legs wider and tried to muffle his moans in the coverlet.

He pushed back as Sy inserted a third finger. His ass was aching to be filled; another first for him. For all he knew, all men getting fucked felt like that, although the sensible part of his brain which was quickly being drowned out in a river of pure sensation knew that wasn't the case. Thinking. Ha. His mind was fractured, and Dakar didn't realize he was humping the pillow under his hips until he felt Sy splay a hand on his lower back.

"I have to." Three simple words but as Dakar felt the push from the blunted head of Sy's cock nudge past his loosened muscles, he was fully on board with the sentiment. *Next time I want to see his face,* Dakar promised himself as Sy groaned and pushed forward. Dakar was surprised he couldn't feel any discomfort and he put it down to Sy's super slick. His mate's cock must have been coated in it because the heat bubbling along Dakar's veins increased. Raising himself on his elbows, mourning the loss of sensation on his nipples, Dakar rocked his body back; his hole finally full.

They had an unspoken accord; Dakar and his mate. Slapping skin increased in speed and rhythm. Dakar gave up trying to hide the feelings Sy was punching from his body with a well-aimed dick. Forget a prostate massage, Dakar's entire channel quivered and flexed under his mate's thrusts. His whole body could feel it. Teeth clenched, the muscles in his arms, down his back and even his toes tensed with the need to come. But...but... "Fuck!"

A ghostly hand wrapped around his dick and that was it for Dakar. He didn't have time to wonder where the hand came from; Sy's hands were leaving bruises on his hips. But he didn't care what magic, spirit or anything else was responsible for that tiny hint of extra pressure he needed to hit his orgasm. He was too busy purging his four-day's worth of frustration, worry, and lust out his cock while his body throbbed and hummed, pushing his orgasm higher.

"I never knew." Sy rested over his back and Dakar became aware of the extra stickiness rolling down the inside of his thigh. Unwilling to dislodge his necromancer, Dakar carefully relaxed his arms out, so his body rested on the bed. Sy's curls tickled his back between his shoulders. He closed his eyes as the curls were followed by soft kisses. "I will love you so hard," Sy whispered as Dakar fell into a dreamless sleep.

Chapter Twenty-Eight

Dining out, or as Dakar had put it, their first official public date, was proving to be an interesting affair. After dithering over his wardrobe for far longer than anyone should, Sy accepted Dakar's opinion and teamed dark gray suit pants and jacket with a soft gray Henley and black ankle boots. It was far removed from his Necromancer garb, yet a surprising number of people recognized him in town and within the restaurant; coming over, shaking his hand and thanking him for whatever service he'd performed for them in the past. Considering he'd only ever thought he was just doing his duty, the thanks were surprising and a little humbling.

Dakar behaved just as Sy always imagined a shifter would around someone important to them. Bristling with protectiveness every time anyone approached, yet almost gloating as different people expressed their thanks; his pride was almost tangible. Sy didn't know enough about interactions in a social setting to know if Dakar should be introduced or even if he wanted to be. But Dakar didn't take offense at his silence on that score. It crossed Sy's mind that some might think he'd finally replaced Brock as his companion but the hand on his lower back, the way Dakar leaned in to whisper in his ear and the smiles were so far removed from the way Brock behaved around him, Sy couldn't think how anyone would doubt that Dakar treated him like someone special. In an alternative universe, Sy would be yelling, "yes, he's my mate," at the top of his lungs, but that just wasn't who he was.

But now they were seated at a delightful restaurant Sy hadn't heard about but instinctively knew from the ambiance he'd enjoy his evening. Their booth was private enough to talk without being overheard by other diners which was probably why Dakar thought to bring up the origin of what he'd called Sy's Super Slick not long after they'd sent the waiter away with their orders.

"I own the company that makes it. I created that particular brand as a private stock and it is only available to select clients." Sy was glad of the dim lighting. His cheeks were scorching. "A single use sachet of that stuff would be worth fifty dollars if you knew where you could buy it from."

"You own a lube company? But you…you…."

Sy's lips curled up at the corners. "I might not have gotten along with my father, but I did listen to his business advice. One of the first things he told me about investing in a company is to make sure the products made are something a person can't do without and need to use regularly. Regardless of the state of the economy, ruling powers or what goes on in a person's life, there are some items they won't go without. I happened to think that lube was one of those things."

Surprisingly, Dakar nodded. "That's good advice. Lube is a consumable product likely to be used by repeat customers, so I can see the thinking behind it. But I've bought all kinds of lube brands before and nothing has ever made me feel like yours. You created a full body experience. What made you think of creating it?"

"Father's second rule of business." Sy's smile widened. "If you're selling a product then you need a unique selling point. I studied the target audience for lube buyers for months; analyzing their various requirements." Sy chuckled. "To be honest, my research told me that most of the differentials in the market were already covered. One-serve sachets were a clever way of increasing the profit per unit. New formulas were created to be more usable in water; flavors were added for the oral market. I decided to create an upmarket range and based on spells I found in ancient texts, I was able to infuse the lube with various ingredients to enhance a person's pleasure."

"Damn babe, you certainly did that." Dakar was leaning close, his voice full of that growl that indicted his wolf was lurking under the surface. "There's someone here who is looking at you like he wants to have you for dessert and it's not me."

"Just keep looking at me like you are," Sy turned so he was staring into Dakar's intense eyes. "I've never dated. This is the first time I've been outside of the house in a social situation without my protective wards."

"You don't need wards. You have me."

Remembering Dakar's aborted PDA demonstration, Sy reached up and stroked along his mate's jaw while he sent his powers floating around the room. "There's another magic user here," he whispered leaning closer. To anyone watching them, there was no denying the intimacy between them, but that was all they'd see. "Norman Gowitch, if I'm not mistaken. He'll be jealous of you, that's all. Or maybe he fancies big strong shifters. Who cares? I'm here with you."

"He's with that journalist, Clive." The jaw under Sy's fingers tightened.

"You no longer work for the Police department. We're here on a date, anyone can see that." Leaning up, Sy whispered in Dakar's ear. "Don't eat them, my mate. Magic leaves a horrible aftertaste and I want to kiss you later."

"I could brush my teeth first," Dakar grumbled, but his tenseness disappeared and by the time the waiter arrived with their first course, he was laughing at some of the tales Sy shared about his misadventures with technology.

/~/~/~/~/

It had been an amazing evening. Dakar would have called it magical under any other circumstances; his rarely used romantic side coming to the fore under the lure of great food, soft lighting, and excellently stimulating company. Dakar had worried that his mate might be too introverted or shy to maintain the warmer side of his personality so few people saw. His worries were baseless. Sy's focus hadn't wavered all evening and by the time the bill was paid, Dakar was looking forward to the rest of their night in a more private setting.

And of course, that's exactly when someone had to go and stuff up his plans. They'd just stepped outside, and Dakar felt an annoying twinge on the back of his head before Clive was up in his face. The look of fury in Sy's eyes could cut marble but before Dakar could ask him what was wrong, Clive was prodding at his chest. "So, this is why you were at the Necromancer's mansion that morning. He's got you in his seductive thrall. It's okay, Detective. My friend Norman here will soon break the torrid connection this evil doer has on you and you'll be back to your old self in no time."

"There is nothing wrong with me and Sy's my true mate." Dakar's hand covered half of Clive's chest as he pushed the human away from him.

"Oh dear, this is worse than I thought. You need to come with us, detective. I'm afraid you're going to have to undergo an intensive spell reversal to clear your mind of this travesty. My efforts to get into your head are being blocked by this monster." Dakar had never met Norman Gowitch, but he'd committed the face to memory when he'd seen the photo early in the police investigations into the serial killer. The skin on his arm itched where

Norman grabbed him, and he pulled away with a snarl.

"You lay your hands on me one more time and I'll rip your throat out and stay the fuck out of my head." Dakar searched for Sy who appeared frozen on the sidewalk. "Babe, let's get out of here. I'm not letting these bozo's ruin our evening."

"Detective, you don't seem to understand." Clive was a persistent bastard; Dakar would give him that. "This...this thing you claim your bonded to isn't a real person." He pointed at Sy. "He was made in his grandfather's lab. He's nothing more than a golem; crafted to channel black magic and carry messages from the spirit world."

Sy's tight lips, closed eyes and pale face was the final straw for Dakar. The hungry leer Norman was wearing as he stared at Sy didn't help. His claws snapped out as he grabbed Clive and Norman around the neck. "Babe, I hate to ask, but we need to discuss some things in private. Would you mind transporting all of us back to the mansion?"

For a long moment Sy seemed locked in his pained statue impersonation, and Dakar thought he'd have to drive the idiots he was holding back to Sy's house. But with a slight shake of his head, Sy's eyes opened and he glared at Clive. "I don't know who the hell you've been talking to, but this time you've gone too far. Hold tight."

The surge of magic fluttered across Dakar's body and he relaxed into it; his wolf confident their mate would never do them any harm. Clive wasn't so sure, his shriek cut off as Sy's magic kicked in. Within the blink of an eye, they were in the Necromancer's mansion. Dakar recognized the basement walls and kept his grin to himself as he released his hold on his two captives. They wouldn't be going anywhere.

"Brock will be here directly," Sy said ignoring the journalist and the magic user. "This concerns him too."

"You know for a big fancy house, you're short of furnishings down here," Clive wandered around although there wasn't much to see. Just four block walls and a concrete floor. The only way in or out was a solid steel door which opened as Brock came in. Norman scuttled back, and Dakar remembered Brock saying the two had had a run in once before.

"Sir, you should've mentioned we had guests." Clive's eyes widened at Brock's formal tones. "I would've prepared the torture racks."

"Torture?" Norman wheezed, clutching at his chest. His podgy face was bright red and Dakar wondered how much of the act was put on.

"You can't hold me against my will," Clive said lifting his chin. He still couldn't look Brock in the eye, but Dakar gave him ten points for trying to brazen things out. "I'm a member of the press."

"With false information you clearly intend on spreading in an effort to discredit the town's leading magic user." Dakar couldn't keep the growl out of his voice if he tried. So, he didn't. "Norman, was this your doing? Are you Clive's informant?"

"Me? No." Norman shook his head. His chest was heaving and suddenly there was a chair behind him which he sank into, pulling an inhaler from the inside pocket of his jacket. After taking a couple of long drags from it, he said, "It's common knowledge Necromancers can't breed and I made my deductions from there. The one who ruled this town before was more a robot than human; especially in his dealings with others. This one," he waved the hand still clutching the inhaler at Sy, "was probably pulled out of a cupboard somewhere where he'd been stashed after his grandfather disappeared. Can't think why, but I imagine the spells on the previous necromancer started to decay over time and he had to be replaced."

There was silence while Sy and Brock exchanged a long look and then Sy said, "You seem surprisingly convinced about your information. Where did you do your magical training, Norman? What coven did you belong to?"

Norman snorted. "I don't like to be tied down. Covens have so many rules and regulations and their ceremonies are just an excuse to get naked. I'm a free spirit."

"A free spirit with lecherous thoughts about a man you claim isn't real," Brock added drily. "Tell me, did you intend to fuck my master, or dissect him and find his source of power?"

Dakar's growl rang around the room and he was by Sy's side in an instant. "MINE!"

Norman's eyes narrowed, and Clive's mouth dropped open. Dakar wondered how much contact the journalist had with paranormals. "The Necromancer is my mate," he clarified, his wolf thrilled at the words. "My wolf never lies and is incapable to being spelled when it comes to mates. That's shifter lore 101; something you should know Norman. But then, if you're a free spirit as you claim, chances are you've never understood anything about the paranormal world you dabble in."

"I understand about power," Norman jumped to his feet. "I've worked my ass off ever since I learned I could do magic. When I was young, it was great. I could feel my powers increasing with every spell I completed. But then zilch. Nothing. The moment I reached twenty-one it was as if my powers suddenly decided to stop growing and nothing I did changed that fact."

"That's perfectly normal," Sy said quietly. Dakar's wolf was still on high alert, but man and wolf appreciated the hand Sy rested on his elbow.

"It's not. It can't be," Norman spluttered. "Look at you. You can't be more than twenty-one yourself and you've got masses of power. I noticed that the first time I came to see you; when your butler threw me out. All I wanted was to ask how you did it. I wanted us to train together, but no. I wasn't good enough for the likes of you. But then I learned how you did it and I want that for myself."

"This is the scoop of a lifetime." Dakar looked over to see Clive scribbling furiously. "I'm going to get a raise and a byline on the front page for this."

The slight shake of Brock's head indicated Clive's hopes for a story were wishful thinking. But Sy spoke again, and Dakar focused on the main action. "Let's suppose, just for a moment, that what you claim you learned is true. That I am just a magically created vessel storing power that's not my own."

"Yes, yes." Greed was etched over Norman's face; it wasn't a good match for the lust in his eyes. "That would mean the power was stored somewhere on your person and it would be transferable."

"Just imagine my body one huge power reservoir." Sy's tone was dry. "What would you do with the additional power if you got your hands on it?"

"Do?" Norman looked around the room. "What do you mean? I won't need to do anything. I'd be the ranking power user in Pedace."

"Aha. There's only one other magic user in Pedace outside of this room, so that in itself really doesn't count. I imagine you think more will come. You'd create your own coven perhaps?"

"Oh yes," Norman stared at the ceiling. "A coven full of lusty young men all drawn to my power. I'd have control over them all."

"And the purpose of your coven? What would it do for the town?" Sy kept his voice low.

"Do? You keep asking that." Norman was pulled from his lustful thoughts. "A coven doesn't have to *do* anything for others. The knowledge of my power alone will keep the town safe."

"My master is a necromancer. If you acquired his powers, then it would behoove upon you to fulfill his duties," Brock said firmly. A large book appeared in his hands and he flipped it open and began to read. "In accordance with the magic council and in consultation with our forebears, the following duties will be undertaken by any and all persons carrying those talents identified under the term necromancy. They include...."

"Bah." Norman interrupted. "You're making that up. I've seen the way you live here. I don't know why we're stuck in this dreary basement, but I've walked the halls of this mansion. I've seen all the gold and fine furnishings. The necromancer does nothing but shut himself away here six days out of seven and barely ever has any visitors. I'm sure I could do a lot better than that."

"You've been spying on him?" Dakar's claws dug into his palm and only Sy's hand on his arm stopped him from leaping for Norman's throat.

"Oh no," Clive piped up, still scribbling madly. "That was me. I'm researching for a story. My editor wants me to write this huge expose." He waved his hand through the air. "The secret lives of Necromancers. I've been working on it for weeks. Not that much happens around here," he shook his head. "The detectives turning up at the mansion was the most exciting thing to happen in months. That's how I met Norman. He's been filling me on the good stuff."

"We'll discuss what you think you've learned shortly, Clive," Sy's voice took that hardened edge that set Dakar's balls tingling. "Norman. You claim I'm not human; that I was created for the sole purpose of dispensing magic justice and providing a conduit for the people of Pedace to speak with the dead. Is that right?"

"That's what I was told."

"Did you happen to come by your information from the demon captain of the police department by any chance?"

"Yes." Norman frowned. "He had a complete dossier on you. I had no reason to think he was lying."

"Of course not," Sy demurred. Dakar glanced down at his mate to see him smiling. "Do you have your license?"

The furrows in Norman's forehead deepened. "License? My driver's license?" He reached into his pants pocket.

"No, no. Your magic license. The one given to all magic users once they've reached a certain level of proficiency. It will contain your photo, personal details and the level of magic you've attained during your training. If you are going to take my powers, then your license will need updating. Brock can take care of that for you."

"I've never needed a license." Norman took another deep puff of his inhaler. "My magic comes from experience, instinct, and my own innate ability."

"Oh dear." Sy looked across at Brock who shook his head as though disappointed. Even Clive stopped scribbling long enough, trying to work out why the tension in the room just increased tenfold. "We'll just have to do this the old-fashioned way."

"What do you mean? Are you giving me your powers?"

"I can't give them to you." Sy shook his head. "I mean, I would, if I could. You seem a nice guy and all and the necromancer garb would definitely be slimming on you. But without a license the only way you can get my powers is if you take them. There're rules about this sort of thing. Brock will tell you."

"Take them?"

Sy nodded.

Norman's Adam's apple bounced up and down. "Where are they?" His voice had dropped to a whisper.

"In me." Sy pointed to his chest. "I mean, where are your powers?"

"I was born with them. But you...but you...you've been made. You must have some idea where...."

"When a golem is created they have no idea the origin of their creation or their makeup," Brock intoned. Dakar was amazed there wasn't a thread of deceit in the butler's voice but then the guy did like to talk as though reading from a text book.

"So, I just...look?" Norman moved closer, holding out his hands. Dakar noticed he was still holding his inhaler.

"Use your magic. Those instincts you told me about," Sy confided. "You might not think that this Detective is my mate, but his wolf believes it with everything he is. It'd be a shame to see your throat clawed out before you got the power you think you deserve."

"Magic, right." Norman stepped back. "So, I just do, like a siphon spell or something?"

"Just throw all your magic at me," Sy's grip on Dakar's arm tightened and he realized his fangs were showing. "It will mix with mine and then you just call it back."

He's lying, Dakar realized, wondering what on earth was going on. All his wolf knew was they didn't like the idea of anyone throwing anything at their mate, but he had to trust Sy knew what he was doing.

"Okay." Norman tucked his inhaler back in his jacket and spread his legs and arms apart. "Watch this kid," he said to Clive. "You're about to see some real magic in action."

Brock quietly tugged Clive closer to the door. "In case there's any fallout," he said with a completely straight face. Dakar wanted to laugh out loud at the look of wonder on Clive's face.

"Are you ready?" Norman asked.

Sy held up one finger and then stood on tiptoes and brushed a kiss along Dakar's jaw. "Don't flinch." Dakar barely caught the whisper before Sy was facing Norman once more.

"Ready."

Norman's whole body started to shake, and Dakar felt a surge of magic in the air. But unlike when Sy used his, which felt as though the air was infused with a dynamic storm cloud, Norman's felt clunky, unused, almost as if it were broken; like a car trying to run with a piston missing. Norman's arms were flying about in the air, as though he was herding cats. Dakar didn't realize the man was trying to corral his own power until Norman yelled, "Excalibur" and flung his arms in Sy's direction.

Dakar jumped, but managed to contain himself. Sy hadn't moved, but suddenly the wicked looking staff with the skull on top was in his hands; the skull ablaze with light as the power levels in the air suddenly dropped.

"What? No! No! No!" Norman yelled. "Come back. Stop. Give them back. What are you doing?"

"I'm not doing anything," Sy said quietly, resting his head on Dakar's arm. "I'm just standing here, waiting for you to take the powers you claim I wasn't born with."

"But your stick...that skull...GIVE IT TO ME." Norman lunged for the staff, grabbing the oak and tugging it out of Sy's hands. "I did it." Norman danced around the room holding the stick aloft. "The necromancer's power is all mine." Then his feet faltered and he stumbled, using the staff to hold him upright. "What's happening to me," he cried, holding his head with one hand. "I don't feel so good. Fates save me. I'm fading. Someone do something. Help. I'm fading." He fell face down on the floor, the staff rolling out of his hand until it reached Sy's feet.

"Take a note, young journalist," Brock said sternly as he went over and retrieved Sy's staff, holding it away from him. "Rule 42; subsection 27, b. In the matters relating to necromancy, no person or persons, by magical or physical means may or should be permitted to ever touch the staff, skull, and any accessories belonging to a necromancer unless they too carry the blood from a necromancer family line. Seriously, kid. It'll give you a headache."

"Is he dead?" Clive asked, looking over at Norman's slumped body.

Even though he wasn't employed as a detective any more, Dakar strode over to check. Feeling for a pulse, he shook his head. "He's still breathing. It's as though he's asleep."

"He is," Sy said. "Does Norman have family, do we know? It's going to take a while for him to adjust to life without his magic. Someone should have taught him never to just throw it away."

"I'll contact Detective Summerfield and ask," Brock said. "Don't worry, sir, I will take care of all the arrangements."

"Thank you." Sy yawned and covered his mouth with his hand. "Clive, you will be staying here tonight. That's not negotiable. Brock will see to your accommodations. I would advise against snooping. You never know what might happen to you in a magic user's house. Even the most innocent of objects can contain great powers."

"Yeah. Right." Clive stuffed his notepad in his pocket. "I'll just…I'll just follow him then." He pointed at Brock who was heading out the door, still holding the magic infused staff. "I'll see you guys at breakfast."

"I thought we'd never be alone," Sy smiled when they finally left.

Dakar looked down at the body on the floor and then stepped over it, holding out his arms for his mate to fall into. "I had so many romantic plans for this evening," he grumbled as Sy leaned on his chest.

"I figure that's why the Fates give us forever," Sy chuckled. "It will probably take that long to actually get through a whole date without interruptions."

Chapter Twenty-Nine

Sy moaned as he heard the unsubtle knock on his bedroom door. "I don't want to get up," he mumbled, rolling over and curling into the heat of Dakar's body. "Can't the most powerful magic user in Pedace get a day off once in a while?"

Dakar huffed in his face. "I've got another thrilling day to look forward to watching my brilliant mate work wonders with the misunderstood, while I stand around looking like a muscle-bound pin-up and about as useful."

"You do that really well." Sy smiled hesitantly and when Dakar didn't return it, a shaft of pain ran through his heart. "Are you tired of me already? We've barely been claimed a week and four days of that I was unconscious."

"I love being with you," Dakar said quickly, and his strong arms wrapped around Sy and pulled him close. "I just wonder, I can't help it really, but I wonder what my role will be in your life. All I seem to be able to do is stand around and look intimidating."

"I don't think we've really had a chance to stop and think about it, have we?" Sy didn't like the anxious feeling he got when he thought his mate was unhappy. "Did you want to get your job back? I'm sure they'd take you if you asked."

"No, no, no," Dakar's arms tightened. "Don't ever think I don't want to be with you. I've wanted to find my mate from the moment I understood what a gift they were from the Fates. I'm not sorry I met you at all. I'm ecstatic we're together. I gave up my job because I knew it would pull me away from you. Well, that and I wasn't about to work for anyone who didn't believe in you and the work you do. Which reminds me. Brock invited Brad for breakfast, didn't he?"

"Brad's going to want a statement and he's going to smell a lie." Sy sighed. He should have stayed asleep. But if he was asleep, he couldn't appreciate Dakar's heat, the feel of his body, or the simple pleasure that came from being held by someone who cared for him. "I'm happy to tell him the truth, but he's no more going to believe me now, than he did before. All he's going to see is that I summoned the Captain for the express purpose of killing him."

"It was self-defense." At least Dakar believed in him and that went a long way towards lessening the anxiety in Sy's heart. "Babe," Sy looked up. The intensity and possessiveness in Dakar's eyes never failed to thrill him. "Please don't doubt my desire to be with you. When you meet my mom, she'll tell you I insisted on sleeping in a double bed from when I was six years old, just so I would have room for my mate when he came. Of course, at six I had no idea mates didn't come along until you were an adult, and my six-year old mind never thought we'd do anything more than sleep in that bed. But finding you genuinely is a dream come true for me."

"I've always slept in this bed, from as far back as I can remember," Sy turned, pressing his back against Dakar's chest. "I remember when I was little, Brock hung curtains up on huge posts and encouraged me to think of this as my safe place. My fort he used to call it. I used to hide in here whenever my parents were yelling at each other or if Father wanted to present me to his friends. I never realized how much I needed that safe place until my father took the curtains away one day when I was ten."

"Why'd he do that, babe?"

"I accidentally set fire to them." Sy chuckled. "I was practicing that fancy entrance you saw when you and Brad first came to this house. It took years of scorching furnishings and walls before I got that right."

"You were using your powers at ten. That's impressive."

"Necromancer's are born with elements of their power." Sy closed his eyes remembering his childhood. "I was talking to roaming spirits in this house from when I was three. I thought they were alive and talked to them just like I'm talking to you. I remember Brock's face when I tried to introduce him to my 'friends'. Apparently, I was a magical prodigy." Something his father took advantage of and that wasn't something Sy wanted to talk about.

It seemed Dakar understood because he didn't press the issue. "My forts involved sheets and branches from the trees in the woods around our pack house. Mom used to yell every time me and my cousins would drag the sheets back home again, never thinking of the mud and twigs we'd be dragging with us. Those were fun times."

Sy turned his head, intent on asking Dakar if he missed his family. But his lips were claimed before they opened and as he rolled over and welcomed Dakar moving on top of him, anything he wanted to say was swallowed in his moans.

/~/~/~/~/

For Dakar, walking in on Brock in the kitchen, cradling Brad in his arms as though he was a lover was a shock; more because he didn't think Brock was the type of guy to incite intimacies where food was prepared. Even more of a shock was Brad's disheveled appearance. Then Brad compounded everything by leaving Brock's arms and ending up in his.

"I'm so glad you're all right. I thought you'd died," Brad blubbered, clinging onto Dakar like a limpet. "I've been worried sick; you didn't call and no one in the house would tell me what happened. Fuck, why didn't you call?"

"I quit the force, remember?" Dakar carefully disengaged himself and sat down next to Sy who'd stayed silent through Brad's mini-outburst. "I told you, told you and told you again. Sy's my mate. He wouldn't hurt me."

"I know that now," Brad sat across from him, wiping his face with his hands. "And that's not what I meant. Brock told me about the fight with the Captain. You could've been killed. Both of you."

"I could've been dragged across the veil never to return," Sy said, his hand a warm comfort on Dakar's leg. "But Dakar was never in danger. Neither Brock nor I would've allowed that. As it was, Dakar saved me and gave me the strength to do what I had to do. I'd be lost on the other side of the veil if it hadn't been for him."

"It was that serious?" Strange, Dakar hadn't even considered that. On the night in question, he'd spent what felt like hours trying to get out of the guest house he'd found himself in. Something that wasn't possible with two legs or four given the magic that sealed the windows and fused the door shut. Then, just as suddenly, he was transported into the basement; into a scene that was the stuff of nightmares with Brock's voice in his head urging him to hold onto Sy and never let go. Which he did. And here they were a week later all having breakfast. "Fuck. You could've been trapped? Essentially dead? I'd have lost you!"

Pulling Sy off his chair, Dakar held the smaller man on his lap, inhaling huge doses of Sy's scent as his body trembled and his wolf howled in outrage and despair. Why hadn't they known the situation had been so dire? Sy huffed but thankfully allowed it because Dakar didn't think he'd be letting go anytime soon.

"Now you see why I didn't want to talk to you about all of this before," Sy said to Brad. "Dakar wasn't there for most of it. He was safe in the guest suite. Brock only pulled him to us when he knew I needed one final boost to my powers. Brock was injured, I'd used too much power and while Brock gave me all the energies he could, it wasn't enough for me to fight the lure of the veil, the demon, and the ghouls he'd called from the underworld. But Dakar was always safe because by then Baltoc, your Captain was too far gone to cause him any harm."

"So, it's all true then." Brad accepted a cup of coffee from Brock, giving him a shy smile. "Brock told me the Captain was ultimately behind the murders of those young men and that it was all an elaborate way of doing away with you."

"A plan that was twenty years in the making, based on a need for revenge that he'd held onto for three hundred years," Sy said. "Can I have eggs for breakfast please Brock, and I think Dakar would enjoy steak and bacon."

Breakfast. Such a mundane thing after so much misery and terror and yet Dakar knew it was his mate's way of trying to put what happened behind him. The demon was vanquished, they were all safe. The police were able to close the case on the young men's death and eight potential victims had been saved. But there was one more thing Dakar needed to know.

Lifting his head, he saw Brad was watching him. "Why didn't you believe in Sy when you knew he was my mate. Why were you so worried about the Captain when all the evidence pointed to him being the one behind the murders and the threats on Sy?"

The skin above Brad's beard reddened but the bear met Dakar's eyes without flinching. "I was wrong. I know that. From the moment we met, I've considered us friends. Good friends. But I owed the Captain. Ten years ago, when I first joined the force, I was just a cublet really. I'd not been long away from my family; I didn't know anyone in Pedace and the captain took me under his wing."

"I'd not been on the force very long when I got a call from my sister. She was in trouble. Nothing major, but she was pregnant, the guy responsible wasn't her mate. He didn't even know she was a shifter and when he found out he didn't take it well. He attacked her with a knife, trying to end her pregnancy. My sister didn't have insurance; I hadn't thought to include her on mine when I started work. I didn't have the money for the medical bills, and my sister would need somewhere to stay…."

"And the Captain helped you with it all." Dakar nodded.

"He told me at the time he was rewarding my loyalty. Since then…fuck." Brad rubbed his hands over his face. "I used to see things, you know. Nothing major. Not even criminal, but over the years I used to wonder just how loyal the Captain was to his position and the town he swore to protect. But there was no hard evidence to ever prove he did anything wrong. He never asked for the money back; he didn't try and take anything out of my wages. When I asked him about it, all he kept saying was that my loyalty was enough. So, I kept quiet. I did my job, kept my head down and rose through the ranks. My sister finally met her true mate and her and my nephew have been happy for years. The captain never asked me to do anything illegal and until this business with the serial killer I never realized how much he hated Sy."

"The fact that we'd never met, and yet we both came to the police department about the same time, should have been a clue. Most police departments use their consultants on a regular basis." Sy nodded at Brock as he placed steaming food in front of all of them. Dakar's stomach rumbled appreciatively as he eyed the three steaks and at least half a pound of bacon piled on his plate.

"Will you still be working with us?" Brad asked Sy, as he tucked into his plate that looked as full as Dakar's. "The work you did with those cold cases was amazing. There are countless other families that'd appreciate knowing what's happened to their loved ones over the years."

Sy didn't answer immediately, giving Dakar the opportunity to enjoy his meal. It was only after the plates were cleared that Sy reached over and took Dakar's hand in his. "I definitely want to help the police, but it will have to be around the work I do here. I still see families three days a week for two hours at a time. It's an important part of being a necromancer, being available to the families during their time of grief. But something my wonderful mate said this morning has had me thinking about what else we could do, going forward."

"You could have your job back at the department any time, Dakar," Brad said quickly. "The place is in a bit of an uproar at the moment. The local council has advertised for a new Captain, but they've assured us all, the Necromancer will be part of the vetting process. Steve took the detective's exam and he's been partnered with me since you've been gone, but I know you'd be hired back if that's what you wanted."

"And I'd support you, if that's what you wanted." Sy turned and Dakar's heart bloomed. When Sy smiled Dakar knew it was just for him. "But I was wondering how you'd feel if we set up something for ourselves instead. Became private investigators. Between your detective skills and my magic, we could work together to clear the backlog of cold cases at the department and take on other cases the police don't have the resources for or enough evidence to pursue. What do you say?"

Dakar felt his own smile forming as the idea took hold. "I think it's a great idea. I was worried I would miss my work, but I couldn't be a detective working on new cases, and still be with you. This is the perfect solution."

"It wouldn't just be us two," Sy warned. "Brock would be a crucial part of our team, of course, and I imagine Clive and Connor would want to be involved once they hear about this."

"Where are the little miscreants?" Dakar looked around, finally remembering their existence. "Has Clive been dissuaded from writing his expose?"

"I offered him a job this morning, Sir," Brock replied. "Clive is now the Necromancer's official biographer. He gets to work with and learn about the paranormal world and best of all, everything he learns is tied up in an air-tight confidentiality agreement. He's ecstatic. He gets a healthy salary; he and Connor are already redesigning the guest wing, because they will both live on site and best of all, he can quench his insatiable quest for truthful answers without causing us any problems."

"And if we require any help from law enforcement, we have a very good friend on the police department. Isn't that right?" Dakar winked at Brad who reached over and shook Dakar's hand.

"You all have a best friend in the police department. Of course, if that means I get invited over for meals more often, then I'll be all the happier."

Laughter rang around the table; even Brock joining in and when Dakar caught his eye, the formidable man nodded slightly in his direction. Dakar got the impression Brock was pleased there was finally going to be some life around the mansion again and as Sy leaned over and pecked him on the cheek, he basked in the warm glow that came with that feeling that everything was going to be all right.

Epilogue

Three weeks later

"I'm genuinely not a party person," Sy tugged at the ends of his bow tie and attempted to tie it in some facsimile of a bow.

"Our in-house writer made a valid argument, sir," Brock said firmly, plucking the tie ends out of Sy's fingers and creating a perfect bow. "One of the reasons so much misinformation exists about you and Necromancers in general is because they don't get a chance to meet and interact with you unless they need your services. Hosting a party in your own house, inviting people from all walks of life to attend is a creative way of correcting misinformation."

"I'm not going downstairs until Dakar gets here," Sy said stubbornly. "I might not get hives anymore with people around, but…." He looked up to see Brock watching him closely.

"Don't you ever wish things were back the way they were?"

Brock offered one of his rare smiles. "You mean the days when you used to spend six days out of seven trying to work out ways of circumventing our social agreement?"

Sy chuckled. "And researching for hours on historical topics which have no real basis in today's world. Every day seems so busy now. I do miss those quiet times."

"That detective does make you happy, doesn't he?" No matter how much Dakar pleaded, Brock only ever referred to him as the detective or sir. "I assumed he did. I've longed for ear plugs on more than one occasion walking down the hallway past your bedroom door."

"Yeah." Sy nodded. "I didn't think it was possible to care for anyone apart from you. You've been my family for so long. But Dakar's amazing. Attentive, annoying, possessive, and so damn curious about everything I do. My heart would be empty without him. And my two C's." He smiled as he thought of Connor and Clive. They were like a pair of mischievous cats most of the time. "We've come a long way in a short time."

"That we have, sir," Brock patted him on the shoulder. "And before you ask, yes I am happy too. I see you grow more and more settled in your role every day. I'd have to be blind to miss the feelings between you and your mate. The patience you show Connor and Clive astounds me. I'm proud of you."

Sy gave in and hugged Brock quickly before the man could object. "Are you sure it's got nothing to do with our friendly bear shifter?" He asked as he stepped back and smoothed down his jacket. "I'm sure I've seen your detective's car still in the driveway many a morning."

"Detective Summerfield is interesting and surprisingly creative when you get him alone," Brock said stiffly. "Besides, I am sure he only stays because of the range of honey's I procure for his breakfast."

"Don't put yourself down, Brock," Sy said quietly. "You have a lot to offer the right man." Checking himself in the mirror, Sy held out his arms. "Will I do?"

"Your detective will be suitably impressed," Brock nodded approvingly. "Many of the guests have started to arrive and people will be wondering where you are."

"I do wish Dakar hadn't chosen this evening to go for a run with that new detective Steve. Wolves can't tell the time. I just knew he'd be late."

"Nevertheless, once he realizes you're mingling in public and being ogled by so many of this town's fine citizens, I am sure he'll want nothing more than to glower at your side. Shall we go down?"

I can do this, I can do this, Sy chanted to himself. He was aware Dakar was near and he only hoped the man remembered to get dressed before coming down to the large ballroom. Dakar's wolf was as keen on Sy as the two-footed version was, and Sy was often picking himself up after being leapt on by the exuberant animal who seemed to want to cover him in hair all the time.

/~/~/~/~/

Shit, I'm late. Dakar ran onto the main gardens around the mansion seeing all the cars, and chatter of people in the huge ballroom Brock had decked out for the evening. The party was a great idea. Although the police officers were now friendlier when Sy was around, Dakar still wanted his mate to be more comfortable out in public. This party was one way of showing the Necromancer that not everyone thought he was sacrificing babies to some ancient dark lord in a black magic ritual.

The party appeared to be in full swing. Music tinkled out across the lawn and everywhere clumps of people were laughing and talking among themselves. Moving closer to the windows, Dakar spotted Sy standing by the entrance, Brock and Brad hovering behind him. *I'd better get my ass in there,* he thought, turning to find the door Sy always left ajar for him. But then he stopped and watched as a long black limousine cruised up the driveway. The car stopped right out the front of the ballroom's French doors and a capped driver got out smartly and opened the back-passenger door.

The hair on the back of Dakar's neck rose as a tall, elegantly dressed and totally arrogant man stepped out and looked around. "Park around the back and find food in the kitchens," the fancy man ordered, waiting until the car moved away before turning towards the main doors to the ballroom. As he moved into the light, Dakar realized he was seeing a familial resemblance to his precious mate. Fur forgotten he moved forward. If this was who he thought it was….

Dakar watched as Sy's smile died and his eyes widened slightly before his face settled into the mask Dakar worked so hard to get rid of. His mate's focus was entirely on the elegantly dressed man.

"Father. I wasn't aware you'd been sent an invitation."

"I hardly need an invitation to visit my son." The two men were standing at least five feet apart and made no move towards each other. *What kind of fucked up reunion is this?* Dakar crept around the door.

"As you can see, I have guests to attend to this evening. Perhaps we can meet at your convenience some time tomorrow? You can let Brock know where and when." Sy turned away.

"I'm sure you'll want to discuss things with me before then, son," Sy's father sounded like he had a baseball bat up his ass. "Your mother and fiancé arrive in the morning to get this place ready for your wedding set for two weeks time. We will need to go over your expected behavior before you will be allowed to meet your intended."

Intended? Fiancé? Like fucking hell. Ignoring the swarms of brightly dressed guests and the fact he was still in fur, Dakar raced to his mate's side, knocking him over in the process. *Oh well, no matter, easier to protect this way.* Straddling Sy's body, Dakar lifted his teeth and snarled at the intruder.

"What nonsense is this. Since when did you have a pet?"

Sy's arms came up around Dakar's neck but he wouldn't stop snarling. "I don't have a pet father, and I have no need for a fiancé either. I'd like you to meet Dakar, my fated mate. As you can see, he's very protective."

"A wolf shifter as a mate? We'll soon see about that."

I can see me and the father in law are just not going to get along.

To be continued.

Thank you for taking the chance on yet another new series. I do hope you enjoyed learning about Sy and Dakar, and Brock and Brad of course, in this new world of mine. Unlike all my other series, this one is planned as a trilogy, meaning there will be two more books where we learn more about Sy and Dakar and the progress of their relationship as they solve new cases together and learn to cope with family interferences and magical criminals. Something told me when they first started talking in my head, that one book was never going to be enough for this couple and I hope you are as keen to enjoy their future adventures as I am.

If you did enjoy this story, please consider leaving me a review. They really do make a difference, especially on sites like Amazon, so even a few words will be really helpful. My contact details are all listed under my bio page – I love to hear from readers so don't be shy and if you are a fan of knowing more about what's coming out before it happens, make sure you check out my personal teaser group on Facebook.

Have an amazing day and as always, hug the one you love. You can never have too many hugs.

Hugs

Lisa xx

Other Books By Lisa/Lee Oliver

Please note, I have now marked the books that contain mpreg for those of you who don't like to read those type of stories. Hope that helps ☺

Cloverleah Pack

Book 1 – The Reluctant Wolf – Kane and Shawn

Book 2 – The Runaway Cat – Griff and Diablo

Book 3 – When No Doesn't Cut It – Damien and Scott

Book 3.5 – Never Go Back – Scott and Damien's Trip and a free story about Malacai and Elijah

Book 4 – Calming the Enforcer – Troy and Anton

Book 5 – Getting Close to the Omega – Dean and Matthew

Book 6 – Fae for All – Jax, Aelfric and Fafnir (M/M/M)

Book 7 – Watching Out for Fangs – Josh and Vadim

Book 8 – Tangling with Bears – Tobias, Luke and Kurt (M/M/M)

Book 9 – Angel in Black Leather – Adair and Vassago

Book 9.5 – Scenes from Cloverleah – four short stories featuring the men we've come to love

Book 10 – On The Brink – Teilo, Raff and Nereus (M/M/M)

Book 11 – Don't Tempt Fate – Marius and Cathair

Book 12 which is Thomas's story will be out soon.

The Gods Made Me Do It (Cloverleah spin off series)

Get Over It – Madison and Sebastian's story

You've Got to be Kidding – Poseidon and Claude (mpreg)

Book Three – Just One Bite – Lasse and (shush, it's a secret) (Coming soon)

Bound and Bonded Series

Book One – Don't Touch – Levi and Steel

Book Two – Topping the Dom – Pearson and Dante

Book Three – Total Submission – Kyle and Teric

Book Four – Fighting Fangs – Ace and Devin

Book Five – No Mate of Mine – Roger and Cam

Book Six – Undesirable Mate – Phillip and Kellen

Stockton Wolves Series

Book One – Get off My Case – Shane and Dimitri

Book Two – Copping a Lot of Sin – Ben, Sin and Gabriel (M/M/M)

Book Three – Mace's Awakening – Mace and Roan

Book Four – Don't Bite – Trent and Alexi

Book Five – Tell Me the Truth – Captain Reynolds and Nico (mpreg)

This series is now finished, but I have promised a couple of short stories about the characters in book 5 so watch for those.

Alpha and Omega Series

Book One – The Biker's Omega – Marly and Trent

Book Two – Dance Around the Cop – Zander and Terry

Book 2.5 – Change of Plans - Q and Sully

Book Three – The Artist and His Alpha – Caden and Sean

Book Four – Harder in Heels – Ronan and Asaph

Book 4.5 – A Touch of Spring – Bronson and Harley

Book Five – If You Can't Stand The Heat – Wyatt and Stone (Previously published in an anthology)

There will be more A&O books – I have had one teasing my brain for months, so stay tuned for that one.

Balance – Angels and Demons

The Viper's Heart – Raziel and Botis

Passion Punched King – Anael and Zagan

(Uriel and Haures's story will be coming soon)

Arrowtown

A Tiger's Tale – Ra and Seth (mpreg)

Snake Snack – Simon and Darwin (mpreg)

Liam's Lament – Liam Beau and Trent (MMM) (Mpreg)

(Deputy Joe and Doc's story will be coming soon)

NEW Series – City Dragons

Dragon's Heat – Dirk and Jon

Dragon's Fire – Samuel and...wait and see ☺ (coming soon)

Also under the penname Lee Oliver

Northern States Pack Series

Book One – Ranger's End Game – Ranger and Aiden

Book Two – Cam's Promise – Cam and Levi

Book Three – Under Sean's Protection – Sean and Kyle – (Coming soon)

Standalone:

The Power of the Bite – Dax and Zane

One Wrong Step – Robert and Syron

A number of readers have asked me if Balthazar will get his own story. I am not ruling it out, but that is likely to be a short story rather than turn this into a full series.

Shifter's Uprising Series – Lisa Oliver in conjunction with Thomas J. Oliver

Book One – Uncaged – Carlin and Lucas

About the Author

Lisa Oliver had been writing non-fiction books for years when visions of half dressed, buff men started invading her dreams. Unable to resist the lure of her stories, Lisa decided to switch to fiction books, and now stories about her men clamor to get out from under her fingertips.

When Lisa is not writing, she is usually reading with a cup of tea always at hand. Her grown children and grandchildren sometimes try and pry her away from the computer and have found that the best way to do it is to promise her chocolate. Lisa will do anything for chocolate.

Lisa loves to hear from her readers and other writers (I really do, lol). You can catch up with her on any of the social media links below.

Facebook –
http://www.facebook.com/lisaoliverauthor

Official Author page –
https://www.facebook.com/LisaOliverManloveAuthor/

My new private teaser group -
https://www.facebook.com/groups/540361549650663/

(You will need to be familiar with my books or a friend of mine on Facebook to join, as there are questions to be answered to get into the group. It helps prevent the group being invaded by people who monitor and report posts.)

My blog - (http://www.supernaturalsmut.com)

Twitter –
http://www.twitter.com/wisecrone333

Email me directly at yoursintuitively@gmail.com.

Made in the USA
Coppell, TX
05 November 2024

39650437R10275